The Nectar of Surrender: Queer Kink Erotica

by Jezebel Jett

Maverick
PRESS

Contents

Content Note

All characters in this book are consenting adults and are eighteen years of age or older. Any resemblance to real persons or other real life entities is purely coincidental.

These stories are from the dominant's perspective: *Loaning Out The Girl, The Girl & The Diner, Touch Yourself, Daddy Wants To Watch, You'll Pay For It Later, The Next Time I See You, Paint Me Indigo, Control, I Want To Taste You On My Fingers, Criminal, Here's What's Going To Happen, Communion, Divinity, I Could Fall Into You Like A Crash, Between My Teeth*

These stories are from the submissive's perspective: *Yours Before I Knew You, The Pulp Of A Peach, Hold On, Worthy, Knife In Your Gaze, Dark Like A Dahlia, Break Me Past My Promise, Open Your Mouth, Road Trip, Come Here, No Rest For The Wicked, Rabid, Make Me Hurt, Unbaptism, Ritual, Her, Triptych, I Like It When It Hurts, You Like Me Broken, Little Deaths, I Dream About You, I Want You To Watch While I Hit You, I Needed You More Than Breathing, Be Good, Spread Your Legs, Charcoal, A Case Of You, Sofia, Sticky And Sweet, Greedy Little Thing, I Got Off To You Tonight, Let The Simmer Steam, The Exquisite, Holy Ache, The Sharp & The Soft*

Both the Dominant and the submissive's perspective are included in: *Just Be A Hole, Kidnapped At The Bar, Breaking The Rules*

Because this is a kinky erotica book, be advised this text does include things that could be upsetting for some readers. If you might be disturbed by this content, please don't read it.

This book includes mentions or actions of the following:
- D/s (dominance and submission) power dynamics
- drug references
- fisting
- sensory deprivation (gags, blindfolds)
- cuffs
- impact play (floggers, crops, belts)
- vibrators
- voyeurism/exhibition
- being consensually loaned out
- dacryphilia (crying)
- rough body play
- strap on sex
- oral sex
- knife play
- fear play
- daddy/girl dynamics
- blood
- dirty talk
- consensual non-consent (CNC)
- bondage in water
- religious reclamation & play
- choking
- breath play
- orgasm control & denial
- cigar play

- caging/confinement
- punishment

Introduction

This book has been a labor of deep love and care. It wouldn't have come to fruition without the education I was privileged to have and receive, from grammar school to college. I was afforded many spectacularly passionate teachers who encouraged me, gave me validation, showed up for me, and nurtured my deep thirst to learn. Because of them, my work as a creative writer bloomed. Under their teachings, I was exposed to so many wonderful writers and poets. They encouraged me to take risks, and I stayed excited about learning, and more than anything else, writing. That access and privilege does not go unrecognized nor do I ever intend on taking it for granted.

I grew up in a stringent religious environment, came out as queer when I was twenty four, and learned about my kink side when I was twenty seven. I wish that I had grown up with more queer, kinky voices around me, not just in literature, but also film and mainstream media. I also wish much of what I had fought to expose myself to hadn't primarily been crafted by a male gaze. The world needs queer people telling queer stories, for queer folks.

Erotica was my first doorway to feeling a deep sense of freedom about myself. When I got my first iPhone, I started buying the *Best Of* erotica compilations Cleis Press had to purchase through Apple Books. I started reading smut on a tiny screen, but the gifts it gave me were more impactful than I could have imagined. It made me feel less alone in my sexuality, and even though I had to hide it initially, it helped my confidence and sense of self broaden. When this happened, I started gaining agency about my sexual identity. I had voices speaking to me that desired the things I hadn't ever been able to put my words into, I had access to a new language of the self. Reading erotica was revelatory to me.

Putting my first book out to the light feels like I am part of that circle of voices that enveloped its arms around me and gave me solace when not much else could. I am endlessly grateful for having those voices and hope whoever this reaches, it is able to offer you a small sense of that solidarity and agency in your own identity and sexuality. Self-expression is resistance — as is creating — in a time of genocide.

There was a time in my life where doing something like this would have terrified me, when I was stifled and lost and not ready to process the shame and oppression thrust against me as a queer, disabled woman in the clutches of the Christofascism patriarchy inside of which I grew up. I encourage anyone who reads erotica to share it, talk about it, and find solace here. You are not alone. You are loved and I beg you: please *normalize your desires and tackle your pleasure unapologetically*. You are beautiful and deserve to celebrate sexuality, kink, eros, intimacy, and queer joy.

✦✦✦

Much of the commercialized erotica that is inclusive of kink that is sold at corporate bookstores or online platforms doesn't feel like the brand of kink I've been involved in, or adjacent to, as a queer, femme-identified person. This is not intended to shame or demean those readers who get something out of those texts and enjoy more mainstream kink — but as a writer, it felt incredibly important to me to not water down or shrink lived experiences, or fantasies of them. Some of what I've learned has come from practice, being around veterans of the Bay Area kink communities, attending events, munches, and kink conventions.

My kink knowledge isn't yours, and vice-versa, and in that fact, there is beauty.

As a writer, I write what I know — and what I deeply want to know. For me, kink is a million different things and shades and tones of emotions. It is vulnerable, potent, and connected. It is also political, raw, healing, terrifying, triumphant, poignant, tepid, taciturn, trusting, and turbulent.

For you, dear reader, it can be anything you want and more.

This book is from one voice, one gaze, one lens of catharsis and curiosity and passion. It is a personal darling because in many non-indie erotica texts, I never saw myself, my desires, or my needs. Often, I have felt that much discourse or visibility when it comes to accessible and lived, experienced kink has had to be excavated. Much of what is commercially acceptable seems to play it safe, play it hetero-normative and is based in white supremacy and patriarchal values and systems that leave little to no room for otherness. Kink to me hasn't ever been a contract with almost zero negotiations, one-sided rules of demands that are blindly followed. The female-identified folks aren't always the bottom, or a masochist, or timid with zero agency. My kink has never included cis men.

My kink is messy, honest, trauma-informed, full of a myriad of awkwardness and unlearning and subverting systems that have been built to confine, conform, and contain. My kink is full of strap ons and 2 a.m. phone sex my neighbors can hear. My kink is full of unashamed squirting and beautiful t-dicks, and scars and bruises and skin that holds stories. My kink includes bodies of all sizes and colors that were born to feel joy and visibility and pleasure. My kink believes in equity, risk awareness, boundaries, consent, and whimsy. It supports the indie content creator, the sex workers, and the voices silenced by the mainstream. My kink recognizes all who came before, especially the trans dyke activists that elevated queer rights and freedoms first.

I know very little about many things at the end of the day and in that humility, there is always so much to learn and so many branches of myself that need and want to grow outward. I do hope that in this text, it is able to resonate with other queers and not play it as safe when it comes to spelling out the eros and desire and edges I sought after and have found. I hope it makes you, dear reader, feel less alone and more understood. I hope above all this text reminds you that what you want isn't wrong or shameful.

Your desires are gorgeous and valid, and magnificently special.

Loaning Out The Girl

D/s, dirty talk, being consensually loaned out, strap on, bruising, spanking

O*wner:*

I was anxious about this conversation but I'd spent the weekend meditating on it and felt secure in my decision. She knew she could say no to me anytime or refuse me. The trust we had built over the years spoke to this, and the fact that she almost never did deny me anymore. I knew her limits well, where her boundaries lay and where I could push them to the edge of her reds.

This would be new for both of us. We'd done a lot over the years in the small community of kink family we'd grown and bloomed with together, but I hadn't loaned her out. Yet. I had some amazing Dominants as friends and that wasn't the issue. I'd contemplated this before; entrusting her with one of them for a day or a weekend but I hadn't ever relinquished that control.

She played with other bottoms well, but I hadn't let another top touch her yet. We'd discussed it a lot over the last year and we were both equally intrigued on where such an experiment would go, what it would feel like before, during and after, who we knew that would be willing to gift that to, but also who she desired in that way. She was still shy about that, thinking admitting her crushes would make me feel less for her when in truth, it made me so fucking aroused.

I liked the idea of her surrendering to a confidant, opening to them and days later having a conversation about her in front of them, a verbal report of how she'd done. I liked the idea of a foreplay meeting with whomever doing the same, negotiating her limits with them while she sat in my lap and I massaged her hair and shoulders, letting them take her body in and inspect her after.

I liked imagining her missing me inside her but also needing someone else to fill that space in the meantime. I liked thinking of her having to be open and vulnerable to another force of power that was both novel and foreign to her. She was so used to me, my ways, my responses and the fixated read we had on one another was so acute. I wanted to challenge her with her own vulnerability too, see how far she could fly if I pushed her.

It was between one of two people for me and I allowed her to choose that night as I called her over to the couch. Her head was in my lap looking up at me and she was in her collar and nothing else. I was playing with her hair tenderly and grazing her nipples and breasts with my hands, mixing softness and squeezes and making her wet. She looked so beautiful tonight, luminous in the mild light of the room and her expression had that peace to it that displayed itself potently whenever she was close to me like this.

"I am going to be doing some traveling."

I stated it bluntly and noticed concern in her eyes immediately.

"You are? Am I coming too?"

"No. Not this time. I've had a death in my family and there are things I need to attend to back east, four days give or take. I've mentioned how they are to you before and rather than subject both of us to their ways and conservatism, I'd rather just go and handle it and come back to you. I don't want the muddle of that and the stress of it on us or our dynamic. I don't want to disrupt anymore of my world I've built over here safely for myself. Does that make sense?"

"It does. I wish I could be there for you more and soothe you though, but if you feel like that's the best way for you to get through this, I support it."

Her responses were always dignified and clear. She made it easy to sort things out and never added labor to my shoulders in moments when I felt I was carrying a lot. The first part had gone well. Now for the kicker.

"I don't want to leave you by yourself here. I have been considering other options and I'd like to propose one to you."

Her body turned to its side and her head was facing my stomach a little protectively now. Her slender fingers played with my belt loop and then started gripping the hem of my jeans a bit. Her knees rose closer to her chest and she looked smaller than usual. She was smart enough to know what was coming, stayed quiet and let me continue.

"I've talked to two friends, both of whom you know very well. Both have seen me top and play with you. The two of them have both spent time with us outside of kink. I know there's a comfort level there with you and these two people and I'd like for you to decide who you want to stay with those four days. We can negotiate tonight about barriers and concerns we may have, fail-safes and a check-in schedule that suits us both to feel connected while I'm away.

I feel like it's time to try this on my end, we've discussed and danced around it for some time now, I feel you're ready. I feel we have the trust and closeness and I also deeply trust either of these friends with you, body and mind. I'd also like to say, if your gut reaction on this is just a solid no, that is completely alright and you can just stay here solo and we don't have to explore it in this moment.

I've given this deep thought and I wanted to bring it to you tonight to see how you feel."

She'd stopped fidgeting and was now holding my hand sweetly and had her other arm around my waist. I let the silence of the room hold us and waited patiently for her to process and respond. My fingers danced along her rounded little shoulders and back, massaging warmth into her skin while she took her time, then spoke.

"Who are the two friends?"

"Sir M or Sir J."

I knew she adored both of them but also knew she felt more desire for Sir M by how she behaved around them. It was obvious to me but I knew she had a deep comfort with both, and their play styles aligned with hers as well as their sadism and emotional intellect.

"Sir M and you spoke, and they expressed interest?"

"Yes. A very deep interest. I trust them completely."

Her cheeks flushed a little at that last statement and her hand squeezed mine a little.

"What terms are you thinking you'd want?"

I inhaled deeply and continued massaging her. So far it wasn't a no, especially if she was asking about terms. She was at least interested and even more so, considering this.

"We will have a meeting the morning of where I'd hand you off to them in person. We would go over everything together while you are between us on their couch. This is a collective negotiation but also one I want to remind you at any point in those four days, you can at any time, be brought back here by them and end it with zero hard feelings.

They also proposed if you needed to halt anything beyond platonic they'd still be happy to host you and just have your company in itself. As far as what I, your Owner would like, similar to what we do here but with some limits. Full access to you for play but no deep abrasions of your skin or blood play. They have your current checklist and know your limits and what you enjoy. They'd be allowed to fuck your mouth and your pussy only. I would be alright with you sleeping in their bed overnight, showering together, kissing, being close and tender.

I know you will miss the intimacy of us and the closeness. I trust them so immensely and I've witnessed how they've cared for their own in the past and we share so many of the same ethics and morals so I know deeply you'd be safe and kept well. I leave in three days time and I've taken the week off so you and I have time to discuss this more at length before Wednesday, when we'd have our meeting and I'd leave early morning Thursday to Sunday ... please tell me how you're feeling right now. Don't hold back, I need to know."

She turned back over to sit up and leaned against my shoulder, nuzzling in closer to my face. There was a slight cling to her energy since hearing this and it was understandable. I was all she'd known for so long now and we hadn't spent a lot of time apart. I could feel her in that small space from knowing I'd be absent that way for the first time and already missing me and a little emotional about things. I was too.

"I'm a little shocked but not in a bad way. I'm surprised you did this much legwork so far ahead but I know how thorough you are, especially when it comes to us. I'm relieved about the two you've chosen and I think you know I desire and connect a little deeper with Sir M, and I'd feel more natural with them overall? I'm concerned about pace and how I'm expected to ease into things with them and physicality. It does give me a lot of peace that you trust them, that they're into the idea of me being with them those ways, and that either way if it's platonic or not, they'd still like my company. That feels soothing and calms me. I also know they look up to you a lot and there'd be respect there and lot of aftercare and just general mindfulness to my needs. Still, I'm nervous about the reality. I'm not worried about disappointing you but I'm maybe more worried about being vulnerable with someone all those ways and hoping I can and it just flows? But I also can't control that. There's a ton here I can't control, but the big things I still can ... so it's making me feel willing to try."

She was in my lap now, facing me with her little knees bent against my thighs and we were kissing slow, in that sacred way where our spirits felt like they were aligned. I squeezed her close in my arms and she sighed, moaned and melted into me and gripped my face in that girlish way caressing the light stubble on my chin.

***

Sir M:

I wouldn't admit this to many, but I was actually a little thrown when the door shut and it was just me and her, alone in here. We had the next four days just for us, and she looked more beautiful than usual. She'd dressed for the occasion, as I requested. She was in a shorter dress that hugged her curves in all the right places, a softer red lipstick on that pout of hers I was always distracted by. Her nails were manicured in a glossy shade of black. Her hair looked so soft and framed her face in shorter waves I couldn't wait to pull with my fists. A waft of her scent hit me when the air from the door closing whooshed between us, and I almost felt like rolling my eyes back.

She was fidgeting a lot while both of us took in the silence between us, that moment before all the other moments. I could tell she didn't know what to do with her hands, or her gaze. She was playing with the handle of her roll-away suitcase and she was looking everywhere but directly at me. It was different, to be gifted power over someone I hadn't really earned or worked for. While I knew her and her Owner for years, and we'd spent a great deal of time around each other, it wasn't anything like this. This intimacy in the air felt weighted, sacred, and deeply vulnerable for both of us.

I hadn't planned for anything other than to just continually respond to her energy while she was here. I enjoyed the hyper focus part of power-exchange most, tuning in to where to take her and keep checking in attentively while she let go. I already felt myself inwardly trying to scale back desire. The wall behind her was perfect to slam her lightly into, push my weight into her and wrap her neck in my hand.

She wasn't ready for that yet. It was amusing in a way, I hadn't seen her skittish like this or flustered to this degree. Her cheeks were flush and I noticed her breasts rising and falling. My penetrative stares that didn't let up were making that a bit more real.

I stepped toward her slowly and felt her body respond, backing up a foot or so until she was against the wall. I moved close enough but left a few inches between her chest and mine, not touching her yet. I reached down and caressed her hand, still anxiously squeezing the handle of her bag. I lowered the tone of my voice,

"Can I take this to the bedroom for you?"

Smiling softly back at me, she nodded, still uncertain of how and when I was going to make the first move, and wondering when my aggression would reveal itself.

"Is that a yes?"

"Yes. I'd ... like that. Thank you."

"Thank you ... ?"

"*Sir*. Thank you, Sir. Yes."

I leaned closer and kissed her cheek tenderly, feeling the heat between us heady and high, whispered in her ear,

"Very good girl. Follow me."

A large part of me wanted to keep her on edge until we went to bed tonight, take the time to learn her skin and her body and the ways she loved and needed to be touched, then denied. Another part of me just wanted to shock her into her submission, abruptly putting her on her knees so she couldn't overthink and she was just where I put her, below me and ready to take what I decided to give.

Then of course, we got to my bedroom and she saw the equipment I had, my open toy closet and implements, cuffs hanging at the ready around the canopy frame. I'd even placed her favorite kind of dark chocolates on her side table and laid out a new robe on her side of the bed. This was special and I wanted her to feel that I understood that, before I even touched her.

She paused to take it all in, scanning the details. There's something about having a girl in your bedroom for the first time, being perceived and watching her eye the furniture and tools I had. She leaned against the width of my dresser and the backless part of her dress reflected back to me in the mirror behind her body. I imagined where I'd leave my teeth-marks, bruises that would get her whimpering. I was so fucking hard, having her in here. I also knew she wasn't wearing panties.

I left her bag in the corner and sat on the padded bench at the foot of my bed in front of her.

"Do you like what you see?"

She was twirling her fingers in her hair, looking back at my eyes finally, a little unsteady but trying to connect. I kept my voice soft for her, my body language open and smiled back with my eyes, conveying she was safe.

"I do ... Sir."

"Tell me what you're feeling, let's not pretend this isn't new. Come here. Sit on my lap and tell me."

I saw some relief ease her shoulders down and her posture relax, she started to slip her heels off, and then raised her brows to me, seeking permission. I nodded and watched her come to me, sitting down gently on my lap.

I rested my hand on her thigh and held her back with my other and just took her in. She was shy about being studied, being noticed acutely, especially knowing she couldn't hide. She was here now, and she was mine, and we both knew it and I was finally touching her. The need in her was obvious, that acquiescence against my hands sunk hard and fast and her hands started exploring me some too. They found my hair first, tangled her fingers in it the way I loved and watched me close my eyes allowing her to explore. She touched the outline of my shoulders, spread the collar of my shirt and went beneath the fabric, skin on my skin. My hand found the back of her neck and pulled her in, fizzing to taste her and she gave in, took my tongue like it was a second pair of lungs. She elicited a soft moan when I broke away and still had her lip in my teeth.

Sweetly, she wrapped her hands around my neck and let me pull her in deeper, my palms scraping the fabric of her dress against her hips and ribs and squeezing her tits. I slid up and took her neck with strength, giving her that structure her spine needed. I squeezed, testing how hard I could be with her, watched her lips tremble. I fed her two fingers tenderly, slowly. Her mouth was small, I couldn't wait to stretch it with my cock. Our kissing went from sweet and deep to ravenous and brutal, my strength bullying her, molding her and pulling her fully into my lap, pushing her to grind against me thick and low.

I could feel how bad she'd been wanting this, hoped she could feel my hunger too. Something about her sweetness right now mixed with the things I'd seen her do, the ways I'd seen her open and stretched and fucked and obedient to her Owner woke an animal in me.

Her body and sounds and taste were even more delicious than I could have dreamed, and I felt that yearning she'd been carrying for me, exhaling, being met with fervor. I kept talking to her through it all, close and deep staying in her head as much as I wanted to be in her body.

"You've been wanting this, haven't you, sweet girl? I know. I already know how wet you are. You need to get fucked, don't you? Mmhm, I wore my best cock for you tonight. It's going to hurt so good. Put your hand on it ... there you go. I'm going to spread you so good, so wide, make you come 'til you're sore and aching, wake you up in the dark and slide back inside because you're mine tonight, aren't you? Say it. Say it back to me like a good little girl."

"I'm yours tonight. Yours."

She was breathless while I picked her up by her cute little ass and laid us on the bed side by side. My legs wrapped around hers and she was grinding against my thigh and I pushed back. Her little moans were erratic and she was shivering when my teeth got to her collarbone and clamped down. I wanted my marks all over her, wanted her to keep her hands behind her back so I could feel her just taking it, just letting me use her.

Her dress was scrunched up past her tummy at that point and my palms started warming up her ass with some light spanks. When I ramped up my rhythm, she shrunk into my neck, needing that closeness with the pain. Even though we were both grazing the edges of touch and intimacy and sex, I could feel in my chest how much we both had behind our desire. It felt like an ocean with each wave higher than the last. The more I tried to take the more she lowered herself to give it over.

I took breaks and squeezed and gripped and slapped her thighs, mixing that with soft caresses, deep encapsulating kisses. I was touching her everywhere but her pussy. I slid her dress up so it was across her eyes like a blindfold of sorts, holding her arms above her head together. My teeth went for her tits, my tongue against her nipples like I was starving to taste them.

Her back bent like she was a willing sacrifice, like she wanted to disappear beneath the vapor of my hunger. That's when she started begging, pleading really for me to touch her, to fuck her, squeezing her own hands and trying to buck into my whispered touches of her upper thighs. She was so wet for me, so lost between tensing and releasing while I threw her back and forth with my voice and touch.

"Such a needy little thing, aren't you? I like it when you beg. It makes my dick hard. Keep going. Maybe I'll give in. Shhh. I know. You need it right there. I'm gonna fill you so good tonight. Maybe I'll just keep you tied to my headboard until your Owner comes back Sunday. Watch them fuck the mess I make of you make of this submissive little body and holes. Yeah, I know you want that too. Greedy little toy."

She was whimpering so hard now, and little bruises from my mouth and jaw were already popping up all over her chest and her neck, her shoulders that kept trying to get closer to mine. I slid the rest of her dress off over her head and brushed her hair away from her face, took her hand and unzipped my jeans and slid it inside my boxers, tight and letting her feel the swell and throb of my cock. She started stroking it as much as she could between the fabric, scraping her little wrist on the zipper.

My neck lobbed back from the pleasure of it, from the hunger to slide inside her deep and pound her through her orgasms, not giving her a break in between.

I knelt over both of us and slid my jeans past my knees, feeling the thick fabric bunched below my calves awkwardly. I took her ankles and pulled them so they rested on my shoulders and she was trembling, clinging to both sides of my pillow and looking up at me with lidded eyes as I stroked myself over her. I slid my fingers along the warm slit of pussy and put two inside, feeling her clench around me. She was tight, so I fingered her deep and slow until I could put three inside her. Her ass was rising off the bed and her mouth was dry from begging and breathing in gasps, her brow furrowed in frustration and her little fists tried to pull me into her by my ass, to no avail.

I slicked my cock with the honey of her cunt and let her feel the head of me pushing into her; slow, but firm. I watched her face squint as I pushed her open, deep and long and certain. Before long, I was slamming into her hard, kissing and sucking on the places I'd left her bruised. Her lips were swollen from my teeth and we both came in violent waves, wrapped up in the salt and water of our bodies.

I pulled out much later and crawled down her quivering body, exhausted but needing the taste of us running down my throat like nectar. My tongue dove inside her and sucked tenderly on the bud of her clit. She held onto the storm of me and I was lost, while she spun round and round in my riptide.

Yours Before I Knew You

edging, daddy/girl, crying, choking, dominance & submission

I felt like I was yours before I knew you. I used to look at your pictures and stare at your hands in them, imagine what they could do to me, how they could decimate and worship, turn me into a symphony or a scream.

Before this I was shaking inside. Before this, the ache in me had roots, until tonight. Tonight your eyes found my body in the dark of your room and your voice ran down my neck like a winding river that made my spine sway.

Now we are in church, and you're spreading my thighs like a book of prayers. You're tasting me like communion and the warmth in me is falling down you like rain, like soft sheets of secrets I keep inside until you pull them from me.

It is Sunday and the light coming in your window makes me squint, dances on your shoulders in stripes and my fingers are combing through your hair with love.

I look down and see your hips rise with need while you're spilling sonnets over my clit with your dandelion tongue. I catch a glimpse of your cock between your legs and my mouth waters. I suck on my own fingers wishing I could have every piece of you at once.

I moan rampantly while you edge me, while you're unraveling the knots inside my body, while the pressure is building and starved to surge. Just give me the word. The command. Your words drive me.

My calves caress the sheets impatiently when that crest peaks and my nails scrape your shoulders in frustration. I want to mark you, too. I want you to leave the steam of your shower tomorrow and remember how I burned for you, how I tried to be good, to be the girl you deserve.

I want to be your waterfall. My clit kisses the ocean of your mouth while I wrap my legs around you like a riptide. A stutter moans out of my throat, matching the tremors my thighs rattle in your warm palms. Your grip is brutal right now, commanding a stillness I never seem to have against you.

This is how tides dance. This is the pearl of me blooming beneath your tongue. This is all the shades of crimson rising to the flush in my cheeks. I want to bleed just for you.

I beg you between cries to stop, to keep going, to let the rise in me fall while I half run, half plummet into you. The amount I'm fighting myself makes your cock throb; the goodness in me comes alive below you. I am the sacrifice.

Your tongue slows, leaves the rabid pulse you made, leaving me shaking. My whimpers fall in salt down the corner of my eyes. You swell and the pierce of your gaze halts my breath as you stare up, turn me to stone.

"Come for Daddy."

The second my favorite word leaves your lips, I let go and the fever of you fills itself, carries the waves with the weight of your murmurs. Your shoulders heave and revel in the mess you made of me. Your voice in the air is my sunrise.

The warmth of your breath is still cooler than the swollen mess of my cunt. The slow rake of your tongue, the way your hands grip as much of my ass as you can hold while I rise off the bed, this is the way we dance, decadence blanketing itself.

You elicit a growl as I pull you over me needing your weight, needing the strength of you to pin me when I'm small. Your chest on mine rises in gusts and I suck on your lips while my own chatter, those wavered blips of pleasure-exhaustion beating back into you.

Your cock is thick between us now, while your hand is around my neck. The volume coming off you is all bass, all beat and thrum rooted in your hips waiting for a flare to fire. I am sweetly quiet in a state of satiated hunger, breathing deep before the hurricane comes.

Your eyes tell me you're nowhere near done. I moan into your mouth like I'm yours more than anyone else's, like the emptiness in my holes hurt when you're not there, buried.

I smirk against your mouth as my legs open wide and you feed me your fingers, watch me suck the storm of my taste away gratefully.

This is how we dance. And fuck, do we dance so well.

The Girl & The Diner

D/s, exhibition, fear play, edging, vibrator

I'd go out sometimes like this. I loved the walk around the corner and up the block to our favorite diner that served breakfast all day and was open twenty-four hours. Sometimes we'd come here at 4 a.m., after a night of voracious fucking and play, the sweat still on the back of our necks. I loved watching her smile gingerly, wincing when she'd ease herself into the booth with the purple I just painted her ass with, look at the waitress innocently with those big eyes and then back at me while I stared at her, knowing. Sometimes she'd stutter through her order, so I'd order for us, get her more bothered with that tone of control in my voice, knowing she could take more; she always did, from me.

We met her for the first time about a year ago. She was in that red sundress that fell just above her knees like I'd asked her to wear, already obedient, a little shy about it being perceived as she sat down and smoothed out the fabric on her lap. She was flustered, fidgety, tits reflecting her quickened breathing and that tinge of pink on her cheeks as she fumbled with the laminated menu. Her eyes kept ping-ponging from mine to the table, the sugar to mine, the menu and back at me.

I smiled warmly, sensing it might help, and leaned back with one arm extending out on my side of the booth, opening my body to her. That calmed her some. Her gaze started to rest in mine more steadily, her voice a little less shaky, making me think of how she'd react if I eased my cock into her all at once. She smelled like sweet fruit, peaches, maybe apricots? Her hands were slender and I assessed they would look small against mine, on my chest, holding my shoulders.

We didn't fuck until the second date, even though I knew by the end of the first she wanted to. I'd walked her to her car parked down a side-alley, not far away. It was dark out by then, well past it and like a gentleman, I'd hooked her arm around mine protectively. I listened to the sound of my boots and her heels on the sidewalk, pleased at the rhythm of us together, already dancing.

We had that awkward moment where it was clear we wanted to kiss and I'd gotten close enough to her face the more we drew out our goodnight. She was doing that obvious thing where she was staring at my lips, a wicked gleam in her eyes I could still see in the dark under the streetlight. I moved into her until she was backed up and her shoulders were pressed against the driver-seat window.

I gripped her waist possessively and heard her inhale, and as that little gasp opened her mouth, I slid between her lips, tasted her deep. She had to stand on her toes slightly to reach me, that felt good, made me swell even taller. I pinned her hips with mine keeping her in place, tangling my fingers in her hair and gripping her neck, controlling her to move into and against me. It made my cock hard, that kiss. I know it made her wet. When we came up for air she was hazy, lost, her little hands squeezing the fabric of the hem of my shirt sweetly, the smallness in her coming out already.

I murmured a low growl against her neck followed by a soft laugh and she started massaging my head, playing with my hair, tugging a little. My fist tapped on the roof in mild frustration and I bit down, moved my hand to her throat, still an inch of space between my skin and hers. She whimpered before I finished getting to her, and that anticipation and slight fear made my hips jerk forward unconsciously. I let myself grip her neck, gently, staring at her intently, putting my forehead to hers and feeling her lean her spine toward me in my quiet patience. I squeezed a little and her hand came to my wrist, pushing it forward. This little girl.

I bit her lip and pulled my hand away slowly then, overshadowing her sense of control she was sure she had. She actually pouted at me after that, grunting a little. I kept my forehead to hers still, and between us, whispered, "I want you wet and wanting. I want you starved for it until next time. You're such a good girl, I know you want to be good, don't you, sweet thing."

She bounced a little up at me at that last phrase, nodded against my shoulder and we kissed again, tender and full of longing. I could still see her fumbling with her keys and driving away, knowing we had a vast landscape in front of us to explore.

Tonight, back at the diner, I was alone. It was around 7 p.m. on a Tuesday so it was fairly dead in here. A few others were scattered around, in-betweeners early for a date or wrapped up on their laptop finishing up here before heading home. Still, it was quiet, and me wearing my wireless earbuds was normal, so was staring at my phone absentmindedly in the corner booth that sheltered my back above my head. I ordered tea and pretended to be interested in the menu, feigning needing more time.

The waitress was cute tonight, tight ass and those curved calves I love with that sweet musculature that always felt good in my strong hands. I was still hard, aching really.

I stared back at my phone, opening to the camera in the corner of the room I'd left her in the center of, cuffed to my cross by her ankles and wrists, her cunt buzzing lightly with the curved vibrator I'd left on the lowest setting. It was enough to her annoy her and do almost nothing, and I'd set the rhythm to sporadic, a mix of beats and lines she wouldn't be able to follow. Her brow was a little furrowed and she was wriggling around a bit dramatically. My tea came and I sipped it deep, spilling a little on the saucer and handing the waitress my menu, ordering a club sandwich and fries.

I could hear her very clearly and caught her saying, "Seriously, fuck you." Which incited the sadist in me even more.

I turned it on high and steady, and she yelped and I saw her little tummy start to shake some. I'd warned her strictly before leaving if she came there would be deep consequences that would have longer ripples in our play than she was probably not prepared to face.

This current predicament she was in, was already a consequence of her arriving fifteen minutes late tonight, blaming traffic and setting her purse down on the floor with an attitude expecting me not to be as decisive as I was.

I'd made her crawl to the bedroom, got her naked and warmed up and writhing for me to fuck her, taunting her grinding my cock against her thighs, her ass, teeth all over her skin and my palm cupping her cunt feeling it grow warm and starved with need.

Then I stopped, cuffed her hands and wrapped my belt around her neck and half kicked, half led her down the hall to the cross until I put her against it a bit roughly. I heard the wind knock itself from her lungs, and I so heavily wanted to put my mouth on her right then, fuck her and edge her until she was crying, but this seemed more fun.

I stepped away from her and her look professed a mix of shock, slight concern and deep frustration. I stroked my cock and let her watch, told her I didn't want to hear a word from her dirty little mouth, reminded her this is what happens to girls who misbehave, who don't listen, who make excuses I don't give a fuck about.

Once my tone changed, it always shut her up. She was a lot of bark until the primal in me came out and then she would shrink, hard and fast and solemn. This was the game between us. The best punishments with her were always like this too; she shrunk from the distance, the loss of my tenderness, the rise of my stoicism and being left alone without me, her head and worried thoughts the only things to keep her company.

I got on my knees then and caressed her legs, reached behind her ankle and fished for the pink curved vibrator I later slid inside her like a glove.

Her cunt was so wet already. It wasn't going to take long before she came. She'd have to try really fucking hard not to tonight.

I stood up and grabbed my cell, turning on the app and she watched me, fearful and noticing I still hadn't turned the light on, noticing I'd slipped my cock off and my shorts were back on my hips. I wasn't staying. Her breathing resonated with this and she started whimpering a little as I turned the vibrator on high, making her jolt.

I turned it off unceremoniously after.

"This isn't for your enjoyment tonight. This is what happens when girls show up late with a shitty fucking attitude. You can't actually believe I was going to reward you with a good fuck? You'll be lucky tonight if I don't leave you here until you're crying about it."

She knew I'd probably never do that, but I let my rage rise high enough that I felt her uncertainty. My fists were balled and I was pacing around her heavily and sort of heaving. I noticed her lower lip tremble a little and could see the tension in her body building, aware she might be here for a longer haul. She swallowed deep.

"You are not allowed to come. I'm leaving. I'll be back … at some point tonight. The camera is on and I will be listening. I will know if you come. And whenever I get back, you better pray hard you don't. Goodnight."

As I closed the door harder than I needed to, she was moaning as loud as she could, thinking it would earn her some sort of atonement or mercy. She'd never learn that way. And I'd never enjoy it half as much. It was better like this, and much more fun.

Back at the diner, my plate had emptied a bit ago, and she was now shivering to come. It was more than clear she was now suffering, begging, apologizing, tugging on her restraints loudly, pleading to come, sniffling at that brink of tears trying to be tougher than I knew she was.

I could feel her pure effort for me, the trying and fear that I'd built the wall too high before she could climb it. Her hips were wriggling almost as if that would get her away from the vibrations I was joyfully edging her with hard now, and the grin I must have had painted on me made the waitress reflect it back at me amused while collecting my second cup of tea and bringing me the bill.

My fingers still smelled like her pussy when I fed myself the last fry and something in me gave in. I left a twenty dollar bill on the table and shimmied myself out of the booth giving the waitress a nod goodbye.

I walked brusquely up my steps and opened my front door quietly to her soft little cries, a little pathetic and a little lonely and sorrowful. She hadn't even heard me come in the apartment she was making such a fuss. I slowly turned the vibrator down on my phone until it was off, easing her down all those levels, and slammed the front door shut again so she could hear me definitively announce my presence.

She let out a guttural cry then that ended in a half sob that trailed into shaky and needy. "Sir!?"

Before she could see through her tears my body was against her kissing the salt from her cheeks and uncuffing her sore little wrists. She fell against me limply in a puddle, still crying with her arms tangled around my neck. I carried her like that the few feet to the bedroom and kissed her until she was slightly calm again. I rubbed her soaked little pussy tenderly pulling out the toy.

She was swollen and writhing and gripping my skin trying to kiss me back in her exhaustion to show me she was sorry. I put her hand between my legs so she could feel my cock there again, and at the end of one of her gasps she whispered a throat-cracking "please" so dimly it almost made me laugh.

"You were so good, baby. I know. You did so good. You won't be late like that again, will you?"

She nodded against my chest as I played with her soft hair.

"Good girl. You can have it all tonight … all your come, just for me. Always."

The Pulp Of A Peach

daddy/girl, riding crop, knife play, oral sex

"**Y**ou're going to regret that later, girl."

A ding on my cell followed by a text on my screen with their name made my head sense something. I looked peripherally and was met with a penetrating stare from across the backyard. They were standing there under the sun at the annual barbecue of a close friend's, holding court with some butch buddies of theirs. The sun made their dimples even more prominent, the slight red in their auburn hair was luminous today.

Between us, there was a crowd of exuberant chatter from a mix of strangers and loved ones we hadn't seen in ages, all wearing neon swimwear and smelling like sunblock and sweat. Everyone had their mid-July tans, reflecting through the light of the willow trees that hung lazily over the yard. The border of the fence was littered with tables of sangria in glass jars, dripping dew on confetti-patterned tablecloths. The smell of charcoal and meat and watermelon wafted through the air.

We'd left late, hurried and frantic from fucking too long and losing track of time. The flush in my cheeks mimicked a mild sunburn but it was really from your glorious mouth between my thighs, your talented tongue, your hunger that never seemed to fill for me.

Still, I managed to find one of my cuter new outfits in a rush, as I'd tossed a yellow sundress on, sandals that matched, and sunglasses that still had the tag on that needed your knife to cut through. It was the one you kept on your belt at all times, clipped and ready for any scenario, like my skin in an alleyway.

Just before we left the car, I kissed you deep and casually mentioned I'd forgotten to wear panties. Then I slammed the door before you could react, rushed ahead of you to greet the hosts with brownies I'd made yesterday. I didn't look back, didn't notice that glimmer of menace in your eyes growing slow.

In the yard now, I set my cell back into the pocket of my sundress and caught your smirk. Even though both of us were wearing shades, I knew what your eyes looked like. You met the flash of my smile and sipped on the IPA you were nursing. You ran your other hand through your short hair, the way I liked to tug on it in the dark.

The conversation I was in was still flowing and I leaned down and pulled my dress more than halfway up my thigh, pretending to itch a non-existent mosquito bite. I gave you my eyes through the top of my sunglasses and knew it would remind you of the way I looked when I was on my knees for you.

We loved this game, the lock and key of the animals inside us pretending they didn't want to run wild in public, the wordless exchanges that rose between us to hide in plain sight in whatever crowd we found ourselves in. I saw you watching me and took my phone out, pretended to text in deep concentration and I bit my lip. The cherry earrings I had on were swaying the same way my ass did when I tried to run from your crop earlier. My skin was still on fire from you. I was already having deep regrets wearing the yellow dress I'd chosen; the harsh sun was going straight through it to burn the streaks on my ass that were swollen and still growing dark.

When I put my cell away, you immediately went for yours in your back pocket and stared into the screen, waiting for something I'd never sent. You looked back at me and crossed your arms, jawline tightening like the strain in your jeans. I blew you a kiss, bold now but knowing I'd pay for teasing you later. Hard.

My best friend grabbed my hand then, led me toward you smiling.

"That sun is really starting to get your shoulders, hon, and your cheeks. Let's get you over here where your cutie is, in the shade."

Before I knew it, I was beside you again and the air between us smelled like your cologne, my peach hand-lotion and the wilting lemons floating in what was left of my sangria. You took my hand by the wrist and nodded at my best friend, thanking her silently. You moved us so our backs were against the high fence and discretely ran your hand over my ass and squeezed right where you'd marked me the hardest. Knowing I'd probably yelp, you leaned in to kiss me and swallow it. You murmured a primal "Mmm" from your throat to mine. Satisfied at the tone you were resetting, you squeezed me even harder just before breaking our lips apart.

You looked around briefly to ensure no one was within earshot, then tilted your sunglasses down enough so I could see the dilation of your pupils, pulsing at me like a threat. Subconsciously, I backed away from the energy of you and felt my back hit the fence. I shrunk down against your changed presence, as if I'd never felt tall before. You sucked on the edge of my ear and broke away before I shivered against your palm at the bottom of my back. Your whisper broke our silence,

"I can't wait until we're back home and I have you to myself. We'll see how bold you feel then, when you're bent over every surface and you're regretting being a brat. The only thing that pretty little mouth will be full of tonight is me, and the words you're going to have to find when you beg me to stop."

Touch Yourself, Daddy Wants To Watch

biting, blood, bruises, cigar play, crying, daddy/girl, masturbation, oral sex, orgasm control, primal, strap on

Watch me while you touch yourself, while I sit at the end of the bed, in my chair. Watch me while my boots rest on the cedar chest, the one I keep the more menacing toys in. Prop your head up, look at me. Don't break your gaze. Good girl. Make my hunger root itself here, in the candlelight of the room while the rhythm of our ceiling fan above your skin mixes with your small little sounds. Look up at me, girl, while the cream of your body melts from my stare.

***

I stretch my arms over my head and fold them at the back of my scalp. I lean back, take in the display, touch what's growing beneath my jeans. I love the moment when your legs spread, wide for Daddy, pink, swollen. I love the climb of your desire where you squeeze your little hand like a vice, because it is starting to be too much. You are not allowed to come, not until I say so, not until it's permitted. You are not allowed to stop, either, or beg, tonight. I want to bring you that point where the crest of you needs to fall like avalanche. I want you in that sweet spot where you can barely graze the bud of your clit, and you suffer for me. I love watching you try, just for me. Just for Daddy.

I want the touch to hurt, so I can see it on your skin like rapture and tears. I get up from my chair and saunter over to your side of the bed, unable to be a passive viewer any longer. I take my cock out and stroke it, front row seat to your destruction. Your little mouth is parched from the staccato of your breathing, and your glistening cunt is soaked. I stand above you, demand your unbroken gaze, command you to go faster, do it harder and before I finish, as that little whimper in your eyes tries to break me. You stare at my cock like you've never seen it before, like tasting it could give you life. I know, girl. Daddy knows.

You hurt so good for me. You are so fragile on the edge of your want, to the point I know if I kiss you or add teeth, lips, fingers, you'd lose this game. I can see how hard it is, to hold it in, to act like breathing is easy. I can feel you pretending that the air over the heat of you and the murmur of my filthy voice in your ear, isn't just plain cruel, it's menacing.

It is, but if you lose this, there is something far worse waiting for you. My punishments have been more brutal lately; the last time is still resting in scattered shades of purple on your ass and inner thighs. You are tender tonight and tearful, thinner in your resolve. I can tell it hurts, see it. I notice you starting to pull away from yourself like your hips are scared of your own touch.

You stare up between moments to pinch your little eyelids shut, try to beg me with your big brown eyes in silence. I pull my chair up to your side of the bed and I light a cigar casually. I blow smoke over your soaked fingers, adding more fever to your cunt. The way I watch you is aggressive, unbending, spectating with intent to harm. At points, you have trouble holding my gaze. You shrink every now and then and try to come back strong, when you notice your own shrinking.

I smirk and squint at you, wafting wisps of smoke close to your mouth so you can taste the bourbon on my breath, the heady tobacco. The curls of it meet your eyes and burn, waterlog your vulnerability even more. It is taking deep focus for you to stay open, stay present, not stop your hand from meeting your sensitive little clit. Circles are your nemesis now, and the muscles in your tummy shiver when I let the condensation from the ice in my glass drip down onto you. I gang bang you with sensation, while the volume of your whimpers rise as high as the heat of your cunt.

I set my glass down and make use of my fingers, now cold and damp. I take your wrist and place your arm to your side, climb on the bed next to you, just one knee, still half standing. I put your little hand around my cock, command you to stroke it while you edge yourself more. I lean down into the softness of your lips and kiss you deep. Your lips shake against my mouth and it makes me growl.

Your need is coming off of you in pulses. Your breathing is erratic through the kiss and elicits something guttural as I touch where you just were. You are soaked in your suffering as I place my palm face down on your cunt, push heavy and feel the button of your clit meet me. Your hunger feels violent, the pain in your eyes desperately tender. There is disbelief in your gaze when I go inside and your eyes roll back in a praised exhale. Your sweet spine leaves the sheets. Every tendril of your nerves rush up into me.

I know right now it's taking everything you have to obey, to keep the promise between us. Your racing thoughts are heady, and at the edge, looking over. Your neck rises up to devour my mouth as I add a third finger, swirl my thumb against the bud of you and pull away rapidly.

"Come."

Immediately, you burst open like the sun. Light pours from all your cracks and your arms and legs pull me from my stance straight on top of you. You squeeze me hard so I can feel the quaking of your swollen walls, in the thicket of your pleasure with you. I feel every piece of you let go of what you were white-knuckling. I kiss and bite your shoulders and neck like an animal both making wounds and then licking the same spots I made bleed. Adding the pain of my teeth to your delicate reality makes you release again. And again.

Your limbs pull me all the way down as they cling to me desperately. The sweetness of that makes my cock twitch, that need of yours is still growing when you are broken and shattered, when you are syrupy and weak but still find that power to hold onto me, tight as a vice.

Your little mewls and moans push me too hard and I take my cock out and slide my sticky fingers along it. I stare down at your eyes still pinched closed in pleasure and graze the head of it along the wetness of you, clit to hole. I like taking it and setting the length of it against you, so you can feel where it will be, know how deep Daddy will go. You shiver and hook your little fingers in my belt loops in an attempt to show you're still starving. You always want it. There's never a moment you're not open to me fully and the reality of that alone is almost enough to make me come. I suck on your lower lip and bite down and your hot little gasp rises as I slide every inch in at once. You moan in that guttural way while I invade you, while I take you over and remind you it's my hole, always.

I fuck you until the wet spot below your bruised little ass is as big as your body. I fuck you while I come endlessly from the thrill of you squeezing my cock and how it shoots straight to my cunt. We are connected by flesh and wetness and sucking each others sighs, feeding and full and the pinkness of you rising up my swollen chest.

We are here and we are always, and the way your cheekbone fits against my palm feels like a decision the universe made before we were breathing.

Hold On: Lover Letter #1

primal, fucking

I love the ritual, the rug burn on my knees from the pull of your walk, leading me to the room where your toys hang on the wall. I want you to hang me from the heavens tonight. I want you to grip the Morse code of my thighs against your neck while they scream so loud you climb back up to me and leave sirens in my mouth. I want to ride you until dawn, run down you like a river while my hands rush like split currents through your hair.

Hold on.

Hold back.

Hold me down.

We put each other to bed last night and lay there humming with the window cracked open. The night air and that smell of honeysuckle fell asleep on your tongue and my teeth chattered from the stardust in your palm, lingering on my hipbone like a dream.

Does the sky look at us and see a constellation?

Our limbs rest messy, gathered like the pulp of broken cherries being swept up by hunger. I fall asleep to the notes running down my cunt, songs you left inside of me that made me dance and reach for you, songs my hips spelled out in sacrilegious circles when you met my fall with your rise. We come up in the morning the same as the sun, the sweet circles of our sighs still dancing above us like stars until the next time when the lights go out.

Worthy

daddy/girl, boot play, dirty talk, masturbation, mild humiliation, spanking, oral sex, primal

"How do you want to prove your mouth is deserving of my cock?"

Your voice echoed between the wooden floors I'd just cleaned, while the vaulted ceiling resting over both our heads looked like a steeple. All the sacrilegious things in this room that ever happened echoed in vignettes to me, corners where we both learned exactly who we were, what demons we'd exorcise that day.

It was a Sunday afternoon and we were lounging quietly at your desk. Rather, I was laying nude beneath it, staring at your boots planted on the floor. The tread of them had marked me deliciously last night. Still, I wanted more, always did.

You were working on a passion project of some sort. Even though I couldn't see your face, I knew that your concentration wasn't breaking between the beat of what you said, and what you were working on. I loved how your brow always furrowed, how your lips curled like even they could taste the thought you'd just had. You looked the same when you were inside me, the same when you were hunting me.

It was raining and the skylight above us was flecked in hollow circles, similar to the ones your mouth liked leaving on my breasts. The rhythm of the raindrops changed as the storm came closer. I could feel the occasional thunder in my chest, like the bass of your boot tapping, waiting for my answer.

Roses appeared on my cheeks as I contemplated. The pen you'd been using was no longer scratching furiously on your notepad. Again, the silence was interrupted, "I asked you a question and I expect an answer."

The brass wheels in your office chair glided back, far enough so the cavern of space between my nakedness and your legs opened up. You meditated, let out a deep exhale as my limbs used the expanded space to stretch sensually. I turned to my side, staring up at you and holding my cheek in my palm. The curves and lines of me were magnificent in the mix of shadow and light dancing in the fire of your gaze.

You loved this, pivoting the energy of the room, snapping me back to reality with the flick of your words. You liked watching me try to form a worthy response while my mind ran uphill to reach you. The control in you was so steady, so daunting, gloriously tall in its power.

I didn't have the right words today for how I felt about wanting you, for how your stare pieced through all of the layers of my body, or how it shot straight through me to the back of the desk. I was already wet, already hungry. My eyes peered up at you while you took your hand and rubbed the outside of your jeans. Deliberate pressure. Your neck bowed back some and a smirk painted itself across your face. Now I was starving.

You noticed everything; the rise and fall of my chest quickening, the flush that had appeared along my collarbone, my thighs squeezing shut in small tremors. Then there was my hand, now moving down my stomach until it was resting just above my cunt, trepidation to go further, to fly without your permission. I stared back at you like the holes in me could only be filled by you. I stared as my hips began grinding slightly into the air, reaching for any font of "yes" they could find.

You let me be that way, for some time. My body stretched taut, moving in waves, begging up at you through my current of want. I stared at you intently and moaned in small syllables. You stroked yourself over the denim, building your need until your ass left the chair at points. Biting your own lips, your other hand tugged on your hair the way I did when I came for you.

Your voice broke the silence in the room again, "You can touch yourself. Daddy wants to see. Show me how you want it, pretty girl. Show Daddy your secret. "

My eyes slammed shut in a silent prayer of relief. I exhaled something I hadn't realized I was holding while my body shifted. I moved myself so my head was against the back of the desk, opening my legs to give you a show. My arousal glistened in the shadows and the wetness of my clit meeting my fingers sounded obscene. I heard you start to moan while I went inside myself with two fingers. I heard your zipper go down and your cock come out. I craned my neck to see a flash of it and whimpered with need as my ass rose off the ground, going deeper.

That's when you really started talking. Any filter in you had completely gone and left only the arousal behind, governing what was leaving your mouth, dribbling down the floor like marbles that rolled over the heat of me, incendiary, climbing toward a release only you could allow me to have.

Your voice was husky and primal, sentences matching the rhythm of your strokes, "Do you think you deserve to come? When you haven't done a thing to earn it, girl. When you haven't even let me use that dirty little mouth my way, wrap it around my cock. Until I say stop. Until your jaw is sore. Until your greedy little body begs for it in your other holes. Does it feel empty with just those two fingers? So much smaller than Daddy. You need something bigger. Something you'll remember tomorrow and the day after. Something that hurts so good, don't you, girl? It's okay to tell Daddy your secret."

I was on the verge now, shaking and touching myself in the lightest of grazes, your words and thoughts and change in your tone driving me there faster. I was already close. Easy. For you. Your energy was a hurricane that bent me in half. You saw it, too, that point where I'd lose this game if I kept going, those muscles in my calves shaking and my hips rising off the floor, even more than their contact with the ground.

The rain was pouring now, mimicking the storm in the room. Lightning flashed and lit you up in your chair, your eyes pools of charcoal and the muscles in your forearms tightly wound. You gripped the chair as your cock stood there, thick and perfect. You spoke again, in that thick whisper that made me weak,

"Come here."

I pulled out of my body and cried aloud at the loss. I crawled to you on all fours slowly, watching you roll away until you were on the other side of the room, making me work to reach you, which drove me as crazy as it did you. By the time I was knelt at your feet, your fist found my hair, and you pulled me up further to meet your mouth. There was a viciousness in your kiss, your tongue giving mine no chance to dance with you, sweeping me up so my neck craned. My scalp burned from your grip.

I moaned against your lips and the sound of my pleasure fed yours, fed the animal in you. Your hands found my ass and started squeezing, slapping me while your tongue danced with mine. I was in your lap now, grinding on your cock desperately waiting for you to let me have it, warm and wet and shaking against you. My small hands tangled around your neck sweetly, my eyes were pinched shut and you watched me unravel.

My ass was pink now, starting to welt and fill with heat below your sore palms. I was in that delicate place between need and retreat, carnal fervor and melting confidence. You could feel me shrinking against your harsh touch, feel me holding on a little harder, whimpering a little louder, grinding my clit to try and find that balance of pleasure.

Your hands stopped abruptly, eliciting a jolt from my belly that escaped my lips in a deep gasp. You put your hand on your cock and guided it into my cunt; my whole body received it in one pathetic tremor. You fed me your fingers to suck on, your lips, your tongue, filling every part of me you could reach as I rode you in deep waves with my hips. My hands were everywhere, looking for yours, holding you by the hair, touching your cheeks while my forehead was tenderly resting against your racing thoughts.

It was too much in this chair, in this dark room during the rainstorm outside. My starvation for you finally met with the uncompromising end of your sweet torture. The denim of your pants scraped my thighs just right. The angle of riding you was hitting me so deep, in that perfect spot where heaven opens its gate. I opened my eyes and found yours staring back at me, noticing everything in me lost in you, against you. You used your hands and started guiding my hips down on you harder, thrusting into me mercilessly.

The sun in you ripened me. You were everywhere at once while we were nowhere together. Your teeth clamped down on my lower lip and I was powerless. My cunt spasmed around, running down your cock into your own body and you released just as hard with me. You gripped the sweat at the back of my neck and pulled me into you so hard as my tension melted into your power.

Breathless and static from a satiated hunger, we kissed languidly, potently.

Your hand took my throat tenderly and you growled, "All mine."

As your soft cheek sleepily met the flush of my own, I purred against you with my body and listened to the rain, the beat of your heart against mine. The thunder between our bodies cracked as the sky above heard our storm.

Knife In Your Gaze

daddy/girl, biting, blindfolds, blood, choking, crying, dirty talk, fear, knives, rough body play

We are back on the naked island of your bed and the heat between us is coming to a boil. I ache for the indigo current of your touch. The sharpness of your stare wraps me tight, pricks my skin like thorns.

Your palms coil around my neck. The sting of my fragility is obvious, as your nails dig crescent moons over my pulse. Your knees squeeze my ribs while you flash your eyes down and hold me like a prayer. You settle me in the velvet of your mouth and roll my mind in undertows from the assault of your tongue. My fingers stutter against you. My fear is desperate and you swallow it down in gulps.

"Breathe," you say.

I return to the ground. Nerves unwound as your fingers comb through my hair, book-ending brutality with tenderness. The bud of my clit pulses like my heartbeat and your next kiss levels what was left of my standing empire.

Your palms breeze along my breasts, following trails your mouth and teeth leave. I scrape your shoulders and you answer by breaking my skin. I cry out while you suck crimson past your lips. We sink below the surface together.

You push your thigh into my cunt like mercy, like it better be enough. My hips talk back to you in tongues while your fingers climb my neck like a ladder, opening my lips, stretching my throat. You shove my own iron and salt back into me as I whimper. The liquor of my voice coats your insides.

My lips vacuum in panic as you find my end, and keep pushing. My eyes beg a yield; I grind against you harder. You pull your fingers from my mouth roughly and feed me with a kiss as deep as my hunger. This is a minor distraction as your fists start falling on me like hail. Your thigh echoes the rhythm of my cunt, rewarding my surrender. I am lost in you. My running in place still feels like running.

You take your shirt off abruptly, lift my head long enough to wrap it around me tight. The knot of fabric pulls some hair from my scalp and the sting of not seeing you makes my fear spike.

Halted breaths release as I squeeze the sheets. You leave the bed. The absence of your weight feels as violent as my forming bruises, but my blood is still on your tongue. It's too late now.

"Don't move, baby.", you whisper.

I strain to listen, my senses more acute than ever. Minutes drag and the dead metronome picks back up from the rhythm of your steps, determined yet soft. Your body settles against me. Lips greet my cheek, kissing me like a send-off to sea.

"Open your legs." you say.

I purr when your chest touches my side, inhaling the scent of you: evergreens mixed with the fire you made before, still seeped in your pores, your hair.

"Hold still, baby. Hold very. Fucking. Still."

Icy metal greets my thigh. I stiffen like a corpse and you drizzle whispers down my shoulder. Coaxing me, you let me feel both sides of the blade, ending with the tip dragging lines from my stomach to my nipple, and back.

I am a body of tremors as sliding turns to scraping, scraping turns to scratching. Then you dig and my skin breaks. You drag until staccato lines appear, Morse code marks that mimic the trembling of my lips against your neck. I am small, murmuring syllables against your thrumming pulse. My tears fall on your shoulder, imprints of my pain like wakes left by waves.

The air stings. Your words cradle. The cotton over my eyes grows damp. Your voice is a savior.

"Show me how it hurts. I'm so proud of you."

The tenderness in you is a lighthouse for my fear. I waver between trust and terror. You suck on my trembles. We collide violence with vulnerability.

After a while, you slow to a stop; you sense my safeword peeking through the curtain of my mouth. You drop the knife, and it signals a breathy sob I'd been holding deep in my gut. You answer, curl your fingers inside my cunt, firm like a riptide. You kiss my catharsis. Pull my pain back to you.

I slide the blindfold off, meeting the cut of your gaze. You overflow into me and you feel like what I think of when I look at the moon.

I'm marked everywhere, like something unholy happened, like the aftermath of a hurricane and no piece of me where I started, like the sky opened and struck us into becoming.

I am a splash of scarlet against your alabaster, pure because you broke me. We are here and your rolling waves are kissing my shore.

The curtains in our bedroom open with a whisper. I show you my wholeness, puzzled together by the sounds you sigh down my throat, proud, drowning me in mirth.

My hands clasp around your neck with a new font of love, swollen and thick, same as the walls of my cunt you languidly stroke. I wrap my legs between yours like taffy. You anchor me with your eyes, looking down at me like I'm a constellation god forgot to make.

My pulse quiets and we drift to sleep. In the morning, the sun comes through our window, just to watch us rise.

Dark Like A Dahlia

water bondage, drowning play, femdom/girl, D/s, blindfold, chains

I was already blindfolded, left alone in the dark, in a large upstairs bathroom and kneeling for her. The square of the tiles made small patterns on my knees and shins. I was slightly chilled, but distracted by the sensations in the room she'd meticulously arranged to calm me. Wood crackling wicks of candles had been placed in practically every corner, my favorite scents of pine and dark cranberry she'd lit before bringing me up here, to keep my nakedness warm, to soothe my mind.

The room's scent was already heady from the bowls of burnt cedar and crushed rose petals she always kept between the hers and hers sinks. Near the claw-foot tub, my breasts grazed the cold porcelain and I inhaled her body wash, orange ginger pressed into the wallpaper from years of shower steam. The slow flicker of the candle wicks cracked and my shadow danced taller on the ceiling.

It was a spacious room but I felt small, already wishing myself against the crescent curves of her pale body. It was difficult to discern time in here. There was no light, no windows, no moving wind. I was solitary on this floor of the house, waiting for the silence to be sliced by her heels caressing the wooden staircase toward me. This was followed by her rhythm in the hallway, then her hand on the brass doorknob.

She was always so measured, her actions so thoughtfully calculated, like all things she did that shadowed the animal in her that wanted to devour in cannibalistic gulps. Eventually, I turned my head toward the sound of brass turning, along with the muscles in my shoulders and stomach; the tension in me released while my breathing became tighter.

I'd negotiated this. She'd taken training classes extensively, we went to demos together. She'd sit at her desk afterward, going straight back to her online work while my own paintings kept me preoccupied in the sunroom downstairs. My favorite space in the house; it smelled like lineament from old books she'd often read to me, and my drying canvas and oils. I felt like a painting tonight; I always did with her. I was always waiting to see what colors she'd find below my skin with her nails and teeth, the menace of her violet voice.

I wasn't afraid of the water, I wasn't afraid of the sound of the womb I got from being beneath. I'd grown up swimming and my limbs were agile from the many days as a child I'd bury myself beneath the surface to push my lungs. I loved that feel of the push, that breathless gasp of undeniable triumph when making it another lap and holding out for one more round of kicks and splashes toward the deep end. Then I'd rush back to the shallows, then back again. My calves would push off and back into the blue painted walls until my muscles burned, killing doubts in my mind with my agility.

Water had always been my sanctum, my connection with infinity, a source of peace. No, I wasn't scared of the water. I was scared of what I would push myself to do for her, while she held me beneath it. Part of me already felt like crying. Part of me felt hysterical from the waiting. Part of me couldn't wait to know what would come from this, between her body and mine, the air and walls that listened, and the after. I knew I'd be a wreck after this, in that beautiful way I needed to be. I knew she'd be the cradle she always was, unflinchingly holding me while my fear and breaths came in bursts like the only word my body knew was "expel".

***

I had asked for this, after all, on a walk with her weeks ago, by a brook that ran along a path behind her home. We both stood in the quiet of that day and just listened, listened to water breaking down rocks. I smelled the way the dampness of the earth was a different fragrance along its edge. I stood there for a while trying to tell her, knowing the sentences intimately in my throat were wanting to be known. Eventually, I asked.

I loved her deeply, out of respect for her ferocity. I loved her gleaming edges that were as sharp as glass, her smile that could roll my eyelids down like a curtain call. I was mad for her amaranth words that ran down my shoulder in the dark, the ones that could send me to the all the spaces between the stars.

Her hands always knew just how to hurt and make it last, make me speak in only vowel sounds, turn my body a kaleidoscope of shivers. I loved that her moving into me made tears fall down my face in streams, after a particularly harsh round of her hunger. Even more, I loved that the soft cave of her neck fit my head so sweetly, and I'd kiss her pulse to show her.

She loved your pain as much as she loved me and it still scared me to know that, but I liked the fear, needed it. It gathered me back together, the broken train tracks inside my belly, the tulip shades my chest would flash and the way her palms felt made for cupping my chin, the way my throat felt sculpted for her fingers and cock.

So I asked her if she could; I asked her if she'd want to bind me in water and hold me below for her pleasure.

When I finally mustered up my courage, I was unable to look at her. I could only stare down into the moving water, until she found the blade of my shoulder with the pads of her fingers and touched me softly where my shirt left my skin.. Her hand deftly climbed up the back of my neck and slowly fisted her palm through my hair, squeezing gently. I released and tensed, as I always did when she touched me, with that sly but knowing tone, like she put this in my mind and she had just been waiting. Bemused, she replied,

"We can do that, darling."

***

Then she was there, opening the door. My limbs were sore from the waiting, and a rush of her scent came toward me in the pressure of the door closing behind her. The rhythm of her heels on the tiles were like pearls spilling on marble, like a shadow shutting off an echo. I wasn't supposed to speak tonight, while I could feel her form standing over me, like a cat that just found it's cream for the night.

My own hands rested on my thighs, electric to hold her legs like like the prey you always were, because whenever she was near, I wanted to be swallowed and held. I understood her power because I knew my own. She knew it, too. I could smell her new stockings, her perfume, leather, the expensive shampoo she used. That Pavlovian headiness was already making me wet, when the water from the tub turned on loudly. My heart felt like thunder, beating only to her name.

One of her knees grazed mine as she knelt down slowly before me. I listened while the thick gush of water slowed to her liking, continuing to fill the tub longer than I'd hoped for. I bit my lip wondering if she was leaving extra room for splashing, wondering how rough this was going to get. She saw my face shift and touched my cheek and I flinched from sheer nervousness. Soothingly, she brushed my hair away and ran her palm against me with adoration. I calmed then, the heat of her body radiating into mine. These empty rooms were always warmer once she was in them with me.

Her fingers traced the line of my jaw to my collarbone and scraped deeper between my breasts, eliciting a soft noise from me and a break in my statued posture. Then, her lips fell close to my ear just enough to feel the sweet moisture of her breath,

"Hello, lovely."

I elicited a full-body sigh into her words, breathing quicker now because my heartbeat was hammering my ribcage. Her hand went from sweet to merciless as she cupped my chin abruptly, pulling me closer to meet her lips. I could feel her steady breathing waiting to syncopate with the tremor of mine. She wanted this too, maybe just as much if not more, and there was something feral in her tongue when she finally kissed me. The end of my spine arched as far as it could, out and up to meet her, craving the consumption. I gave every drop of what I felt for her to that kiss, to her mouth, knowing she'd take and take and take, and it would only build her ache.

Pulling away before I got half of what I wanted,

"I just wanted you to have some of me on your tongue when you're down there, fighting, desperate. Tonight I'm going to lick your tears away, darling."

My stomach jumped at that, reacting to the immediate sound of heavy metal falling in sheets beside my thigh.

Chains.

Not just chains. Weight. Cold weight.

The end of the long braid of metal held by her firm grip began to run along my neck like a cold snake, then my shoulders, down my spine making me shiver from the heavy chill, followed by the saccharine blackness of her voice, in leveled commands:

"Stand."

"Turn."

"Cross your arms."

"Wrist over wrist."

"Breathe."

"Good girl."

I shivering now, wishing my body would warm to the metal, knowing how I must look from the waist up. I was wrapped up like a medieval present, for her, for the push that I knew was coming. I was unable to fight back in this strange harness she'd fashioned. The hanging lock between my breasts was a stronghold for her to push and pull, coupled with the d-ring around my slender neck that her graceful fingers looped so perfectly inside.

She came around behind me, inspecting. She took her time caressing and kissing my back and shoulders, biting, holding and grabbing me possessively. She was studying and spotlighting me, testing the firmness of her work, of my willingness to be tested. My strength searched for her sympathy, her need hunted my nectar. She was measuring and feeling my shifting mood into that universe where I could be small, but simultaneously the most powerful I ever was.

Eventually she pressed into me tight, with an arm around my neck allowing my weight to be held the way I loved. She tightened her strength around my throat, giving me a taste and testing my breathing out, like a bully who wanted to see what I'd be able to bring to the schoolyard after hours, like a predator that has it's dinner by the neck and playfully shakes just to hear it whimper.

My thighs were moist and I could smell my own arousal; the room was slightly humid from both my body-heat and the warm water entwining in the atmosphere. She held the singular thickened piece of my hair, now fixed by her in a tight ponytail and being used to lead me toward the tub. She let my knees hit the deep edge of the claw-foot and kissed my neck tenderly as I arched into her for more contact, craving silk before the hurricane.

She held me there with temperance, patient and knowing. This wasn't the time to be abrupt just yet. These were the moments before the moment. Sensing the hesitance in your growing quiet that I knew how close it all was now, she reminded me this is what I wanted. She bit me gently, then hard enough to get me to break my silence with whimpers and shakes. She held my breasts as soft anchors to pull me back into her so I could feel her skin; her lace bra, her stockings and garter, the thin lines of it all giving me envy they weren't her lips and tongue. She whispered then,

"Climb in first, slowly. And kneel like you mean it."

I followed as she gave me her hands for guidance. She positioned me so my back was at the tub's back, and she slid in to face me after. Her hands deftly found the fold of my knees and pulled me by my collar, until the water touched my nose.

The blindfold was lifted now, so I could see her. My face was inches from her and her expression was waiting to measure mine. Her smile was tender but her brows and demeanor and voice had that primal tone of readiness, that eager animal that was tired of it's cage and hungry.

The chains felt incredibly heavy in the water. Her gaze felt like it was trying to remind me this was where I belonged. She caressed my shoulders with the warm water, grabbed me by my collar and pressed her forehead to mine. My breathing had quickened and she needed me calmer, like a slow river.

She wanted this to last, wanted us to grow together, to feel me pushing outside myself with her, for her.. She kissed me sweetly and grabbed the lock, waiting for my breaths to syncopate with hers. She calmed me with her eyes, touching me everywhere she could with her body. She reminded of the double-punch of the tub's side to safeword out. She reminded me that being here with her made her so proud. I gave myself to the silence, to her, and closed my eyes.

"Are you ready?"

I nodded halfway, between the fear in my mind and the trust in my head, forgetting words for a moment.

"I need to hear you say it. Tell me you're ready."

I take a deep inhale. Still nodding, "I'm ready." The last syllable leaves my lips with certainty, and then my head goes under.

The grip she has on my hair is tight, firm and weighted, keeping me low while between her legs. The echo of both bodies shifting in the tub is loud at first, then quiet, until I can hear my own heartbeat. I can hold my breath a long time when I'm calm, when I'm steady. Tonight I'm on edge and desperate to show her how far I can push.

She is my breath tonight, deciding when I rise and fall, trusting herself to sense when that is and listening keenly for my palm to hit the porcelain in case I need to stop. The longer I'm under, the tighter my lungs become.

My eyes tighten in the silken warmth of the water and I try to center myself. This is as mental as it is physical. The more relaxed I am, the less intimidating the seconds seem. Her fist tightens and her legs gather around my shoulders, anchoring me down here, grounding me further.

I want — no, I *need* — to push myself for her tonight. There is a deep need to prove my worth, stretch those miles of devotion out in front of her. I'm at the point now where the inches of air above the surface feel romantic. I fantasize about that first gasp I'm going to suck in and how good it will feel. I think about the pride in her voice while my body stretches toward a place it isn't meant to go.

That tightness in my chest feels taut as bubbles rise to the surface, a brief signal that I'm are close to being done. They are loud when they break the water in this strange white silence of the room and she sees them. I know she sees them because she dips me even deeper with her palm around the back of my neck. This is met with some murmured whimpers and my hand clenches tight in panic, ready to slam the side of the tub.

Just before I can, she pulls me up heavy from the chains, violent in her grip while I gasp the nectar of the room deep into my lungs. The humidity and steam and the scent of the candles is thick, the same as her voice over the water in my ears until I can tell she's saying "good girl" over and over until I come down.

I meet her like a waterfall falling back into the body that made it churn. I meet her like her praise is filling my lungs as much as the air. The delicate power of her hands pulls me in while my hair drips down both of our bodies. Her tongue swallows the rivers in me that are still rushing. That stammer of heartbeat in my chest slows against her pink lips.

I look at her and see the flame of the candles reflecting in her eyes. She looks back and pulls me closer while our shadows dance on the wall as one shape. The ripples below our breasts are now still, and with her hand hooked in my collar, her voice breaks the quiet of the room.

"Again, sweet girl. Again."

My eyes could see hers through the my own tears, dark like a dahlia, poison holding me down.

Just Be A Hole

D/s, anal, daddy/girl, strap on, bruising, oral sex, crying, blindfold, dirty talk, choking, belt, rough body play

Melody:

Sometimes when I was here like this, I thought about cranes. I thought about felled trees that had to be wedged into to drop, carved and chipped at slowly, to break. I'd think about flowers leaning toward the sun, the one piece that held them up craving heat so bad it would bow, even split for it. I thought about the angle of the vertebrae at the top of your spine when you stared down at me hazily, below you while you rose up my skin. I remembered it sweetly, how I arched my cries to reach you, curved my neck while you opened me, how I let you bow my hips like the knees of a saint, begging for forgiveness.

This was tonight. This was now in the dark. This was you coming back from drinks at the bar and my cell still bannering your text from twenty minutes ago before you'd left:

"When I'm back I want you naked, bent over the dining table, your cheek and palms pressed flat on the wood, and my silk tie around your eyes. No questions. And not a sound from you when I'm home. Now."

It was so quiet in here I could hear the grandfather clock ticking at the end of the hall, my heartbeat going faster, and my moist breath hitting the cool wood below my lips.

You'd left me home alone hours ago, having a night with the boys and handing me a list of chores too lengthy to finish, even if you'd been gone twice as long. I'd completed just over half, and had negotiated my time as concisely but also as thoroughly as I could. I wanted it to be enough, but I knew it might fall short of your expectations.

I was unaware of how much time I'd have or when you'd come bursting through the door with that pace of energy you always came in with after seeing them. I wondered what you talked about, sometimes wishing I could come too, or sit at the end of the bar and eavesdrop while I left lipstick on the edge of a glass, similar to the scarlet imprint on the head of your cock I'd made last night.

Was it all sex talk and cigars? Was it the tight shirts across your broad chests and everyone in black and the smell of fresh polish on your leather boots? Was it the linger of perfume you all had a whisper of on your collars, left behind from when you hugged your girls goodbye? I wanted to know so desperately sometimes.

Mostly I just liked imagining you there, talking with your hands, your different smiles you reserved for different things, that bawdy volume you all bounced off each other that made me feel like a cheerleader squeezing my thighs on the bleachers, staring intently at that primal energy I wanted to tackle me later.

I wondered if you went in the bathroom and stroked your cock slowly, staring at yourself in the mirror just as you had days before when you fucked my ass over the sink, my small handprints still on the mirror after our shower. I wondered if you thought of me when you were gone, saw other women at the bar and missed the way I laughed when your palms playfully smacked my ass after fucking it senseless.

I wonder if when your teeth broke through the cherry in your drink, you thought of my swollen lips sucking on your tongue.

Something about this bent over position made me feel so vulnerable, my tits pressed against a hard surface, legs spread open, the inability to see, my face down and my ass up, hearing the echo of everything from a lower point in the room, you above me, soon.

I'd gotten wet while doing my chores thinking of you in all of those ways with your friends, wistful and aroused and fantasizing about when you'd return. Would you call me or just burst through the door hungry?

Sometimes you came home and ignored me for a good while, listening to my breathing change it's rhythm when you'd stand up and move around me, plucking at my anticipation. Sometimes you'd come through the door calm and quiet, until you called me over to the floor below your chair. I'd rest my head on the curve of your boot while you sat silent and read or worked. Sometimes that would last hours and you'd pull me up and use my mouth, just for you, all for you. Then you'd put me to bed ignoring my ache, but knowing you'd push it further in the morning.

Other times you'd return and I'd decided not to follow any of your directions. I'd watch a movie, take a bubble bath and put on loud music, pretend it was a good idea saying hello when you got home, so casual it drove you up the wall.

Sometimes I wanted to incite that side of you that would pull me down the hall by my wet hair and edge me until I was crying, breaking blood vessels on your hands from how big of a mistake I'd made. After, you'd put me to bed in the guest room alone, come back to me before dawn pushing your cock in me while I was half asleep.

Tonight I couldn't predict the temperature of you, but my ass was still bruised from last time, so I was decisive and listened to everything, choosing obedience tonight.

My grip on time was starting to falter and I couldn't tell if it had been minutes or hours. It felt so much longer when I was wet and antsy, uncertain of your mood. My palms were slightly damp now from nerves; they were mildly shaking and sticking to the table. I could feel the cool air from the overhead vent brushing soft across my back, grateful for small comforts that may soon be stripped away entirely.

Then my muscles tensed, as I heard the deadbolt unlock and the air change in the room when you stepped back inside. I heard your boots cross the floor, felt your body heat close in on me. You smelled like whiskey and sweat and leather and the boys I was warned about in high school. You smelled like all your dirty thoughts were written on your skin ready to spill onto me. You smelled like you. You smelled like home.

***

Max:

I loved how much of a slut she was. For me. Against me. I loved how anytime I whispered to her cravings, they spilled back over me in her needy little whimpers, her tightened fists, her furrowed little brow, always so desperate to be filled and used.

I needed a toy tonight, pliable and bending to my will, something to chase and catch and loom my shadow over slowly while she shrunk. Let her cry. Let her beg me to stop. Let her break below my boots on the floor like a sad little puddle. I wanted to lick the salt of her tears tonight, chase them with the liquor of her swollen little cunt, so greedy and hopeful and hurting to be touched. Let her wait.

I felt like I'd been gnawing at the bars of a cage as I drove home. I wanted to be fed by her cries tonight, her needy little protests; I wanted to kick her thighs open so wide her hips would hurt, slam into her and crush her shaky little body so her tits would be bruised the next week. She needed it like that. Make her prove she deserves it.

When the door slammed behind me it was quite the pathetic little display to take in.

Our longer dining table lays parallel to the front door so when I stepped over the threshold, her greedy little holes were right there glistening back at me, presenting themselves and her ass was still so fucking bruised from the beating I gave her last night. I ran my eyes over them again, noticed what would be tender, what could take more. How could I push her? Where would she run?

I advanced closer and noticed her calves tense, her breathing quickened slightly. I unbuckled my belt slowly, pulling it out of each loop like a snake that was restless to wrap her up in scarlet streaks. She was keeping quiet, holding it in, pushing it back.

I wanted that space in her chest, wanted the bass of me thundering her out of her little mind so she was all body, all mine.

I wanted to be the Daddy tonight that made her wait, kept her anxious, built her fear with my energy and echoes dancing around her, pathetic in her stance all open and quiet and nervous. Just a toy. Just my holes. I wasn't there tonight. I didn't have the patience or the time to draw this out.

I wanted it now, rough, toxic; the sheath of her aching holes forced to take, accept the use. Say thank you. Say it again. Make me believe you love this. Keep crying. You know how much I love that.

My cock could already feel it as I palmed the length of it below the tight denim I had on. This was all for me. Her God. My pleasure. She wasn't allowed to speak so I spoke for us,

"Look at you down there for Daddy. So small. I can smell your cunt through the door, you know. Already such a greedy little brat when I gave you everything I had last night. Did you already forget?"

I cracked my belt across the bruises on her ass and the deep breath she'd been holding burst out of her, eliciting a stubborn moan, making me laugh and waking the sadist up all over again.

I kicked at her ankles, spreading her open as the sting of leather on skin snapped in the room, too hard, too fast for her, her hips already pushing themselves into the table as if doing that would save her when she had nowhere to go.

Once the tears came, my hands touched the heat of her skin, welts already forming and her ass trying to grind into my touch, advantageous as soon as she could be. I bit my own lip and bent over her body so I was flush against her. I brushed the hair from her neck and slid the belt around her throat, pulling her back to me so her spine was arched into my chest, making her feel my cock.

I kept one hand on the belt while the other grabbed her weeping cunt possessively.

"Do you know how many good girls there were at the bar tonight? How many of them wanted to sit in my lap secretly instead of listen to their stupid boyfriends. How many of them I could have brought back here and used? How curious they were about what's under my jeans...How they'd kill to be right here, right now? Instead I come home to this toy that's dripping, forgetting its place, forgetting who owns it..."

I squeezed her cunt with my fist hard and she cried out, harder than she needed to and nodding and sniffling in her blindfold.

I unzipped my jeans and ran my cock along the length of her ass, poking her bruises with the thick head.

"You think just because you listened and can bend over for me you earned this, girl? You think these holes are better than theirs? You think you deserve relief for doing half of what I asked? Fucking slut."

I found her oozing cunt and slid two fingers inside her aggressively, feeling that tension in her spine untangle against my chest and biting and sucking on her neck and shoulders, tightening the belt. She was moaning now, acting like she knew I'd fuck her. I pulled my fingers out abruptly and stroked my cock.

"Shut up, greedy girl. That hole didn't earn Daddy tonight. You'll be lucky if I touch it again for a long fucking time."

Another whimper. Let her be scared. She knew. I let the length of me slide up and down her ass and loosened the belt, replacing it with my forearm, skin on skin. The smell of her drove me wild, her hunger, the juicy little ass so sore and hurting for me. Mine. I shoved my still moist fingers in her mouth and pushed the head of my cock against her ass.

"Suck on my fingers, girl. Act like they're Daddy's cock. Deeper. Mhm. Good little slut. Fucking pathetic to be filled. Just here to be used, aren't you? Show me. You can cry, girl. Give Daddy those hungry holes."

She was gagging now and distracted, lost in the push and trying to meet me but failing. She was anxious and the back of her bruised little neck was damp, shoulders shaking. I kept talking, pushing into her tight little ass while she took my fingers down her small little throat. So pathetic. Trying so hard.

"You are a good little slut aren't you? Take it. Open the fuck up. Tell Daddy thank you. Louder. You can talk while you gag. Try again."

Her lips were trembling around me in that sweet moment where I pushed past that bundle of muscles inside her and I was through, past that threshold that always scared her. Her little legs were shaking and I pulled her into me real tight, sucking on her neck and tasting her surrender in primal gulps. My thrusts were shoving her hips into the table with my weight, and she felt so fucking good. Sympathetically, I reached for the bud of her clit and as soon as I touched her, buried in her ass, she squirted all over my hand. I growled and kept going, pulling tantric orgasms from her starved little cunt and pounding her ass.

She was wrapped in me again, all confusion and hurt and pleasure and bundled tension unwinding from my presence, my cock, my touch.

I wanted this to take all night, wanted to exhaust her until she collapsed at my feet in that sweet mess of tears and come and shivers, just how I loved her.

She broke her voice restriction after the third time she came and elicited the smallest whisper of "Daddy" I'd ever heard from her. I turned her neck to the side and kissed her deep.

"Shh. No more thinking. Just be a hole. Open up."

Break Me Past My Promise

daddy/girl, biting, choking, dirty talk, edging, fucking, strap on

I want to wake up with you already inside me, sleep still on the edge of my eyes, wet from dreaming about you.

You spoon me, small puffs of your breath against my shoulder while the light of the morning hasn't filled the room yet. My muscles are pliable, molded against your skin beneath the sheets, raw. Sweet mewls of my dreams collide with your kisses; your lips are two travelers meandering slow along the expanse of my back. I scoot into you tenderly, press myself against you like flowers, while you show me I'm your sunrise.

Your hands trail along my thighs until I stir more, my ass quietly tucked into your hips, not even the space for a shadow exists between our curves and lines. You grip my thigh and wrap a leg around mine, opening my hips wide, craving the depth of me.

I was wet, my eyes still closed but moaning indulgently into your touch. The shapes of us meld and my body feels like mercury in your palm. You made sense inside me, like the face of God, like you'd always been there. My clit began to bud from the warmth of your touch, sunlight through water, pushing below the surface to find the nooks it can illuminate.

You slide into me deep and I feel like a body of clouds. The wisps of your lashes against my cheek when you kiss me make my cunt flutter. Your arm serpents around my throat, gripping me firm. My mouth hollows like a knothole, body rocking against the sturdy branches of your form.

I am lost in you. All it takes is your touch, your presence, your voice. Your eyes run up and down me, pairs of cherries that trigger bell sounds in my blood. We are light now, while the honey of me coats your fingers. Two turn into three and your other hand holds my neck stiff and upright. The pressure of your grip makes my breaths come out in gasps.

"You know how much I fucking love to hear you struggle?" you say.

You tighten against my throat, thicker, meaner, and my mouth waters to taste you just as bad. Barely letting me settle into you opening me, you start to fuck me fast and strong. Your need is insistent tonight, abrupt and washing whatever sleep was left in my body away with your teeth on my neck. You force me to meet you, that racing frequency of you overwhelming me past where I can go.

"You love this, don't you? Being my little morning fucktoy. Swollen and sore for Daddy. Fucked back to sleep. Holding onto me like I'm your gravity. You're not allowed to come. Make me believe you're worthy."

You circle my clit as my hips met your rhythm, desperate for this. It was so easy. I was.

I cry against your arm, your focus intent on edging me and the fear in me rising that I might break our promise and come, without permission, without your command.

"You want Daddy to feel bad for you? For having someone that's so good to you spread you open while you wake up, swallow you as deep as your cunt takes my hand. Should I feel bad when you struggle and beg? You probably don't even deserve the edging today, do you girl?"

My clit swells hard under your thumb, three fingers inside me and I was fucking gone on you. Unable to answer through my moans, your teeth gripped me rabid. I found pieces of your arm around my neck and and sucked, clamping down on anything that could ground me. My thighs trembled, body tethered to you and spine trying to run. Begging was the only music of the room. Your silence ignored it entirely as you tried to break me past my promise.

I started rising louder then, my voice damp against your forearm and your gasps sucked on the shivers on the back of my neck. I was almost crying now, pulling away from your rigid touch, trying to control what I couldn't while you bullied me through this edging session. "Please can I come" was spilling from my lips, spinning in the air like a carousel over our bodies in repeat, desperation, while my calves and thighs tensed.

You nibbled on my earlobe and held onto it with your teeth. Squeezing my neck the hardest you ever had, you spit the word "come" in my ear like a threat and I fell into you. I fell down that mess of stairs as you kept going and my cunt was squirting down your wrist; the warm rush of my release making you grip me like the scruff of a kill.

The current of my body thrashed against the steady shore of yours and you held me like I might disappear. Your arm loosened around me and you pulled my chin sideways until my lips hazily met yours, tongue finding mine and sucking down all the demons you'd exorcised tonight. I came down against you until my cries turned into pleasured moans, then soft nuzzling as I turned into you.

You wrapped me like a present with the ribbons of your limbs and I fell asleep sweetly in your chest while you caressed me like a lullaby.

Open Your Mouth

daddy/girl, dirty talk, mild humiliation, exhibition, voyeurism

"Open your mouth, I have something for you."

You held up one of the raspberry filled truffles on your plate you knew I always wanted. It sat delicately between your fingers, resting in midair while you stayed still. You wanted me to come to you. I always did, especially in the dark, when our clothes were off and I was pressed against your body and the wall like a flower.

You had that self-satisfied smirk painted on you as you stared across the table knowing this would be more of a challenge. This restaurant was formal, conservative, quiet. It would spotlight me to shuffle my chair in bits, even more to stand and rise and meet you to be fed.

Your eyes were amused, but something else was there too, tempered patience waiting for me to decide. The square of the chocolate was getting softer between your thumb and forefinger. You cleared your throat loudly and raised a brow, expectantly.

On that cue, I gripped the bottom of my chair, curling my fingers around it nervously. You stared at me hard, as I short-hopped it's legs toward you pathetically. It took me almost a dozen scoots to get to you and when I finally set myself down, I felt like such a spectacle. It was loud, the metal legs scraping the floor at each pathetic little bounce. Heads rose from their filet mignon, turned toward me like sirens going off. A flush on my skin had developed from feeling all of their eyes on me.

Next to you now, your hand gripped my thigh possessively beneath our table. I looked up from the floor and you were right there, smiling devilishly. The candle in the middle of our table was still dancing frantic from the air of me settling beside you.

Your lips mouthed, "Open up."

You fed me the chocolate slow, making me come to your fingers, pulling it away as I tried to take a bite. This was a show now. The sound of forks stopped dead and a hush settled over the room as they watched you set it on my tongue and push it back with two fingers as my mouth tried to close. You left my mouth ever-so-slow, forcing me to suck the syrup and cream from your fingers as you withdrew from my lips.

This was obscene for somewhere like here. The room's hush had now shifted to an air of discomfort and some of the strangers had elicited whispered gasps. I could hear the moment linen napkins met mouths in an offering of etiquette to mute their own shock.

"Look at me," you said.

A command. Your fingers were now holding my chin and your eyes offered up a resting place for mine. You were always so steady, confidently holding me. Your hand under the tablecloth moved up my thigh like a predator as you watched my eyes widen.

"Shh. No one knows. Just for Daddy."

There was menace in that last sentence as you whispered this was just for us, our secret.

"You forgot to say thank you, girl. Don't you want to show Daddy how grateful you are?"

I looked at you with pause, stunned. I swallowed deep, still tasting the cocoa at the back of my throat. Still tasting you.

"Thank you."

Just above a whisper. Timid. Trying to stay hidden.

"Louder."

My eyes left yours and went peripheral, both sides of the room tuned into us but mimicked gestures at their table to pretend they weren't. Unscrupulous glances darted between us and each other in whispered conversation.

"I want the room to hear it," you smirked.

The heat rose up from my chest, to my collarbone, to my cheeks. My ears were hot and I looked at you with a spit of venom in my eyes. You saw the flash of it and pinched my thigh, making me whimper loudly, my hand flying to my mouth. Even more eyes were watching now.

"Don't make me wait, there will be consequences."

I exhaled the breath I wasn't aware I'd been holding and said it louder, firmer, wanting to melt into a deep hole in the floor.

"Thank you."

Impish from your power, you took the cherry from your drink by the stem and playfully dangled it and bit down hard, satisfying your teeth as you broke through the skin. Your nails climbed higher up my thigh under the table, scraping skin.

"Mmmm. Tastes like how Daddy is going to break you later."

Shock and arousal obvious in my demeanor, the waiter sidled behind us with the check and you handed him your card, not missing a beat, not breaking our gaze. Full control. My clit was pulsing and as he walked away, you slid a finger between my fishnets, grazed the dampness that was growing and laughed in a low hum. You sipped the last bit of your drink, set it down, and licked the same fingers. You winked at me and signed the check when it came back.

The rhythm of your breathing and mine had syncopated to our arousal, eyes lidded at one another in a silent battle. You pulled my chair out and held my jacket up as I slipped my arms inside. Always a gentlemen. You took my hand and as the door to the restaurant closed behind us, we were met with the chill of the autumn night. You pushed me into a brick wall abruptly and kissed me, mixing the whiskey in your mouth with the dark chocolate in mine. Intoxicating.

"I have other things for your mouth tonight, girl. Time to go home."

Because I Want You

biting, blood, bondage, choking, D/s, fear, primal, strap on

She's sleeping now, that sweet constellation of freckles on her shoulder peeking out from the sheet. My cock is still hard, pulsing and pressed tight against that luscious curve where her pale ass meets her thigh.

I never would have known she was into that. I raise my head off the pillow and brush her hair away from her cheek and she purrs; her little hand finds my hipbone and she grinds back into me tight, needy, luscious.

She looked so innocent, when we met for coffee a week ago. She showed up in moto boots and a skater dress, flushed cheeks and her breasts swelling slightly. The less I broke eye contact, the more she fought to try and keep it. She kept drinking and sipping her coffee, even after the cup was empty and I pretended not to notice. Later, when I took our trash away and sat back down, her nerves worsened since she didn't have that to fidget with any longer. She kept touching her hair, bouncing her eyes between mine and my lips, letting that one dimple in her left cheek flash impishly at me.

I wanted to feel my palm fisting her skin. I wanted to put my teeth on her tits, open her thighs under the thin fabric of her dress and watch her eyes widen. My primal side could feel that anxious sensuality coming off her in thick waves. Hey shyness made me want to shove her in my car and take her somewhere dark, somewhere quiet. Her mouth was distracting me. I kept thinking about the pink of it wrapped around my t-dick, then later, my cock, the bigger one I keep for special occasions. Let her try.

She laughed when she was nervous, smiled exclusively with her eyes first, then her little rosebud cheeks. She'd unconsciously moved on to fidgeting with the gold chain on her purse. It made made me want to cuff her delicate little wrists to my headboard.

She was smart in that quiet way; she had that kind of intelligence where when you are across from her one-on-one, all the universes she's taken with her and known and ascended, come out in passionate little bursts. Of course, those trailed off her voice when she looked directly back at me and my eyes were right there, seeing into her.

***

One week later, and her juicy little ass was grinding into me now, a little lazily with that scarlet of hunger behind her waking eyelids, that appetite for me sandwiched below the puddle I'd already made of her.

My hands caressed her wherever I could reach and she arched her neck back into my chest deeper. She moved lower in the bed, took my arm and placed it around her quickening pulse. So decisive in her want, this fucking little girl.

I flexed my forearm making it tighten some, giving over that sweet pressure to show her she was mine in this room. I loved that reminder. My fingers trailed down the falling crest of her hip, taking my time to whisper to the touch she really wanted. The shallow little circles she was making against me deepened, made themselves known as I caught the scent of her. Her want thickened the air, just like her rising moans. My teeth found her neck and scraped her skin as a soft warning, while my palm found its way down, resting perfectly over her cunt. She was still warm and swollen, full of craving in her emptiness.

That pulse of her need dishevels me, makes my cock throb, trades the human in me for animal, and I froth. My ache is always bigger; it sits on a throne intently, watches her crawl her way through my fists and nails and teeth to touch it, only to shrivel at its feet and hold onto the piece she's reached with her sweet little body.

She was getting louder now, that pout of her lower lip trembling against her pillow while I bit too deep, too hard, feeling the muscles in her back tense up at once. She shrunk away instantly and my forearm around her throat tightened in response. Her last moan had that terror at the end of it, that realization of what she'd woken back up to and her shoulders fell closer to her chest in a failed attempt at protection.

I might break skin tonight, might break her. I know she needs it, because I do.

I wanted to shut her up, make her just be my pretty little thing that takes. I shoved two fingers in her mouth and her tongue thickened around me trying to suck while I pushed back roughly. She can't find her rhythm and I'm going too hard, too fast. My hips slam into her simultaneously, making her feel the length of my cock, the violence in my thrusts ready to use her. I push until some little gasps spilled out of her lungs. I push insistently, like I'm seeking all her secrets to swallow, finding all the limits of her little mouth. The syncopated gasps in the air between us get interrupted, by her sputtering in that shocked way that almost never expects (but still aches) to be put right fucking here.

I pull my mouth away and then ascend to a spot on her shoulder I bruised an hour ago that's still tender, growing darker. Her blood is so pretty there, just below and pooling for me, raising itself high for the next week when she's out with her friends in the springtime sun. My cock grinds into her harder so I'm physically pushing and pulling her now. My waves. My control. My law.

She is cowering more, afraid this next mark will be worse and I growl in her ear to make that tension rise. Her little terrified mewls drive me. I suck and kiss instead of bite, and as I feel her hard release of that breath she'd been holding around my fingers, I push it back down her throat, so she's gagging.

Then the whimpers come. The pressure grows. That sweet curve of her ass strokes me, relentless in its beg for pleasure, for distraction, release. I don't acquiesce. I pull my fingers out without warning and her teeth scrape and I growl. I find her dripping cunt and feel her spine turn to taffy when I hit that sweet spot so deep.

I hold still and wait while she pathetically tries to control her body, but I have her, by the throat, by her little neck. She knows better than to really try to fuck herself on my fingers. An frustrated grunt exhales into the pillow and I move just the pads of my fingers, right up against her g-spot and her little bundle of muscles clench me, desperate to keep. I rotate her neck so I can put my tongue in her mouth and taste that surrender. My arm loosens and turns her into me and I grab her hip and stroke my cock so the head teases her clit a little.

My eyes are dilated and the surge in me is ready to burst. My hand takes her throat and keeps her mouth against mine until her breath is shallow, until she needs the air between us to go on for me. I feel it, that moment where something in her breaks from my push and she is small again.

I swell and she crests.

She puts this thing in me that lets me rise like this, lets me heave and bellow and feel her caught between pleasure and acquiescence, orgasm and tears. Not yet. I gave before. Now I was going to take.

Road Trip

strap on, blowjob, rough body play, D/s, dirty talk

We'd settled into a quiet together in your car. After a few hours of being on the road for this trip across states, the radio had taken place of the hum of conversation, our adrenaline now winding down into that eased comfort with one another. It was a brutally hot day where the a.c. had to be kept on full blast and our sun visors felt lifesaving. We were almost to our halfway point by early evening, about to cross into Utah.

The landscape was sparse, everything stone and jagged and different shades of rust. I was staring at you from inside my sunglasses, really looking as a familiar 90's song played and the bass hugged our legs through the low speakers by our calves.

You were in a white tank, black sunglasses, one hand loose around the steering wheel and the other gripping your drink sturdily. Your shoulders and arms were long and tan, thicker at the top the same way your dick was. I glanced down at the shorts you were in today, dark with small white stripes, boyish and fitting you tighter in the crotch where I noticed the outline of your dick as you shifted slightly in your seat.

You had set your drink down and were resting your hand on my thigh now, the pads of your fingers grazing my skin tenderly, sending a shiver to my cunt and putting a blush on my cheeks. The effect you had on my body from just your presence, your touch, and your voice was potent. I uncrossed my ankles and felt that antsy wave in my stomach, eager to get to the hotel and my tongue thick in my mouth to taste you again. I'd had you this morning already (for hours) but that already felt like it was ages ago. The more I had you the more I wanted, the fill always circling back to the deep ache.

The steadiness in you was so measured, your presence so calming and easy to dive into, until you weren't that way at all and that primal side of you switched abruptly. Your voice would drop low and your fist would squeeze my hair in that brutal way while you kept my neck bent back and dug your cock against my ass. The air in the room would fill with your soft threats and your hips deeply grinding into me, pushing my weight lower with your own and my cunt damp and pulsing for you. My resolve was always melting by then, like it was never even there.

I squeezed my thighs together, missing you buried inside, my pussy still sore from this morning and how deep and long you'd had me, digging in hard and firm and relentless and the mattress soaked from how much I'd squirted around your dick. I felt the sun's sting on the parts of my bare legs you'd gripped and bitten, clenched and slapped with your strong hands.

My neck turned toward you then, after your voice broke my thoughts, "You doing okay over there, girl?"

Girl. That's how I felt with you, small, tender and hunted in your gaze, cradled in the swallow of your jaw and the froth of your limbs handling me and wielding me below you just how you wanted to.

I cleared my throat and the "yes, I'm okay" came out much less convincing than it sounded in my head and you laughed, squeezed my thigh and dug your nails in until a breathy moan escaped me. Unconsciously, I leaned my head back and my hips rose up into your touch, a few inches off my seat and the belt around my waist cutting into my stomach.

It was darker now, the sun had settled lower in the sky and those tangerine hues were reflected from the lake we were curving around. It looked like glass almost, like a painting, like the way I felt inside when your fingers gripped the pulse points on my neck and you commanded me to come for you, again.

"How long until we're there?" I asked this politely, trying to restrain the need and hunger for you from being so visible. You knew better. You'd noticed my breathing change miles back, my eyes darting to the outline of your thickest packer and my hand touching my hair in that flustered, tension-filled, girlish way to hide my arousal.

You took my hand then and placed it on your dick, firm and folding my fingers around it outside your shorts. A gasp left my lungs at the abruptness, the rougher way you jerked my shoulder down to feel it all at once and that shift in your voice dropping deep and quiet, almost to a whisper,

"Is this what you can't wait for? I didn't give you enough of a pounding this morning? I'd think your pussy would still be so swollen and sore. You still want more, don't you? Greedy little girl."

I bit my lip and nodded at you, words escaping me and seeing that satisfied smirk painted on your face.

"You can't wait another —" you tapped the screen on your dash from the playlist to the maps app, "Fifty-eight minutes?"

Your hand pushed mine down harder on your dick, menacing, running my palm along the length insistently.

"Use your words, girl."

A small but bluntly honest "no" escaped my lips. and you laughed, that power resting on your shoulders that rose and fell and flexed around the steering wheel harder.

"Good. Let me find a road I can take us down now that it's dark, where I can fill that nasty little mouth of yours, make you gag louder than this morning and remind you that I own that throat, and that it's here for my pleasure and use, isn't it, girl?"

My cunt pulsed and I stared sideways at you needily, nodding and biting my lip, taking your hand and sucking on your fingers, feeling you push past that point and then pulling out after hearing me whimper.

You grabbed my chin roughly after and squeezed the angled bone of my face. "We'll see. If you take it good and deep and make me come hard enough, choke on it just right, maybe you'll get a reward at the hotel. Maybe you'll get my fist."

My body shivered at that and you flicked your turn signal capably, leading us down a dark road that led to a public park, clearly empty and the gravel crunching below your tires loudly.

You pulled into the parking lot sideways, haphazardly, unbuckling your seatbelt and leaning your drivers seat slightly lower.

You slid your shorts below your strong hips and took your dick out, stroked its length proudly, tantalizing me and staring me down like an order, that clouded brutality and haze rising at me, pulling me in like a riptide.

I leaned toward you, overzealous, forgetting I was still buckled in. The strap across my chest stopped me. You grunted in amusement, taking your hand and pushing down on the red button by my thigh with surprising acuity. I giggled at myself, sliding the seatbelt over my body. The metal clattered against the door.

"So eager to please, I like that."

You said this as your hand found the back of my head, palm flat and hovering on it as you felt me bend over you inch by inch, until my mouth was hovering above the head of your cock and I had that breathy desire making my lungs rise and fall harder. You caressed my hair tenderly, letting my head pull your hand with it as I took the tip of you between my lips. I gripped the base of your cock with my hand (as much as I could close around you, anyway) and let some of my spit trickle down, between my palm and the warmth of you.

Your head was lifted slightly, eyes low and watching me intently, that hum in the back of your throat turning to a growl as I slid you inside my mouth and went halfway down. My hand pumped the base of you in synchronicity, tugging rhythmically on you and hitting your t-dick at that angle I knew you loved.

I moaned around you like I'd just swallowed my first gulp of spring, like the ache of you invading me was almost enough to get me off. I hollowed my cheeks around you, still only able to go just halfway on my own, my head working faster and hoping when this was over I could lick you clean, suck on your t-dick at the hotel, like this morning, when you had to push me away and pull me up your body by my neck because you were too sensitive to take anymore.

I loved you like that, shaking in your hands as you held onto me and that deep tension in your thighs and stomach erratic and rumbling; the noises of you loud and hard and thick like an animal.

Just as I was in that rhythm of my wrist and mouth, sucking hard and pulling and grinding the base of your cock against your body just right, I felt your fist tighten in my hair. Your shoulders were off the seat now too, and the windows were moist with the commands of your voice running over my back like a stinging crop.

"You can go further. Take it. There's my good girl. Don't fucking stop. Just my hole. Mmm, fuck. Hands behind your fucking back."

I complied and at that last word and you shoved yourself further, making me gag. You held me there still, the force of your hips thrusting up just enough to make my eyes water, make me whimper, put that fear in me and make my clit pulse harder.

I was struggling tonight, sensitive and whining more than moaning, the water from my eyes now dripping down my cheeks as deep as my saliva messily streaming down your cock.

I was choking now and you could feel it, that contraction at the back of my throat that resisted any more, that met your push with a scared little shudder. I tried to inhale in a panic through my nostrils but it wasn't enough and I pushed up against your fist finally, while you pulled me up and the head of you popped out of my mouth roughly.

"Let me see you. Let me see that greedy little face. Breathe."

I turned to you flushed and my hair gathered in a tangled mess. There were streaks of dampness on my cheeks as I fought through blinking and inhaling the air in the car in desperate gasps, shaking a little from being perceived so close.

You hummed a low laugh and growled in that guttural way, still bucking your hips for more. You looked at me in the dark light of the car with that kerosene in your eyes, pinching your fist through my hair so my scalp burned and placing me back over you once again.

"You're not done until I say you're fucking done."

Before I could take more air in my lungs you shoved me down, harder this time, grinding your hips well off your seat like you were possessed, listening to my gags and spit come out in sad little waves and my whimpers hitting the roof of the car in echoes, tearing up a little, just how you liked me.

"So fucking good. You asked for this. Keep going you can take it. I know it's too big. It's always too big. Don't you fucking slow down. Harder. Fuck."

My hands squeezed themselves behind my own back and my stomach lurched inward as I felt you slam into the very back of my throat. You pulled me back up and slapped my cheek, wet from tears now and my sniffling and gasping scared and small and trembling.

"One more time, girl. You can do it one more time. You want me to come don't you? Worship this fucking cock because it's going to fuck you so good later. Show me how fucking good you are."

You took your hand off my head then and scraped your nails down my back until you untangled my wrists and shoved my hand back toward your crotch. Obediently I started stroking you again and took my small ounce of control back, pumping you hard and desperate and your own gasps dancing with mine. Your legs were wracked now with those familiar tremors and I could feel you about to come so I tugged harder, making the base of your packer slam down on your t-dick just right. I was aching to taste your come and you could feel it, as your upper body sat up and you gripped my small shoulders, pinning me down around you and squeezing my neck with your legs as you came violently.

I tenderly licked the length of you and swirled my tongue ring around the head, slid my fingers down against the wetness of your body and brought them to my mouth and sucked on them moaning, savoring you while I rested against your hip breathless and shaking. Your hand tenderly ran through my damp hair to reveal my eyes fully and you stared down at me, still spasming and murmuring syllables that wanted to be words.

My arm caressed your stomach to your chest lovingly and words weren't needed. Slowly and in phases, we rose back up together, back into our seats and we kissed deep and languid. The aftercare of your mouth sent me. I felt delicate and shivery against the power of you and your shoulders curved inward, until your arms held me like a warm cradle. You soothed me back to myself, the tenderness in you as loud as the primal just was.

After a while, we went back to our respective positions and the hum of your GPS robotically echoed, "Fifty-four mins until your destination."

We both laughed and you turned to me with a satiated grin, "Think you can wait that long for your reward?"

I nodded sheepishly and ran my hand through my hair and exhaled.

"I think I can make it."

With that, you turned back onto the main road, taking us back out into the dark, this time with the windows down and the breeze of our scent dancing between us in the dusk of the night.

Come Here: Lover Letter #2

oral sex, orgasm denial, primal

C ome here. Come lick the liquor of your voice dripping down my spine and make the violent current of my ache thick. I need the heavy insistence of your tongue pushing my breaths back down my throat. I breathe when you let me. I part and bend and shiver, shredded from the gravel of your words scraping me in streaks that leave me scarlet. Tonight we are animals. Tonight the curl of your lips over your teeth suck me through my thrashing. You pull sacred stories from my center while I chew on the meat of your shoulders; the pain of permission stands still like a scream in a dream you won't let me have just yet.

"Don't you fucking come," your cheeks murmur between the buttercream of my thighs. It hurts to hold it. It hurts when your rabid palms keep my pulse pressed between the glass of the sheets and your lips.

I can't stand your voice. It puts everything I hate inside of everything I love and my body becomes a swing set between your rabid eyes and your whispers. You keep me like this in the dark, your words spilling out of my cunt and back down your throat while I lay here and try to invite gravity back in.

In another life, we were waterfalls. In another life, we were two tributaries of a riverbed rushing toward each other just to entwine, just to be the same shade of indigo that reflects constellations back toward the sky.

You'll Pay For It Later

daddy/girl, bratting, slapping, edging, spanking

You were being a brat this weekend, mouthy, pushy, testing me. It was suddenly summer and we had functions to go to, errands to run, the heat to deal with, time constraints.

I hated being late. You knew this. You showed up to my front door Saturday morning in a new sundress that hit you just above the knees. If you bent over far enough, others could see you were wearing nothing underneath. I had plans to put a lot of things low to the ground at the barbecue today and "need your help."

The mood you showed up didn't match mine. You were chewing gum loudly, flopping your body on the couch distracted on your phone while I brought all the things to the car, already sweating. You were half listening to me when I asked if you knew directions, gave me a vacant "mmhm," and went back to texting.

You trailed after me absently, jangling your purse and throwing your mirrored sunglasses on in response to my,

"Car's all packed."

You forgot to bring our waters out, gave me attitude when I set the keys on your lap to go back and get them. If you hadn't looked so fucking pretty today I would have roughed you up before we left, edged you on the counter leaving you wet and wanting the rest of the afternoon, marked your ass so when you sat at the table later, I could watch you squirm.

You came back and were waiting for me to drive while I stared at you, waiting for you to put your seat-belt on like you always remembered to.

I couldn't tell if you were just egging me on today or were truly this distracted. You smelled like your strawberry bubblegum, like innocence, and your small knees resting together made my cock stir.

I pulled the car out and you turned on the radio like you were already bored, pointing the a.c. vent at your head, impatiently waiting for the coolant to do its work. It was 11 a.m. and it was already 92 degrees outside. Thankfully this was at someone's home today, and we weren't hosting.

"Do you have the directions up? Where am I going?"

"Oh yeah ... hang on."

Wow. This had to be intentional. My hand shoved the fabric of your dress up until I was squeezing your upper thigh and you gasped in shock, a bit theatrical almost.

"Are you going to be good for Daddy today?"

A fucking smirk formed on your face as you put in the address between a wince. It took everything in me not to slap it off you. Everything.

My hand gripped you harder and my fingers curled into your skin, digging in my nails and feeling your upper body tense, giving that facade of yours away entirely.

"Don't make me ask again, girl."

I pulled my hand away and removed your sunglasses, grabbed your chin so you had to look at me directly. Your eyes told it all, you were testing me today, spirited and aroused because of summer. I hadn't let you come in days, made you watch me get off last weekend while I kept you tied to a chair with a wand rigged against your cunt. I could still hear your pathetic little pleas, those moans later on from your exhaustion of needing it so bad but not letting go for me. That scream of you turned whisper from how I broke you.

You had no armor today. This was your only weapon.

You stared back at me earnestly and I could see that defiant spark shrink some. You were contemplating how far you should push, nervous to keep going, the frustration in you aware if you didn't behave I might not give you what you want. Then again, even if you were good, I still might not.

Slightly defeated in your stare back you uttered my favorite phrase,

"Yes, Daddy."

"Yes, Daddy. What?"

That spotlight on you hotter than the sun, your cheeks blazed. I could smell your wetness through the thin fabric of your little sundress. You didn't know it but I was going to fuck you all night tonight.

Edging you like this, not having you was admittedly just as hard for me as it was for you. I missed your taste, your shivers, your little hands resting against my chest when it was over, the sweet pulp of your lips and the way you gushed over my cock the moment I told you to.

"Yes Daddy. I'll be your good girl today."

I cut you off at that last word and kissed you with the intent to take your breath away. My hand found your little throat and squeezed until your feared little cry coated my tongue. I swallowed it like I'd been waiting for it all week, pulled away and bit your lower lip until tears welled up.

I put my turn signal on and ignored you while you collected yourself, steered the car in the direction the map on your phone was telling me to go.

I put my own sunglasses on and stared forward,

"Good. You know what fucking happens to girls who are bad. Daddy has rewards for you tonight. So you better be good."

Your little hand slid toward mine in a silent apology, for now, and I grasped it sweetly, turned the radio up for you and drove, thinking of all the filthy ways I'd have you later.

No Rest For The Wicked

daddy/girl, boot play, dirty talk, fear, primal, slapping, ass play, plug, riding crop

You were focused and deep in concentration, lost in the middle of your newest book that was research for the next class you were teaching. You were not to be interrupted, but I was bored. I was hungry, and I fucking wanted you.

I tried staring at you while I flipped through channels on the television with my headphones on, unnoticed. I tried yawning loudly, throwing a blanket off myself and animatedly pulled it back up my body. I made the cat purr loudly as I pet him, giggled heartily at Tik-Tok when I paused the film I was almost through watching. I got up and stretched on my way back from the kitchen, arms high above my head making my tank ride up to show my hips. I made sure to squeeze my ass, arching my back just a little, pointed both towards you.

You gave me nothing. It was irksome. This was our quiet hour, to your decree. I didn't want it tonight. I wanted your attention, your full-bodied gaze that spotlit me in that way I loved most. Tonight the minutes felt like hours. Your quiet was deafening. Tonight my body was rebelling hard enough for me to act, breaking the consistency of my obedience in half. I knew once I stood up, there was no going back.

You had noticed all of it, of course. You kept silent and remained focused, reveling from my obvious frustration. Your breath almost hitched when the periphery of me left my spot on the couch, stood up and moved toward you.

I padded over to you loudly, a few stomps demanding recognition, clearly forgetting my place in this hierarchy. Over your chair now where you were perched comfortably in your quiet, my shadow blocked the words on the page you were intently scanning. Rude. Disruptive. Brazen. Your tongue clicked hard and you continued to stare down,

"Yes?"

A low growl elicited in your tone and that last word rose to a boil. The need to get work done being sacrificed now by the seconds I was taking away from an important task.

"I'm bored."

Your eyes widened at the page, incredulous. You squeezed the binding as you shut the hardcover with some force. The loudest sound in the room echoed in my chest and you gazed up, bolting the bounce right out of me. Maybe this was a mistake?

"You aren't allowed to be bored. You aren't allowed off your side of the couch. Or standing right here, on that part of the carpet, in front of Daddy's chair, while I'm working."

You tossed the book abruptly to the floor, the thud of its weight on the wood echoed in the room. Your hands wrapped around my hips in the silence after, pulled me into your lap possessively, just like I wanted.

I scanned the shift in your demeanor, calm to primal, the pads of your fingers dug into my ribs until they felt bone, then dug harder. You watched regret start to flood my face as you perceived my slow shrinking.

Your hands crawled up my body, noticing the small shivers that formed, desperate for touch, for attention. You pushed the bottom of my tank up as you slid inside, finding my breasts heaving up and down, enough to signal a change in my heart rate.

The ache in me was obvious, and I was honey from the contact of your skin. Your palm reached for my cheek, caressing it, watching the blush form. You watched my head lean and purr into your hand. My eyes closed and were met with the sting of an abrupt slap, waking my jaw. The nerves in my face exploded in shock as you took me by the throat. My eyes watered, slammed open to find you staring at me with the darkness in your gaze prowling toward my discomfort.

My small hands now gripped your shoulders subconsciously, while my ass and thighs tensed in your lap waiting for you to speak, almost flinching for what was to come. I tried not to blink while you spoke in that lowered tone you used when you were Daddy.

"You're going to regret being bored, little girl."

You pushed me off your lap and watched me falter while I tried to right myself. You placed your heavy boot on my back to keep me from rising, nudged my ass with the toe and stood over me. Your shadow eclipsed my body and after an exasperated sigh elicited from your mouth, you paced me in a circle, the way an animal does when it knows it's hunt is running.

A pit of fear grew deeper in my stomach and I peeked back over my shoulder and saw you there, foaming down at my smallness with destruction in your eyes, blood rushing to your cock.

You nodded back at me, looking down the long hallway to the bedroom, a signal of where I was to go next. You kicked me again, harder this time, as if my knees needed that to jump start my crawl.

"Move. Now."

Your cock strained the fabric of your jeans as you watched the perfect curves of me knee-to-palm my way down the hall. I was quiet now, my boldness already silenced and the anxious tension coming off me in waves, a 180-degree shift from moments before. As I crawled, your breaths deepened behind me and then something else, the metal buckle of your belt clicking open. The sound of it was obscene against a whimper that fell out of my mouth on the way to my fate. This was followed by the friction of leather against denim in one swoop.

You turned back and gave a brief gaze at the book on the floor by your chair, meditating momentarily while your eyes rolled back to me. I was knelt at the foot of our bed now, solemn and silent in my brash decision. You could already taste my tears as you rubbed your crotch, as you advanced closer.

All work and no play. It was time now, to play.

"On your fucking feet. Palms on the bed. And don't fucking move," you decreed.

I rose but kept my head down. I didn't dare look over my shoulder, so I kept focus on the geometric patterns of our quilt, the same preview every time until it got too much and I collapsed in defeat from you, from the pain.

We hadn't played in a week or so, and my body was a blank canvas again. You both hated and loved that, especially when you could smell my arousal between my legs, that total loss of control shutting down any resistance I might have left in me. Just a change in your tone could shut that up, or a low growl, or that black that pooled in your eyes when you stood above me seething and swollen to keep me small, keep me scared, keep me yours.

Your boots meandered to the side of the bed and peripherally, the silk blindfold in your hand flashed in my vision. You set it below my nose on the comforter quietly.

I took it along with the silent message of impatience and wrapped it around my head, the tie I was making suddenly interrupted by your firm hands, making the knot hard and tight around my head. You planted a kiss on the back of my neck after running your tongue up my spine and I shivered. Your hands caressed my ass and squeezed and pinched, warming my skin for what was to come.

Then it was quiet again. I never rested well in that space with you. When it was quiet, it meant something was coming. When it was quiet, there would be blunt disruption. I went back to my training, trying to place myself in that meditative state where I was present and trying to find that space you were opening up for me.

You stared at me, taking it all in, the rounded curves of my hips, my pale ass that longed to be marked, my shoulders tense as I held myself up.

My thighs squeezed here and there in anticipation. My breasts rested tight against the mattress

Your belt jingled and something loud hit the floor, making me jump. You snickered and I waited longer, until I felt it, the small glass plug wet with lube pressing into my ass, followed by a slap on each of my inner thighs with your small crop.

I let my muscles open to you, to the toy, and you slowly eased in until my body was gripping the base as it rested there. I exhaled and allowed myself to feel it, going back to my deeper breathing. Then your fists came down. They were wrapped in the leather of two of your belts and the texture of them over your knuckles both stung and pushed my skin forward, testing my steadiness, making my knees buckle awkwardly. Your boots kicked my ankles apart keeping my thighs spread and you punched at me harder, hitting spots that weren't soft, finding bone, feeling me pull into myself like I had somewhere else to go.

I wasn't tied to anything and you liked me like that, liked to feel and see me run, turn, twist so my body might cramp or spasm in its effort to flee where I couldn't. You wouldn't stop until I used my safeword to stop you, and the sadist in you loved to keep pushing me. You loved that fight I had with myself and my body, the sting of your fists and how I kept pushing for you against that moment I didn't want to come, that end where it stopped and I never wanted to be done. I almost always went further than you'd expect, and you always believed you could stop me sooner than the last time.

This was the battle. You kept pummeling me and were adding your boots now, and using the end of your crop against my cunt, the wetness adding to the sting of the leather while I cried out and clenched my thighs again, eliciting a harsh kick from you to keep them open.

You put your weight against me then, feeling that spike of the pain in my body and knowing that the connection of the heat of your body, your sweet breath in my ear, your lips that tenderly met my neck and shoulders;

I'd keep going for you, against you. Your strong arm found my waist and I felt you grinding the shape of your cock against my ass, denim burning my skin as your fists stopped and your teeth started. The crop dropped loudly and your jaw bared down more on my flesh, making me start to cry. You licked the welt that was forming and reached for my clit and slapped it and my head fell against the mattress. It was that point where I could only hold half my weight and my breaths were halted, my whimpering louder as you tugged slightly on the plug and then shoved three fingers inside me, staying still.

"Are you going to be bored anymore, girl?"

"No, Daddy!"

"Are you going to stay here in this room until I'm done with you?"

"Yes, Daddy!"

A grip of your hand scraped my jaw and you bent my neck back to kiss me roughly. You shoved me back down on the bed and flipped me so I was on my back. You slid me back up and stared down at the sight of me all flushed and red and flecked with colors from your fists. My stomach was shaking and fists gripped the comforter as you pushed me to lay flat in the center of it. Then you left me, only to return tying hemp rope around my wrists and ankles, noticing my neck reach for you for a kiss and ignoring me, ignoring my trembling lower lip and little sighs and moans. You slapped my cunt with your hand as you took in the vision of me all messy and scared.

"Daddy needs to go back to work. I hope you don't get bored in here, again. When I'm done, maybe I will come back for you."

I cried out as you shut the light off and the door, heard you sigh in pleasure and mild exasperation, amused at the predicament I had put myself in and stroking the bulge in your pants, thinking about later tonight with that menaced twinkle in your eye.

Kidnapped At The Bar

consensual non-consent, fear play, dirty talk, drug references, gags, crying, riding crop, D/s, slapping

K^{ai:}
        It was late now, getting close to last call at the club and the Friday night crowd had slammed us. My upper arms were burning from the amount of stretching, reaching for all the top-shelf liquor everyone seemed to want tonight. My knees ached from crouching down and trying to fit myself in the small spaces between the other bartenders roving legs and kegs that needed to be switched out hourly. My shoes were sticky and the busboys were doing their final round in hopes people would leave once the tables were wiped down in front of them.

A few patrons were scattered here and there, calling Ubers on their phones or drunk texting a fuck-buddy, coming up to me with slurring words to close out their tabs. Most everyone had that aura to them of arousal, sweaty and satisfied from a night of dancing with friends.

I made great tips tonight. All the men seemed to believe (or want to believe) I was straight, and I dressed accordingly, my cleavage poking out of a low-cut top and my favorite ripped jeans that had frayed holes just below my ass for a nice show. That was the game. It worked well on a Friday night and the wad in my pocket was thick proof.

I eyed my purse under the bar and remembered the joint I'd rolled earlier, thought of the cool evening air in our back alley and that specific quiet of a dying down city that exhaled along with me, settled back into itself sans crowd and noise.

Our club manager was doing their nightly walk-through as I packed my things and closed out the bar. I'd always found them a bit mysterious; they kept to themselves and mostly stayed in their office during busy nights, stood on the second floor balcony with their vape pen pensively watching the dance floor below. They always wore all black to work; I got the sense they enjoyed being a fringe-dweller and didn't enjoy the spotlight much unless it was on their own rigid terms. I never saw them bring anyone home or bring anyone in. We were often the only ones at the end of the night in here together and we shared few exchanges, most of the time.

Tonight their energy seemed a bit frantic, louder than usual as they lifted the chairs and rested them on the tables, tossed sunglasses and photo ID's in the lost and found. Truthfully, I found them a bit intimidating, thinking back to my interview two years ago, alone in their office their energy felt palpable. No one knew anything about their personal life, and they kept to themselves, which piqued my interest even more.

Sometimes the withholding type feels exotic to me. I'm so social and put so much forward and strangers are just comfortable with me, which is such a double-edged sword a lot of the time. I always wondered what it felt like to just be so naturally withholding, and further, wondered what lay behind that veil in others that guarded their autonomy with ease.

A loud crash jolted me as my back was turned away from them and I shrieked. As my hips rotated, I saw the haphazard pile of chairs they thought they'd stacked evenly, that had caught on their shirt as they were walking away. That feeling in my chest was still banging like thunder, and a flush came over my chest. I cleared my throat embarrassingly, tried to calm myself as I turned and their eyes caught mine.

"I'm so sorry! I did not mean to make you jump! Oh fuck, are you okay? I'm just. Someone canceled on an appointment I had tomorrow on my day off and it's the third time it's happened. They just texted me at —" I looked at my watch. "Yeah. 1:30 a.m.? Yeah. I'm just. Upset? Agitated? Also a bit frazzled."

Their brow furrowed a little deeper at the end of the last sentence, looking down forlornly at the pile of chairs. This was probably the most verbose they'd been with me in some time, with anyone in here, honestly. Their strong facade faded while I watched their expression turn from anxiousness to frustration and then when their eyes met mine, something unidentifiable, control? I had the sudden urge to give them a hug, but put some softness in my words instead,

"No worries! I'm so sorry that happened. Sounds like they might be a bit unreliable for your schedule? I can finish the chairs if that helps and you can scoot out of here if you need to. I've closed before a bunch and I can handle it."

They looked up from the ground, collected again, and set the chairs back to how they needed to be. Their arm reached behind their shoulder and rubbed their hair, exhaling a deep sigh.

"No no, that's okay. It's basically done in here. I think I just need maybe, some fresh air? Wanna grab a smoke outside?"

They pulled their vape out of their pocket waving it in the air a little anxiously with a half smile. It made me feel a little fluttery inside.

***

Jude:

I had this all planned out: the sob story about ruined plans, staying in my office prepping during the day, finding out about her private life, knowing she was single, queer, and lonely. I noticed her posting more selfies on her social media lately to get attention. I watched her flirting with the queer patrons at the bar the last few months, many that resembled me. Then tonight, I lingered after closing to put chairs away to get her attention after everyone had gone.

Since I'd hired her I knew we would fuck, and since she never initiated and it hasn't happened "organically," I decided to take this into my own hands. Needless to say, this had taken patience and time, studying her routine and stalking her online presence.

I made blank profiles on the dating apps she talked about with her girlfriends who came out on nights to keep her company during the slower shifts. I read her profiles that feigned her weaknesses for soft masculinity, her indecisive ways she seemed frustrated about internally, how she had to mask at her job all night and needed to come home and turn her brain off. A lot of the profiles that were out there also mentioned a mild curiosity about kink, probably more for intrigue on her end than genuine understanding.

Still, it was enough to know what she needed, more than she knew what she did, anyway. I was tired anyway, of seeing her date clones of toxic energy, the same type of cocky butch, just in a different font. I'd watch her after each breakup, when she'd be sad for weeks and I could feel it, then she'd take a break and try again. I could fix that for her, wear her down in a better way.

Truth be told, I loved a new femme, green around the edges and sucking the air in gasps once she was below me, completely stupefied from what I knew how to do, what I could bring out in their hungry little bodies, their sad little holes that hadn't ever hurt like this before. Even more, I'd live on in their minds long after, break the backbone of their brain so it was stretched where it should have been all along.

I wasn't an asshole, but I also wasn't a nice guy. I chose my moments carefully until I got someone home, had them calm from the pills my pharmacologist at the club made up for me, and that's when the real fun started. Everyone needs a friend who was a former chemistry major. I'm getting ahead of myself though.

I was staring her down in the alley, her small back leaning against the cold brick. She kept tucking her hair behind her ear in the wind instead of just changing direction to stand closer to me. (Bottom.) She wouldn't look me directly in the eye and instead her vision would trail off somewhere in synchronicity like the end of her sentences. (Confidence.) Her skinny jeans she had on had loosened from hours of bending and kept sliding down while she fidgeted from the cold, exposing her hipbone I couldn't wait to mark with my belt. She didn't adjust that as much as her hair in her eyes. (Good little slut.)

She was smaller than me, so this would be easy. Center city was quiet now, everyone was home now hugging their toilets from a night of excess, or passed out in bed, or sexting their exes. There were no cars in the lot behind the club except mine. She lived close, rode in on her bike a lot, especially on a Friday when the night train was a mob; this was another important detail I'd studied well.

The thing about sadists is this: we are experts at waiting. The waiting is the foreplay. That delicious gap between knowing and acting, being the only one that knows what's coming, and then slicing the air of the room in half once that moment presents itself; we live for that shit. When that moment does come, the way it was stoked and re-calibrated and poignantly crafted makes the action so much sweeter, the tastes and touches ten times more decadent.

Then there's the fear, ironing it flat with my power to stretch it and her body in ways she never thought she could. Then it's the fight, the coaxing words and the harsh touch. The slaps of a tear-stained cheek while I'm calling her my sad little slut and she's melting between her legs for more. That's my sweet spot, that's where I shine, when her cheeks are just as wet as her sweet little cunt.

In the alley now, I had her comfortable, had her feeling at ease and safe. I played the part well, the inquisitive Butch who just wants to listen to someone's problems, the strong shoulder ready to take them on with tenacity on her behalf. I was a master at the direct eye contact, the authenticity that ensured things will be alright. Eventually, I'd sidle close enough to place a gentle hand on her small shoulder while she became comfortable and her filter dissipated, both from the weed and the space that's rarely been made for her to be seen. It was easier than it looked.

I took a hearty puff off my vape pen as I watched her stomp delicately, almost tenderly on the joint she'd just finished with her tough girl boot. I smirked inwardly.

I pulled a small bottle of whiskey from my back pocket I had prepped for this very moment, asking if she wanted an end-of-the-night chaser. At first, she adamantly shook her head saying she was sober and needed to bike home, being overly polite to the boss, uncertain if this was a test or not.

I offered her a ride in my truck, feigning ignorance and realizing her place was on my way home and that my flatbed was empty and it was do-able, and it seemed like she'd had a long night and could use it.

She almost declined politely a second time until I started screwing off the lid and handing it to her to hold. She eyeballed me with a mischievous twinkle that made my cock twitch for what I had in store for later, silly little girl taking a drink from someone she barely knew, what a lesson she'd learn tonight.

After she took a more than generous swig, I figured I'd have about thirty minutes before what I'd sprinkled in that bottle kicked in full force; that was adequate time to get her and her bike in my car, lock up the bar, and get her inside my place before she was off to dreamland for a bit.

I winked at her as she gave me back the whiskey and I caught a tinge of a blush before she looked back down at the blacktop shyly, then my boots.

"Let's get you home," I said, holding the door open for her with that brand of chivalry that was masking the monster inside so well. The pads of my fingers thumbed my house key in my pocket with menace, resting duplicitously beside keys that locked other implements that waited patiently for her at my home. My jaw tightened and nostrils flared as a whisper of her perfume wafted over me as she grabbed her purse.

Tonight was the night.

***

Jude:

The drug had taken effect quick, lasted long enough to get you back to mine and ease the small form of you through my door. I set you on the couch at first, posing you to sit, studying you potently in your haze of unconsciousness.

I'd left this morning with the bedroom ready, the scissors on the table to cut off the clothes you'd no longer need, the fabric only a distraction of what was inevitably going to happen to you. I removed everything like a ritual, slicing through the mesh and faux leather like I was unwrapping a present I'd been waiting for for years. Your skin was so soft, your wrists delicate enough I could wrap my fingers there and close around you like a cuff. Your hair smelled like clovers and nectarines and your nipples were slightly upturned and begging for my mouth already. I surveyed the inches of you with my eyes, the deep breathing and peaceful expression on your face, the darling little line of your cunt, every bit of you my land to invade.

I pulled the nakedness of you against me and carried the limp weight of you back to my bedroom, locked your limbs down taut so you were spread-eagled. I put a gag around your pink little mouth and buckled it behind you tenderly. You were still out like a light, affording me time to light a few candles and make myself a whiskey on the rocks, perching myself in a chair adjacent to the bed so you could see who put you here.

I eyed the line of implements and toys behind me on my dresser, higher than the bed so you couldn't see what was waiting for you, but close enough so you could hear when I shuffled them around.

I had to admit, as much as I drank in the form of you at the club every night the past couple years, when the curves of you would paint the bass and the customers gulped down their drinks, when you'd put your hair in that loose ponytail I wanted to drag you across the floor by, when you smiled softly to yourself on your phone; that was decadent but tonight, you looked the prettiest when you were here, finally at my mercy.

***

Kai:

I woke up with a pounding fucking headache, half aware of my body even existing and then everything a blurred focus that seemed to refuse to become clearer to me.

Where the fuck was I? In a room. Not my room. Someone's room.

What was that smell? Candles. Evening air. A window cracked. Leather.

My muscles felt lifeless, sore, tender, exhausted. I couldn't breathe right. Something was across my face. Straps. A wet ball between my jaw I could squeeze, only slightly. My mouth felt like it had been vacuumed dry. My throat hurt. I couldn't move. I could flex my joints but I was tethered. I had the desire to fight, to run, but the energy of a rag-doll to execute any of it.

I was in a large bed. I was naked. Who had undressed me? Where were my clothes? I was covered in a dark sheet. Was I bruised? Was I wet anywhere other than my cheeks? Was I bleeding? Everything hurt. My heartbeat felt slow. I couldn't form words and the room felt hazy. My eyes cracked open and I started to inhale in that panicked way through my nose, muffled whimpers from behind the gag that was around my jaw that were making my head feel like it was vibrating.

Any energy I had seemed to wane almost immediately and even trying to hyperventilate or induce myself with adrenaline exhausted me quickly. I wasn't paralyzed. I was tied down. Why was I so fucking tired? Why did everything hurt? Remember. Try to remember. Your name is Kai. You have 2 cats. You live in the city. You work at a bar.

The rest started to come back after that, in fractured pieces. Sticky shoes. Tip money. Empty bottles of Jameson in a trash can. Someone's vape pen. Chairs falling. Jude. Jude smiling. Smoke in the alley. Nothing. Nothing. Where was the rest?

My eyes hadn't been covered, only my mouth and the fear of what both of those meant made my stomach turn. Whoever did this wanted me to see but keep quiet. They weren't trying to hide. So far all I had the courage to stare at with my heavy eyelids cracked was the white ceiling.

Something about this felt like a ritual; the candles, the position of my body, the silence, the precision of the knots around my extremities, the gag. Was this planned? Pre-meditated. No that's a term for criminals. Murderers. I'd be dead already if that was the end game. My stomach shuddered at that last thought and a cry that scraped the back of my dry throat spilled out and around my gag. Panicking at my own noise, I turned my neck and saw them there, poised and quiet in a chair a few feet to my right, watching me, still in their work t-shirt and jeans, predatory and silent, collected, staring right back.

Jude. The flask. Had they had a drink? I couldn't remember. There was nothing after. My eyes watered over their lids subconsciously trying to discern what this meant. I was tired of keeping my eyes open already. I tried to raise my neck, caught a glimpse of a mirrored bureau in front of me with things laid out in a line on black silk. I let out a sob and my head turned back to Jude quicker than I was ready to, the image of the bureau wavering awkwardly into the image of them and not quite catching up. They sat just as still in their chair like a statue while the feeling of vertigo washed over me and the tunnel of my vision closed again.

***

Jude:

My cock was hard. I'd maybe over-negotiated the dose I'd given for her smaller frame and when I heard her finally stir, whimper, and attempt to move, it made me feel hopeful; two players in this game, finally. She looked truly helpless, all of that badass little moto boot, ripped jeans, attitude stripped from her (literally and figuratively) and just the softness of her pale flesh, the tremors of her muscles reacting to the room, her predicament. Her sounds were small, delicate even, same as her slender wrists which barely had energy to flex let alone pull on the braided knots I'd circled them with. She was mine finally. No power. No fight. No running. The swell in me rose higher at that last bit.

I knew her better, more than she knew herself. I could break the cycle for her, show her how much she was wasting her fucking time on the others; fuckbois and bar-flies so unworthy of her time, her body, her holes. She just needed to be shown. This was the easiest way. I watched her intently, her nipples hard under the sheet, her awareness rising, her confidence crestfallen. After a bit she finally turned and saw me.

I didn't say a word, tried to let her rest in the solemn rule of my eyes, my energy knowing what she knew now and watching the betrayal realize itself into her body. The fear in her eyes was that of a faun before a car is about to scrape it off a pavement, trapped and desperate and terrified, wide-eyed to the inevitable loss of control and even more, trembling at who the universe gave it to.

Just as I was about to stand and advance toward her, she passed back out. The drug was in its early stages of wearing off and this was where I wanted her; docile in her body but becoming more aware in her brain, the spark in her being kept at bay. She could have her words, her emotions, her choices to react how she wanted and needed to, and I could keep the rest.

I decided to lay down next to her, taking my boots off and hearing them thud on the floor in sequence, stirring her some. I kept the sheet over her, my hand deciding to study her face instead, brushing her hair behind her ears the way she had a mere hour ago. I noticed her cheekbones, her lips, swollen and wet around the gag, her breathing quiet and slow, small tattoos on her clavicle and rounded little curves of her right shoulder.

My hands felt like they had static in them, my palms eager to grab and squeeze and thrust and bruise. The force in my body always had that pressure behind it, always that need to exude itself upon smallness or to shrink something that wanted to be bigger than it was. I was built to strip power, to take, to fill and crush and find the right kind of caves to echo my growls into deep.

This was where I put her, and I knew it was a gift. She would find her way to that understanding as well. I slid my palm across the red ball of the gag and cupped it, feeling the moisture of her breath and I lowered my face into that small curve where her neck met her shoulder. I inhaled, felt like the pulp of her was already in my mouth, between my teeth. My arm ran from her throat to her cunt and I held the heat of it harder, possessive. Her eyes fluttered back open and I felt her hips try to press themselves back into the mattress, trying to hide in the corner I already had her in.

A murmur caught in my throat then and I smiled down at her sadistically.

"Shhh, no use fighting. That deep swig you took from my flask. That wasn't all whiskey, honey. I know. Shhh. It's why your body feels so heavy. Why your eyes feel so tired. It's easier this way. Can't have you fighting me, hurting yourself, hurting me."

I adjusted my hips to move closer to her and grazed her thigh with the bulge under my jeans and her eyes moved down and in a failed effort to lift her head fully, it landed back against the pillow heavily.

"Mmmhm. That's for later. My cock. It's gonna hurt so good."

She flinched in response to that, as if I was going to slap her and instead I slid my tongue from her chin to the corner of her eye, tasting the salt of her tears and bucked against her hip a little rougher. My arm leaned across her stomach and I gripped her hipbone aggressively and kept my face close to hers, almost cheek to cheek. I kept my voice low, feeling her elevated breathing in her belly make my forearm rise and fall.

"I suppose now is a good time to explain myself. I have been watching you since I hired you. Watching you flounder. Give your time and romance and body to unworthy parties. I've been watching you break your own heart, repeat the same mistakes. Devalue your self worth for attention and hope that this time it'll be different. You're in a cycle. You are more than this. You want more, too. I've listened to your conversations with your friends, ghosted you on dating apps where you hint at your desire, misunderstand your own submission.

You don't know who you are as well as I do, you don't know how you could fly from someone cutting off your wings. I do. I can see by the confusion in your face and that angry little brow you have zero clue what I'm referring to, which is why we're here. I also know that I'm your type. That you find me attractive, that your body responds to my presence, and that you need this overwhelming brutality against you."

At that last phrase, she attempted to turn her head from me but I caught her jaw in anticipation, keeping her there under my gaze.

"This little fight in you is cute at best," I said.

You growled in response, and I laughed, furthering your anger. I slapped your cheek a little tenderly and reached across your neck, hearing you gasp while I grabbed the large bottle of ice water with a straw that had been perspiring on the side table.

"I would like to remove your gag. I don't enjoy one way conversations with my toys. You know now this is me. You know you have a choice in what you decide to do if I take it off. If you scream I will leave you here alone in the dark with nothing. I'll spend the next few hours making you deeply regret it, and it will break the trust I hope to have and build here. You're fucking mine. I have your phone, your pass-code to respond to your friends. I can tell others you are on vacation at work. No one is going to come looking for you. No one is wondering. It's in your best fucking interest to listen."

At that last sentence, I raised my voice more firmly and noticed her shoulders shudder out a few shivers. She believed me. She saw I'd come this far, gone to these lengths, planned ahead. I wasn't bluffing. I gripped her hair with my fist and told her to nod if she understood and agreed.

Her neck lazily moved up and down as much as she could control it, and my fingers unbuckled the back of the gag in one fell swoop and I removed it, the straps leaving little impressions of tightness across her reddened cheeks and her mouth reaching for the straw quietly.

She sipped almost faster than she could swallow, until her neck got tired again and she stopped herself, needing to take deep inhales to catch her breath. Abruptly, I pulled the sheet from her body so the only fabric between us now was the cotton and denim of my own clothes. She sniffled and sucked in air darting her eyes at mine trying to study what might come next. I felt the tension of her body stiffen on the mattress and ran the warmth of my hand against her stomach, her hips, between her breasts tenderly, exciting her body amidst the fear, muddling her head even further in confusion as to how she could enjoy being both captive and touched like this willingly.

She was a bundle of nerves, fighting herself internally at the pleasure of my touch and the predicament of her ties, her non-consensual choice at being put here naked against my body, being taken away and drugged. As my fingers grazed lower and lower each rise and fall, I finally grabbed her cunt and felt the heat of it, along with her own wetness. I stared down at her knowingly and saw a mix of things spread across her face; shame, objectification, embarrassment, smallness in being perceived so acutely and honestly, and I saw her arousal. Her breasts were rising and her ass even did that thing where it rose from the bed up into me, barely at all but enough. Bodies always tell the truth. I decided to break the silence,

"Tell me, Kai ... has anyone ever cropped your pussy before fucking you?"

***

Kai:

This was not okay. I could feel them feeding off me like some sort of vampire, my fear and anxiety and that penetrating stare of theirs just relentlessly competent and stoic. Why was I getting wet? It was just because they were touching me, right? No one gets off to being drugged and kidnapped. What the actual fuck. They drugged me. They admittedly told me they had and they had planned in advance in a moment of my own vulnerability to do so, and they did that. Yet, here I was, exposed, scared, shivering against them from the presence and the heavy perception of their gaze. No one had ever looked at or into me like this before, even in the most intimate moments I'd ever had with the best lover I had ever been with. No one ever saw me like this; it was if they were gathering all my facets in their dilated pupils and throwing me back at myself to see what I felt. The gulps of water I'd inhaled helped my mind clear some, rose my awareness and the sensations of their touch on my body felt more welcoming than it should. Drugged?! Brought here against my will?! Stripped? I still had no fucking idea where my clothes even were.

Still, their hand over my cunt made me pulse, and the ropes around my ankles when my thighs tensed burned ... good? This had to be the drugs. Maybe they change your personality or something. My body was fighting its own impulses, and in my mind, I was trying to convince myself this was wrong. Bad. Violent. Fucked. Up. I closed my eyes when I felt myself dripping against their palm, ashamed. My lower lip trembled on the edge or more tears as they started grinding against my clit in that way I always craved, deep pressure, power, possessive with a knowing rhythm my body was owned.

Then the question about being cropped arose and I whimpered in response. If I said no did that mean they would do that to me? If I lied and said yes, would they believe it and stop touching me? I didn't want them to stop ... what the actual fuck. Once again, they broke the silence in the room,

"You don't have to answer. I know you haven't. I think I know a lot if not most of the things on that bureau behind us are novel to you. Don't close your eyes and hide. I can feel you liking this. I want you to like it. I want you to enjoy the force of me and the things I'm taking from you tonight. You can cry more. I like your tears. I know, baby. Mmm fuck. I know."

The betrayal of my body was making me almost lightheaded and I opened my eyes back up to meet theirs, finding a tender smile I had trouble believing was just tender. They rose off the bed then, taking their hand with them and subconsciously my hips bucked off the bed to try and follow and they laughed low, a slight menace behind it.

I tried to raise my head and shoulders to watch them move toward the line of things, saw them grab a crop and my stomach dropped. They took their shirt off and the broadness of their chest and shoulders surprised me, always hidden beneath their clothes. Their hand gripped the handle and they moved it in the air a few times, making it whistle. My hips tried to move my thighs closed protectively and forgetting my ankles wouldn't let me, I gasped and exhaled a scared noise similar to that of a victim when she's being chased, hunted. Still, I felt turned on. By violence?

Power?

Helplessness.

"I d-d-don't like pain, please …. don't. I don't w-want this," I blurted this out in a stutter, slow and my motor skills still impaired from the drug.

Jude smirked, seemingly taking that as a challenge instead of a boundary.

"Do you think I care? You're tied down because I knew you'd want to fight. Don't think of it as pain. Think of it as something you're pushing yourself through to get to the pleasure I want to reward you with for being good. You want to be good, don't you? You don't want to imagine what could happen to you if you're bad. Is that shivering from fear or need? Do you know the difference? Is there one?"

My body trembled feverishly, not sure how to fight back without any control, terrified to push them.

"I know you. I see things in you that you aren't aware of. Why do you think you don't hate this right now? Why aren't you fighting more? Why didn't you scream? You could pull on the ropes more. You could have bitten me when we were cheek to cheek, spit water in my face. Cursed me out. You haven't done any of that."

They let the crop start caressing my skin during this speech, tapping lightly and smoothing where I felt myself taut and anxious most; my stomach, shoulders, my neck, my inner thighs. The square of leather grazed my cunt eventually, rubbing the wetness of myself along my quaking calves, my ankles, sliding it in their mouth obscenely. I searched for mercy in the black pierce of their eyes as they held my hips still, wishing my own stasis and silence would save me.

They looked down at me with a bemused grin on their face. "I'm not stopping until I feel like it."

***

Jude:

The drugs were wearing off now, and I could tell she was back in her body and almost back in her mind all the way. She was crying now, full blown sobs and streaming tears; red puffy face and halted breathing mixed with murmured syllables and trembling lips. She didn't want me to stop. I knew I had been right. She always needed it like this.

I started slowly easing her into it and adding some sting about every five slaps, sometimes on her cunt and other times on her tummy, her thigh, her knees, once or twice on the bones of her hips. There was already a wet spot on the bed from her arousal and she'd almost came quite a few times, until I commanded her to not. Her cries swelled louder then and I taunted her that the neighbors around here probably loved the sound of that; a pretty little toy getting beaten as foreplay by someone who finally knew how to control them.

She took it, too. She fought through it hard, grunting and clenching her teeth, seemingly trying to prove something to me, or herself, or both of us that she was tough and I couldn't scare her, making me push her harder until we got into that pretty dance of that ebb and flow, bullying each others senses higher and higher. I could see welts starting to form, bruises thick in spots under her skin where it was hot and the blood of her had pooled to dark violets. Her wrists and ankles had those burn marks from the constrain of the rope.

She was so fucking beautiful, so pliable and in her power because she was in her smallness, below me. Her voice was cracking now in that way I needed to bring her back down to an end, and the bruises were taking up more space now than the unmarked spots of her thighs. I laid one last brutal one right above her clit and she screamed and I laid my body on top of hers, swallowing the noise with the heat of my form and a deep kiss feeling her cry against my lips. My shoulders felt the racking of hers into mine and I spread my arms against her own, tenderly untying her wrists and placing my fingers between hers, keeping her down, holding her steady. That last blow was always the one that released that last bit, that final gush of letting go that was cathartic and tender and terrified to leave a body. She'd needed this for a while.

I slid my jeans down my hips and took my cock out, throbbing and rubbing it gently against her swollen little pussy and exhaled sweet things in her ear.

"You needed this. Needed a good thrashing before a good railing, hmm? You feel that, girl? Feel how fucking hard you made my cock. What are we going to do about that? Those thighs have thought about opening for me before, haven't they?"

I could feel the tension easing from her body, her little cries quieting and turning into hunger, greedy little hips digging back into the length of me, gasping at how thick it felt, sucking on my tongue.

"That's my filthy little toy. So good. It's good when you're obedient like this. Good girls get big rewards. You want me to make you all sore inside now? Yeah. Grind that need on me. Shhh I know."

Before she could answer, still of out of her mind slightly, I felt how damp and messy her little hands locked around my neck sweetly were. I sensed her trying to rise into me desperately with her ankles still tied and forced open wide, I took the thick head of my cock and placed it against her and she shuddered. It was so much thicker than her small little hole. I kissed her deep and swallowed a frustrated moan. Every time I pulled back she tried to take me in. I growled and bit her lip, fisting her hair with my forehead against hers, circling around her cunt, feeling the pull of her wetness trying to bring me in deep.

I kissed a line down her neck then, whispered, "Breathe."

I buried myself in her deep, one thrust that slid past those tight muscles in her that were gripping me violently, shaking around me as she trembled against my chest. My shoulders held her into me, so small under my frame, my power, my hands full of her flesh and her sad little bruises and sighs while I started pounding her through the mattress.

She came once, twice, three times, squirting between our stomachs all the way to the end of my cock soaking us both and the bed. I didn't stop. I kept going until she was almost breathless, until I was smothering her mouth with my tongue and her tits with my rough hands and her neck with my digging teeth. I felt her body weary and limp and her cries mingling with my groans and my fingers shoving themselves down her tiny little throat to shut her up. Mine.

Her little fingers held onto me wherever she could, curled into my hair, scraped my shoulders, gripped the sides of the pillow below her head, gripped my ass that continued to dig and thrust into her until we both came so many times we were drained of each other, collapsed in a sweaty, silent heat with the breeze from the window flowing over our skin in a sheet of cool air that was welcome and soothing.

After a while, I reached down and untied her ankles, rubbed them tenderly and kissed all the marks I'd made, took ice out of the thermos by my side of the bed and soothed them sweetly. She was almost too tired to sigh and we lay there with our legs tangled in each other, in and out of sleep for hours.

***

Jude & Kai:

"So, our very first CNC? How was that for you?" Jude asked.

"I think ... I would like so much more of that. Fuck." Kai giggled.

"I wonder what the rest of the employees at the club would think of us. Still can't believe we've hid this shit this long from everyone. I think it's why our play continues to be hot as fuck though, too."

"I liked pretending to be drugged, the research you had me do beforehand about what that would be like and trying to act like I was. It put me in my head so much more and having to be so silent while you moved me and cut my clothes off. Just. Fuck. This was seriously almost as delicious as our first night together two years ago, when you whisked me away in your truck back here and showed me your little toy bag, like butch show and tell."

"*Big* toy bag, excuse that pretty mouth of yours. I'm so happy you liked this and we did it right with patience and planning and trust, babe."

"Me too. God, this was hot as all hell. This pretty mouth wants to clean your cock off still."

"Are you asking or telling?"

"Asking, of course."

"You're welcome to."

"Can I suck on your t-dick after, Sir?"

"You ask so pretty. You may. Also, we are fucking doing this again. At least once a month."

"Mmm, yes please. Next time, you're a stranger."

"We'll fucking see. Now let me see the that mouth get to work."

Rabid: Lover Letter #3

biting, blood, D/s, edging, masturbation, primal

I got off to you this morning, thinking of your weight on me, thinking of your growl against my neck and the bared teeth of your s. I missed your hands full of my flesh, your fingers opening me like you were rabid for my pleasure. I missed the moment my small hand tried to hold onto the sweat on your neck. I missed the delicacy of my surrender, when my body was a white flag against the rushing battle of yours.

I miss when you spit in my mouth and bite my lip, breaking something in me deeper, licking blood away. I thought of your voice in my ear, reminding me to be grateful, as your cock slides home. The bottom of my spine felt like falling rocks from the depth of you, how you invade.

The braided knots of my nerves were tight, begging for an unravel. I'd been thinking of you all morning. Consumed. Edging myself and never wanting this to end.

Your eyes were the same color as onyx. I missed how the taste of your tongue brutalized my senses. I loved the strain in your expression when I was on my knees and pulling your boxers down, aching for what's there. My throat was always hungry, my neck always begging for the pressure of both your hands guiding me down until you could be swallowed.

You always forced the hollows in me to make space for every bit of you. I didn't need a toy today. By the time I touched myself my thighs were already damp and trembling. I slid inside my cunt, wishing it was you. I'd barely grazed my clit and came violently, immediately. I moaned loud enough for the neighbors to hear, mourning through my pleasure for the absence of your cock.

My calves and thighs were a rave of pulses as I kept going, pushing myself the way you would. Relentless. Governed by ache. Shaking through the dance. The rhythm of my body was like a taffy pull, thick and feeding absence with fullness.

I am laying here breathless from you, thinking of what it would be like to wake you in the morning with my lips, stir you out of sleep and suck on you like a last meal, taste your come running down my throat. Dreams of you are still airbrushed to the lids of my eyes while the nightmare of your hunger takes my pleasure, makes it yours.

Make Me Hurt: Lover Letter #4

belt, bruises, impact, pain play

Make me remember pain from every angle of your choosing. Leave me shuddering in the wake of you. I want you here inside me after, pleasure blanketing my bruises, your cock deeper than my hunger so I can feel you all week long. I want this later, too, in the shower when the jets pulse on my thighs, in bed when I turn too hard on my side, wincing from hitting a mark you made with your belt when it wrapped around my hip and stung me back to being.

You are there like that, a sack of poison beneath. You are far below, crimson running under my curves and lines, part of my blood and part of my bones. You are warm and pulsing and textured. You are menacing in your smile while you brush my body dark with the charcoal of your gaze.

I want this just as bad as your tender touch, just as much as your tongue swallowing my sighs and opening me like a music box. I want you here now, the glare of you peeling me from the inside out, teeth foaming until my skin is settled between your jaw. I want to feel that rigid tension, like the kill I know I am. My fists hold you like a reflection. You are mirror of who I am, from all the angles you allow me to see.

Unbaptism

biting, D/s, dirty talk, fear play, fucking, primal, religious play/reclamation, daddy/girl

"Is that a dare?"

"No, it's a fucking double dare."

They looked at me sideways while sipping their whiskey on our wraparound porch. It was newly autumn outside and we'd taken a trip to the mountains for a long weekend to get away, to have some private time to ourselves where we could engage in some kinky fuckery without noise. We needed this sanctuary, a place without horns going off outside our bedroom window, pedestrians coming out of the belled door of the bodega at all hours below our apartment, cats fighting in the alleyways and drunk girls mumbling slurred words on the corner.

We were lucky to know friends who had this cabin, vacant half the year, waiting in the woods for our return. By early September, we were always clawing to get here, scratching at the fading crimson sunburn on our necks from concerts in the park, the whirlwind of Folsom street fair, and the social commitments we'd made with friends that we deeply tried to keep. It felt like we were always pushing through some form of tiredness to celebrate a birthday or a barbecue or a group trip. We'd missed that energy so dearly and now that we could do that again with more mitigated risk, we tried. While it filled our cup, it also drained our batteries, deeply.

It was so sacred here. We came every year, multiple times, despite what was going on in our lives, promising to make this space for ourselves, our minds, our intimacy, and our bodies.

Everything in the air smelled like different parts of the earth, new parts of the season, different pieces of summer fading into the smell of spruce. Walking up to the cabin, we were hit with the smell of the lake and that forest floor pocket of chill against its body. That scent that rose from the morning fog covered the windows in dew, covered our ravenous hours of fucking and the drunkenness of me between your thighs with a belt around my neck you'd pull on hardest right before you came.

That moment always came when we could feel the shift in both our consciousness. We were part of the stillness, where all the birds were recognizable by chirp, where the water flowed and sounded the way the sharp cold felt up to your ankles, where my knees felt as hard as the pines outside when you pushed yourself deep in my throat.

You talked about things you didn't realize you needed to. We purged among each other and fed on the cyclical energy that gave as hard as it took. Other times, it was just us sharing the solemn quiet, not needing words, only looks between us, flickering like dancing wicks side by side.

Our third evening on the porch, that malaise and comfort had set in deep and our walls had come back down, until your conversation hit religion. You noticed my posture change, my legs cross themselves, and the tension in my palms gripped the Adirondack chair I was on a little tighter.

I had a history with that, very unlike yours, things I'd worked to subvert, things you wanted to erase to create more ease for me. Parts of my youth hurt so hard from it yet, if I flipped the trauma upside down and inside out enough, I'd wanna touch myself in the dark while you watched me intently from a corner, while you did the same, admitting things to you I didn't realize I even had to admit.

On one of these occasions, I told you about the first time I was cuffed to a St. Andrew's cross and I came barely five minutes into being beaten. I shared my fantasy about wanting thorns dragged across my ass drawing blood, like my flesh was the communion and your lips on my cunt were the prayer said before. I wanted to feel your eyes on me holding my head down devoutly while you came hard for the benediction. I wanted the hymns of my moans and the snake of my tongue around you like it was its own unbaptism.

You wanted to spend time creating this for me, wanted to find a cathedral and pulpit, doors with brass knobs to pin me against like I was the stained glass of saints, like I was the tongue you put in me to speak. There were too many options on how to wield this with you, too many ways you could manipulate and torture me if you wanted, to break me and find my tears.

I glanced back at you and could literally feel your gears working in overdrive. Smirking privately to yourself and throwing you the keys on the table between the two of us.

"Fuck it. There's got to be a church out here somewhere that's just old and no one uses much. I doubt Sunday service gets packed around here when there are literally only a few dozen properties spread generously out around this lake. It's also a Tuesday, so there's that."

I swallowed nervously, feeling every muscle of my throat swell with hunger for you to fill it. I turned back to you after scanning the early stars peeking through the darkening sky. You were sipping your drink casually and wiped the flavor from the rim off your lip with your thumb, the one I loved you shoving between my lips when I came.

"You sure you want this? Because our toys are still in the trunk, and it's absolutely trespassing. But fuck if it isn't almost dark out and I know I want to see you on a kneeling bench for me, bound tight and waiting patiently."

I stood up and finished my drink and walked over to you, sat on your lap, facing you shyly. I sucked sweetly on your lower lip and you pulled me in deep, the animal inside waking up again and grinding your thigh between my curves.

Your palm caressed my cheek when I started moaning into your mouth. Your boots stomped on the wooden beams of the porch and your hands crawled sacrilegiously up my shirt. You squeezed my breasts enough to make me whimper, enough to make my lips tremble against your neck.

"Is that how you're going to pray tonight? Like a good girl? Like Daddy's going to take away your sins if you repent hard enough?"

Your hand put mine on your crotch at that last line. My head sweetly nodded, in my quiet, already wet and gone on you.

"You going to confess things to me with that pretty little mouth? Take a vow of silence when it's wrapped around my cock? Covet my fist inside your little hole like you think it belongs to you?"

A slap against my cheek. Once. Twice to make sure I understood. Your hand found my neck after, and I tried to bury my face in you as I went deeper into that space, where the control I always thought I had was stripped away entirely.

Your murmured growl of a laugh both cradled me and terrified me; overwhelming me just how I liked it and unsure at this point how you were even going to break away to walk to the car. We both came up breathless and noticed it was twilight, not even dusk now. The shadows loomed long, the tall pines over the car and the wind scattered leaves past the the steps of the porch. The smell of your skin on my shirt made my cunt pulse. I stared intently at pulp of your lips, still swollen from swallowing the wine of me in gulps.

***

We drove for a while, around the solitude of the lake this time of year. Other houses were dark inside. It was that time between seasons where the summer tourists had left, and the ski crowd was waiting impatiently for white on the mountains. The hum of the music was low on our laps and I watched you shift gears up and down the winding back roads. The way you drove turned me on; you drove like you fucked, with hard intent, fully focused. Still, you held my left hand in yours when you could, attentive to my breath changing, my muscles tensing from overthinking while you stared straight ahead through your high beams.

While many of the lake houses were newer, modern even, the town was older. It was kitschy, in that way that its aesthetic could tell you stories. Many of the walkways were just planked wooden pathways. Lots of the buildings still had cement floors, vaulted ceilings, crown molding done beautifully. Regal lampposts stood like statues on every corner. Shorter headstones rested crooked and faded in the cemetery. The back of summer smell passed between us in a cross-breeze, those cool damp pockets from little creek beds that ran parallel to the road. The air of the mountains blew my hair around my neck in curled wisps that almost stung. Main street was mostly quiet since it was after 10 p.m. Everything felt like it was just for us tonight, us, on our way to fall harder from grace.

Meditative in the rhythm of the drive, the wetness between my legs, and your hand holding mine by my wrist between us, your voice made me jump slightly.

"Could this be the place?"

Pulling off the main highway, the tires crackled loud on gravel, our SUV teetered back and forth down a long hill. The light of us interrupted the stillness while your hand expanded the navigation screen with a green dot marked Mt. Haven Chapel. I became much more aware of the risk this was now that we were enclosing on the small little building, resting quaint and pretty to most. Still, my stomach turned at the cross on top. With a hesitation in my voice,

"So, we're sure about this?"

You slowed in front of a small entrance with red french doors, put the clutch into park, and turned sideways at me,

"If you're having doubts babe, we can turn around, head back now and still have all night to do all the dirty things I want to do back at the cabin? Or ..."

Trepidation on my brow now. "Or?"

You smiled that soft smile, despite the wicked gleam I could see in your eyes, hoping. "Or ... I could go check the doors around the perimeter and if one of them opens, text you to cut the engine and grab my toy bag and follow me. I could take you somewhere tonight. With me. Below me. Against me. It is so dark down here, we'd see anyone that comes down this road far ahead. We'd hear it and we'd have ample time to get back outside excusing ourselves with a need to rest somewhere safe from the drive, which I don't think will even happen. It's the off-season. It's a Tuesday. We were the only car on the road the last twenty-five mins outside of town. And I I really want to watch you take some of this power back. I want to be the person who helps you diminish some of that trauma you had as a child. If you decide tonight is the time you trust me enough with that, I'd love to make that space for you."

I sat there pensive for a moment, studying your expressive eyes and looking down at your hand in mine. I looked toward the building. I had made a hard effort to not set foot in or near a church in ages. None of my friends were practicing Christians anymore, or any religion for that matter. I was all push back, all the time with that. It wasn't welcome in my universe because I had that choice now. I was free and wanted to stay that way with the space between my childhood and that toxicity growing further day by day. The purposeful avoidance constantly rested just below my skin, the rage, ready to put walls up high for anyone who tried to change my mind, challenge me, or test the validity of my trauma.

Still, that wasn't this. That wasn't you and we'd talked about that part of my past together for years now. I'd expressed wanting the planning to be more spontaneous like this too, knowing if we planned far ahead, I'd more than likely bail and be too far inside myself during the length of anticipation. I realized this was fear play, exposure therapy, all mixed with a catharsis scene. This was a lot on your shoulders and you were so willing to take it on.

I was aware of the energy and space you were capable of putting me inside of and there was so much trust here, sacred, deep, full trust. Both of us were so comfortable being vulnerable with each other; there was no one else I'd have considered even discussing this type of scene with, let alone park outside the kind of doors I'd refused to walk through in some twenty years.

I looked back at you, saying more in words with my eyes and my clenched jaw. My delicate fingers felt damp between the steadiness of yours. You felt that gravity, looked back into me telling me you understood. You clicked your seatbelt off and pushed your forehead against mine and my mouth latched onto yours like you were a lifeboat, like I was already sinking and trusted you to pull me in and hold onto me just right.

Your hand slid up my thigh and around my waist and my arms found your neck, holding your shoulders. The brutality of you was at bay for the moment while you swallowed my letting go in measured gulps, feeling my smallness rise. My mind floated toward that heady place, holding your shirt like an anchor, already begging you silently. I felt myself swirling down while your power grew big enough to hold me inside.

Your tongue tasted like sin, like my knees were made for your altar. The serpent of your fingers teased the hem of my jeans. You pulled hymns from my body with your teeth.

The control in you still right on the surface, you pulled away with lidded eyes. My body responded in a pathetic tremor as the driver door closed. I watched the flashlight on your cell abruptly split the darkness while you advanced toward the entrance. Your hand gripped the brass knob confidently, twisting it and pushing.

It opened and my heart almost pounded through my chest. It looked dark as fuck inside. The form of your body made a silhouette in the door-frame and your palm opened to me like an offering, I grabbed your bag before my mind could change and let you pull me inside. Abruptly, you nailed my back against the door as it closed, knocking the wind from my lungs. Your hand cradled the tightrope of my spine, traveled back down and around, gripping my hips with ownership, reminding me I was yours. I felt you possessing me like an animal while your fingers slid inside my tight jeans and opened my cunt like a prayer book.

You growled in satisfaction against my neck. "Tonight I'm taking you to confession."

Sliding inside me deep, my body bloomed into your touch. Your teeth caught the tremble of my mouth and kissed it away as my ass left the wall greedily, wanting more. You pulled out just as I started swelling around your touch, slammed my hips down with your own, thrusting my wetness for you down my throat.

I tasted myself on you and closed my eyes, hummed around your fingers as the door latched shut behind us.

"Tonight you'll only speak in tongues."

You ripped my shirt in half as you said this and before I could finish my gasp, pulled my tank over my head and fashioned it into a blindfold. You knotted it behind me, tightening it aggressively enough so my neck jerked. You hung onto the knot you'd made, leading me in the dark until I heard you flick switches on. The carpet was thin and I could smell that cedar from the pews when we entered a second pair of double doors, guessing we were in the sanctuary.

I could smell the old red felt that held the leather bound hymnals, the brass of the offering plates. That echo of your voice was so specific to a pastor when you sat me down on a stale cushion embedded into wood.

"Stay here until I come back for you. Stay quiet. I'll be in the room with you, I need a moment to prep."

I inhaled deeply and exhaled even louder, nodding quickly like I was in trouble and calming when I felt your lips kiss mine tenderly.

When you walked away, just the sensory experience of being here made a lot of the memories come back. I felt the soreness in my legs from standing so long in rooms like this, no air conditioning in the middle of August, the hours dragging after the monotony of Sunday school. I remembered the panic of not having a pen to write on the church program with, forgetting my Game Boy and getting in trouble for playing it, accidentally having the volume up. I remembered getting caught stealing my Dad's car keys out of his suit jacket so I could sneak off and skip service, only to be hunted after and scolded for embarrassing my family. I remembered trying to hide in the church library during my sunday school and the kids from my class ratting me out because if they had to be there, I should have to be too. I remembered my teacher finding my parents at the end of the afternoon, going home and being grounded the rest of the long weekend.

I remembered going on vacation and getting up so early before any breakfast places were even open, driving another 40 minutes. I remember feeling nauseous while I frantically listened to my parents in the front seat with a spread out map looking for a church where we could still go to a service because god forbid we not attend on a Sunday during vacation. I remember them talking down to us about my Mom and saying it wasn't good of her to not be taking us to church, and feeling they thought they were better than her for it.

I remember feeling just as anxious and holding my brother's hand knowing they'd fight all day if we couldn't find "a place on vacation to worship at" and we'd be forced to do a bible study in the car where they'd grill us with questions I didn't care about at all. I remember having massive difficulty fitting in with other kids who loved being there, and they chastised me for not liking it.

I remembered being pressured to get baptized once my brother did it, and my parents making me sit in our living room telling me it didn't look good that I didn't want to do it and that tomorrow I needed to bring my swimsuit to church because after, we were going to the pastor's house so I could do it with the rest of the youth group. I remember being submerged and hating everyone harder than I hated myself for allowing them to control me. I remembered the hypocrisy of various pastors that performed marriage counseling, how they had multiple affairs and it constantly was swept under the rug. I remember my parents fighting about tithing when they were broke, making us give from ten percent our small allowance to establish a habit like theirs, shaming us if we spent it on an arcade games before we'd even turned ten.

I remembered "forgetting" a dress and only bringing my brother's hand-me-down clothes for the weekend thinking I'd gotten away without having to go to church since I didn't have a "feminine outfit." I remembered my stepmom would start checking my suitcase before she picked me up from my Mom's so I couldn't do that anymore. I remembered hating shaking strangers hands, having to hug too many weird old men, clinically reciting psalms in bible games, thinking a lot of this was stupid and being alone in that. I remembered only being able to watch biblical shows on when my friends were allowed to go to the mall, or the movies. I remembered crying before going to sleep because I had lied so much that day and was sick from the idea I'd be going to hell. I remember our preschool school teacher offering us cookies if we accepted Jesus, and getting none if we didn't.

My thoughts were intercepted by the long creak of a door nearby being pushed shut again and out of instinct, I jumped.

"Just me, baby."

***

Your voice had that echo as it bounced off the wood and glass in here, resonating the power it always had inside me. I heard you shuffling about near the pulpit in front of me some twenty feet away and slowed my breathing. Feeling you near me was soothing, listening to your measured energy and that control that started to overtake your body to hold mine against it made me calm. I let myself feel you and let those memories be what they were, memories far away from my reality.

You came over to me and gripped the knot of the blindfold and began kissing my neck, took my hand and stood me up slowly and turned my body so it was beside yours being led. My steps melted into yours and you squeezed my hand you were holding and it made me feel warm all over.

You stopped me shortly after, and my hips and ass felt wood against me. My hands slid behind my body and I touched a larger table. You knelt down and started kissing along the hemline of my jeans, your fingers digging beneath the denim along my hip bones caressing me like a treasure. My head fell back as your hands dug in, pushed and pulled my body the ways you wanted it, slid my jeans down my thighs and calves and the coolness of the air in here put goosebumps on me as you began covering with your warm mouth. We fed off the headiness of our hunger for one another; that coupled with a low, deep growl made me shrink lower. My panties pooled around my ankles and I slid my bra over my head.

You sinewed up my body like a snake that couldn't stop biting on the way to its constriction. My whimpers echoed and the upturn of your smile on my skin made me shiver in that way that made your cock hard. I caressed your crotch pathetically, breathless already to feel you inside.

You grabbed my hand in synchronicity with my other wrist and laid me down on the large table. It was longer and much wider than my body. Your tongue made me feel like a communion as you tasted my mouth, secured cuffs above my head with an echoing click that resonated off the glass windows surrounding me, somber saints forced to watch depravity. I reveled in that as my tongue licked my own lips to taste the moisture of yours you'd just left behind. My senses were acute behind the blindfold and I was just existing, listening for that reverent silence to be interrupted.

The table below my body had some sort of marble inlays in various patterns and parts of it were chilling the cream of my thighs, my shoulders, my neck. I could feel small flickers of heat wavering toward me at the same time.

You moved away abruptly. You were making me wait, lighting candles around me one by one. The fizz of the wicks igniting felt the same as my cunt felt in the air, throbbing and heated, dripping things that the heat made pool.

I wanted to be this right now, the lamb, the silhouette in the dark with a looming presence hovering over me, meditating quietly and swallowing the bundles of my tightened nerves in hurried gulps.

What happened tonight would be holy. I wanted the hellfire of your tongue on my cunt. I wanted the spread of my thighs to be as feral as I felt growing up, the stifle of my rattling cage cracked open by the head of your cock, opening me to the world I always wanted more of.

You smelled like cinder from matchsticks when you came back and you put your weight on me, buried your teeth in my neck. I cried as loud as I'd always wanted to in this room. I purged against the heaviness that had always held me down, held me back. Your body was freeing me. The hardness of you rested between my legs pointed itself exactly where it was about to go and I felt you stroke yourself with a hunger I'd never felt before. The head of you slid against my wetness and teased, put that sacred ache inside my belly while you sucked on my tongue like everything depraved I always wanted.

You slid inside in one thrust and bit my lip so hard I swore it might bleed.

The body and the blood echoed in my mind like a chorus and your strong hands held my wrists while you fucked me deep and slow, thrusts meant to feel every bundle of nerves inside me that unwound the longer you were there. You made space inside me for the things I didn't know I needed, pulling the tangles of pain and judgment away and putting something else there. I could fly. I was beautiful. This wasn't wrong. My hunger could live. My ache could exist, loudly.

You were edging me now, and my breathy cries were insistent, feral, my hips trying to take what you weren't giving me just yet. You gave me your fingers to suck knowing how bad I needed to wrap my mouth around you, pulled out after a while and kissed my cheeks. Your hands slid the blindfold away and my eyes flashed open and above me, you looked like a god. Your dark hair was messy and damp, your chest swelled around me and the power of your thrusts started losing a rhythm and became manic. You kissed me deep and we moved like animals until we came together, me squirting all over your cock and you coming violently from the sensation of my surrender.

In the end, I forgot where I was because I was with you.

In the end, you leaned your lips into my ear and whispered, "You're not the sacrifice. You're the fucking altar."

Ritual: Love Letter #5

primal, oral

I wanna be your baby. Your ritual. A deep cut you dream about during the heaviest of sleeps. I want you to wake up and still feel me on your skin the rest of the day. I want the sinews in your shoulders to hold me back from running, the tattoos on your body to cradle my cheek in the dark, when I'm streaming my lips over you like a river trying to carve veins into a rock.

I want to make you feel sacred, like deer tracks in snow by a railroad that no one can find, like the whisper between pines that are only meant for a night owl's ears. It is raining tonight and I am watching it fall in bands down my window and I'm thinking of the howls I left against your neck.

I want to take you there, put something in you that's made of stardust. I want to leave parts of me between the freckles on your body and lower the volume of the world, so we're floating in space, so your eyes are all celestial and your thighs are cradled by the curve of my shoulders like they were born to rest there.

I want to linger here for a long time, meditate on you like a prayer I learned to save my life. I want to bite the air when it's over, still taste you in the room. I want to keep you under my tongue like a scream when you knock on my door, feel you in my chest before I see you.

Her

D/s, fucking, oral, femdom/girl

She told me to put my mouth on her, in a tone, one that had been waiting to say it all day out loud. She gazed down at me knowingly, sensing I'd drop to my knees before she was done telling me to. Sometimes I felt like I was breathing all day to get to this.

She tasted like a sunset running down my throat, like all the vibrations of her sweet growls, dancing down into me.

I had driven to her work to take her to dinner. I had dressed in her favorite outfit, wore her favorite scent. Unfortunately, I had gotten there too early, interrupting her last meeting and been told to wait to be buzzed in. This was the game.

The hall to her office was long. The decor was minimal yet imposing, with too many mirrors on the way, to make you see yourself clearer before you saw her.

I turned the knob and she was waiting. The entirety of the floor was almost empty, save for one secretary rushing to pick her kid up from daycare and already running late. She leaned against the desk in the dark, didn't say a word but I could feel her seeing me. I stared at her pursed smile, amused I was being spontaneous by being there, yet under full awareness of what I was up to. Her energy was already charging in to take the reins before I could grip them at all.

She had her skirt pushed to the side with both graceful hands. Her legs were in black pumps, stemming from the shiny wood floor, calves just muscular enough to tell she wore heels more than anything. The soft curves of her thighs were already kissing my cheeks like two peaches while she coated my fingers, like warm honey.

I wanted my knees to hurt from the flood. I wanted my hair to feel her still clenching it, tomorrow morning when I'd wake up after, remembering it was real and not just a dream. I wanted to get off to this in the shower alone, wanted to paint this again in the days to follow and have the urge to touch myself, if she allowed it.

I dropped to the floor before she could tell me to. I let her pelvic bone grind hungrily against my nose and hold me there, small bursts of air coming to me as I'd gasp. Her heels hit her mahogany desk at first, then perched on my back stabbing me harder when her spine would leave the surface. The more her legs stiffened, the more I'd push. Her clit was a bulb only I could flicker and burn out, between my lips tenderly, then with my tongue ring dancing around it to make her spin.

I wanted to conquer her control, or at least try. I wanted to watch it fade and dim and still feel her wrists, voice, and thrusts grab it back, holding it against me like revenge for the vulnerability and softness she'd given to me in the dark. Soon even her ass was edging up the table, her heels carved into the blades of my shoulders, desperate to still leave me with marks that reminded me I was owned. I wanted to taste the hum of her nerves, feel the pain in my back from arching into any angle she could make me follow in her need.

Her legs were flush off the floor now, body on the desk making me rise to meet her like a predator, following until my breasts hit the sharp edge of the desk and still pushing to bruise them to grip her, to keep her, to pursue and hunt her pleasure no matter how deep it took me.

She'd been stifled all day, in her meticulously planned outfit, her charisma for her clients worn thin. Her glossy black nails haphazardly flew up toward my hands on her tits, knocking her stationary to the floor. She giggled at that, grinding harder into my mouth with a pleasured purr.

She was close, sensitive to the point where she couldn't decide to push or pull me, and breathless while her body was aerobically trying to meet the sensations faster than her lungs could take in air. My fingers were in her deep and my was tongue was bullying her at the edge, curled inside reaching for it and soothing her with my hands, running along her skin like marbles and finding those small grooves to leave my own marks. I was just as eager for her comedown to make her shiver, to make her echo hit the hall, to grab her ass and pull her back down, so I could look up at her, looking down at me.

The Next Time I See You: Lover Letter #6

blindfold, biting, oral sex, sensory deprivation

The next time I see you, I want to blindfold you and feed you black cherries. I want to watch your teeth break skin while I tighten my necktie around your eyes, deliberate force chasing little gasps you funnel down my shoulder.

I want the dark on your tongue to compliment the scarlet mess I'm going to make you, left on your skin like the wake of a heavy tide on white sand. I want to taste the pink of you, savor the soft parts in your center and and keep some of your surrender in my mouth, for later.

Show me how it feels. Louder. Let me wrap you in the ribbon of my arms while I feel your spine rise and break the tide in my chest. Rage with me. Ache while my lips find the poems in your veins, and I pull you out of the womb you hide in, with nothing but my teeth.

Tryptich

biting, blindfolds, choking, dirty talk, fucking, oral sex, slapping, threesome, vibrators, daddy/girl/girl

Y ou're in an Uber on the way to their house. You weren't supposed to see them until Friday, but they wanted your company Wednesday because the texts and calls were bubbling to the surface the past week with so much energy, something had boiled over.

The foreplay of your three-way conversation was feeling stretched flat, and it had only been a matter of weeks. There was a connection building here that was more than growing rapidly; with a deep appreciation for exploration, depravity, curiosity. The three of you were in a place in your lives where you were all learning about your kinky selves independently, but discovering together. It felt novel and exciting, but potent, too.

You were nervous; chewing gum a little frantically, clutching your overnight bag in the backseat, weaving the strap around your fingers already wishing it was her palomino hair. You didn't know exactly what was going to unfold when you arrived, but you needed to. You'd never done anything with a queer couple, other than flirt or display your dimpled smile from across the room from compersion of how cute they were together.

The circumstance had simply never presented itself, and even if it had, the desire for the pair had to vibrate loud enough to turn your head and theirs in synchronicity seemed rare. You had to feel safe, and of course, feel desired by them. It was hard enough to meet one person that shared your hunger for kink, eros, and sensuality. Because of this, it felt hotter between your legs when the car pulled up to their driveway.

You'd talked to Evan more than Tina throughout the week. Their hours at work were ever changing and afforded them more free time in the day. Tina's conversations with you happened mostly at night or when you'd go out with them to dungeons and watch others play together, share meals at restaurants and talk about nerdy, kinky, poly things. Evan was also an east coaster like you, and Tina was always amused and giggly listening to you both reminisce about hyper-specific parts of your past.

You knew her and had known her from years before; you'd met through mutual friends at queer parties you'd bartended, but never played at. Some of your anxiety often kept you on the fringe, observing and absorbing the changing energies around you all night.

Even at those events, you remembered always asking her close friends if she would be there, if she was going to show up later. Something magnetized you to her, but nothing had ever quite sank into a resting place with connecting physically before. In time back then, the friendship had fizzled out from a divorce on her end, a chronically ill kid of hers she had to pause and focus on, and your father becoming sick. The fading out wasn't intentional as much as it was circumstantial. There'd be texts here and there but less presence and in-person contact.

***

Until recently, it had been a few years and you reconnected through a local poly group you had rejoined. Unknowingly, she was also a member. You let a month go by and, and you saw an event she was attending that her pocket of folks would be at. You'd not yet interacted with them and you decided to try and go after a few friendly exchanges in text beforehand. You wanted to branch out, meet new people. You were hungry for spontaneity, maybe even a little danger.

You went to a sushi restaurant and she was there with friends, social butterflying still, same as when you'd known her before. You saw her before she saw you, orchestrating her energy between tables bringing that light she had all over, like a lantern bug that can't sit still.

You had always been deeply attracted to her, her sensuous cappuccino eyes surrounded by naturally wavy black hair that went to the bottom of her shoulders. She was always in red lipstick and had lacquered black nails, always winking at you. She smelled of decadence, of plum and freesias and leather. You'd kissed before (for hours) and she'd tasted of black cherries, When she looked at you she was always smiling with her eyes. She wore a lot of backless dresses, tops where her shoulders were exposed and you wondered what her skin would feel like between your teeth.

Not knowing how many people would be there for the event but knowing she'd be one of them, you made sure to dress in your cutest outfit. You wore your leather jacket, your fishnets and pencil skirt, moto boots that gave you a little extra height, and perfume you'd worn once you remembered she'd loved.

When you walked in the door, a pianist was performing eighties cover songs and a long table stretched out with about twenty people, some heads turned. Standing taller, you walked along it and found her, politely tapped her shoulder. Setting down her drink, she turned and squealed excitedly meeting your gaze, shoved her chair back, bopping over to hug you deep and long. She somehow looked even more gorgeous than before, that spark in her eyes dancing when she mentioned how hot you looked tonight. Before you could reply she grabbed your hand and put a chair beside hers and handed you a loose menu, placing her palm on your leg saying how glad she was to see you.

You still felt naked when you talked to her and met her gaze. She still gave you that feeling where she held all the cards and you were always wanting to know what was in her hand. She oozed sensuality, drinking whiskey or wine, almost ready to tell that secret in her eyes but even more, make you dig for it.

At one point she was finishing the last sip of a drink, she set her glass down, dangling something in front of you,

"Do you want my cherry? I think you should have it. Seems like it should be yours. "

You almost choked on your own drink and as you composed yourself, you took it with your fingers touching hers and sucked on it gently, then bit into it, using every fiber of your being to keep eye contact.

"Mmm. Good girl."

Fuck. You were going to die tonight.

You wanted to trail after her like a puppy and hear about her life now, have her to yourself. Being back inside her forcefield of vivacious energy made you understand something about your own nature at the same time. You didn't realize at the time some of this was you feeling submissive and even now, you were just starting to piece that together; when you were close to that untamed vibe, you'd revert to your own inclinations and instincts to worship and service it from a lower gaze.

Before your food came, she reapplied some lipstick and noticed you refilling her empty water glass, amused. She smirked and asked you to the bathroom with her. On the way, she told you about her new poly person she was seeing. They weren't here tonight but she was about to give them a check-in call and as she dialed, she began animatedly raving about how lovely they were and how she knew you'd get along and how she'd already told them about you.

When they answered her call, she winked at you and stared, leaning against a wall. She began gushing to Evan about how you showed up tonight, as promised. She joked to them about how good you were, kissing the air in your direction making you blush. Abruptly, she headed into the ladies room, handed you her cell in a bubbly manner telling you to say hello to Evan, after explaining they were from back east where you'd grown up, articulating other things about their experience in kink and how they would soon be moving here for her.

You liked how her eyes looked like two stallions running side by side when she mentioned their name. They'd been dating long distance a while. They'd met her son, felt very protective but at ease about themselves, and sounded like they just had been infused and entranced with her energy, which you more than understood. They talked about each other the same way. There was something sacred there you sensed, something untouchable, a bubble they lived in no one could penetrate and you felt it from both sides when you spoke to them. Both of them were absolutely more dominant than you.

You got on with Evan more than well on the phone and it surprised you. They were charismatic, similar to her: funny, intelligent, unashamedly and bluntly honest, bold. You sequestered yourself in the bathroom hall for almost twenty minutes, not even noticing she'd been back at the table without you. Listening to them gush about her in all the ways made you want to fuck her more. Even more, it made you want to fuck them too. It felt good to hand her back the phone when you finally did hang up. Unexpected conversations were so fucking rare, especially stimulating ones where you felt nervous but also wanted to laugh and bond like that. She whooshed past you to collect you back to the table of friends she was with, urging you with those red lips.

You were sitting next to her the last hour of the night and she kept putting her hand on your knee. Every time she did, your stomach dropped. What the hell was it about black nails and femme hands? You were taking selfies with her, being playful, and then she flocked to others, sweetly kissing a few women on the cheek goodbye when they left. You wished they were you. You squeezed your thighs together, wondered what else you could manifest, if you had the power to even do that. Sometimes when she'd giggle, you felt like that was one of the laughs you'd hear if she came. It was all you could do to imagine your tongue inside her while ripping those stockings off her legs in pieces, or being below her on the floor, edging yourself with the point of her heel on your neck.

You knew the bar was closing soon and she offered to drive you home. Sweet relief. You just wanted more time with her, more mischief, more unearthing where she'd been and who she was now and what had changed. The openness and trust was still there between you, dancing from topic to topic with ease. She drove a sports car (in her heels) with a stick shift and it was all black inside. She switched the gears firmly, sped a little too. You wondered if she fucked like she drove.

You made plans to see one another soon as Evan moved here and got settled; plans which you kept; the three of you finding that rare sort of kismet comfort and playfulness. Then there was the shared adoration for her as a baseline of bonding with them, which felt incredibly flirty to partake in.

***

Now, some months later, here you were in an Uber on your way to their place, from one decision to rejoin a poly group. Wild.

Something different the last few weeks had been happening, though. You'd taken them to some trusted playspaces, introduced them both to the local community, they made other friends but always wanted to go to things as your little triad. You watched scenes together, gathered at munches and discussed desire. You talked about milestones you'd been through, how you came to discover those parts of yourselves, what you wanted to learn and what you felt you understood. Evan had been practicing lifestyle kink for over twenty years, but Tina was newer. She was fascinated, engaged and hungry to learn and ask questions, thirsting for experience. She wanted to explore her top side with someone and Evan was interested in seeing that happen, but guarded and watchful of who she connected with, understanding how that newness often got taken advantage of. Evan was protective and cautious, which honestly served as a good balance, because her whimsy was untamed at times, but with kink that could pose as a threat. You understood this as a bottom yourself.

The desire was there but unspoken at first, to be a part of an experience for each other, to grow and learn something together; there was also the fantasy fulfillment of what you all had been wanting and dancing around, too timid to mention it that it felt like cruel edging, until one night, when they drove you home after a party. They both got out of the car to open your door for you, and she pinned you against the car by your jacket collar, loudly closing it behind you. Evan stood there with a suppressed grin, all-knowing, while she moved into you close enough that your noses were touching.

You held your breath.

She asked, "Can I kiss you?"

Then you were gone, your hand around the back of her neck and her mouth like another world making your knees weak. Your palms grabbed her supple ass and her fingers tangled in your hair, gripping you like she already owned you. She was still intoxicating, still kissed like you, her entire body leaving itself through her mouth.

You felt like every nerve you had was fizzing after, and when you both came up for air, Evan was biting their lip and grinning wide, full of deep-lidded arousal. "Okay, so that was Really. Fucking. Hot. Jesus. Fucking. Christ."

The two of you giggled in response. Tina spoke, "Daddy, I want her. She is really fun to kiss. Can we take her home with us?"

Your cunt throbbed hearing her talk like that, vaguely objectifying you. You gazed at Evan take on that energy suddenly, the shift in them making you wet. It made sense now hearing her call them that, made her more powerful than ever to you. Your cheeks were flushed and your eyes darted back and forth unsure what to say or do, but also still realizing you still had the fabric of her dress bunched between your palms hungrily, even though you'd both pulled away a bit ago.

Evan smirked and waited a moment, staring into her with command and presence. Her hands were still on the collar of your bomber jacket and her breasts were moving from her breathlessness still.

"Not tonight. I think we spend the week discussing and negotiating this together. I want to make sure we all feel safe and get what we want. I can see between the two of you the more time you have to wait, the more entertaining this will be for me. Let's do this the right way, yes?"

She pouted slightly and turned back searching your eyes, seemingly looking for support to change their mind.

Their demeanor changed and lost some of that softness. "You're not about to challenge Daddy, are you? You know good girls don't get to decide what they get and Daddies have to choose for them if they're being bad."

She planted a tender kiss on your cheek and turned full body toward Evan. "I can be so, so good! I'll be good, I swear!"

Evan and you shared a laugh at her immediate change in attitude and you kissed her on the lips again sweetly. They came up to hug you goodbye as well, and stopped and looked at you, studying quietly. You felt that dominance still emanating from them and wanted to melt against it. You wore it on your face and they saw it and took your jaw endearingly,

"Don't worry. I know you're a good girl, too."

At that, they waved goodbye and left you standing there fumbling with your keys desperate to be inside so you could get off all night. After the third or fourth orgasm your cell dinged and on the screen a text,

"Our place next Friday? Six pm? Would love to have you come."

***

You didn't make it to Friday.

Shocker.

By Wednesday, the group texts had become incredibly erotic and raw, and at a point late in the afternoon you joked about wanting to teleport to them so you could straddle her and just kiss for hours.

This was followed by a few minutes of silence where you wondered if that was too forward, and then a response: *Come now. Bring an overnight bag. We will be up late.*

You reread it and felt your adrenaline spike. You missed nights like these and felt like you were in your twenties again, with no script but that sort of anticipation that had your cunt pulsing, your mind running, and your skin vibrating from energy exchange. You craved the unexpected, mystique behind the desire. At times, you were too timid to put it out there. Sometimes your shyness needed that bold push, and Evan and her both had more aggressive personalities than you that seemed to understand. They understood the trust building, the creation of that space to make you feel secure and hungry and present. They leaned into their top sides to catalyze it all, too.

You were coaching yourself on the drive to not overthink even though you could feel your heart in your chest, even though you hoped you were ready for this, whatever this night even was. You kept glancing at your phone as the map showed the minutes to their place falling lower and lower. You squeezed the chain on your purse wondering if the driver could sense you were aroused and heady.

When the car finally pulled up, you stepped outside and went in a french door entrance, into a mudroom. Evan was standing inside to greet you with a warm smile and took your bag sweetly. In the tight space, they came into you for a full bodied hug. They smelled like evergreen and the light stubble on their cheek scraped yours, and you felt warm all over.

They were just as attractive as Tina, taller than both of you with eyes the color of a fresh pool. They had dimples on both their cheeks and strong shoulders, a sharp jawline, and tattoos on their sculpted calves. They had that soft masculinity that you always adored, moreover that impish boi energy that knew how to tease and flirt, beckon and wrangle femininity confidently. It made you feel feverish. Tina radiated in that light of theirs and from how they were looking at you right now, you felt just as flustered but could sense they enjoyed that, too.

Once your shoes were off, they held the second pair of doors open on one side and stood sideways for you to pass, so you had to brush against their chest tightly. The body on body energy of that second you sensed the primal in them, resting patiently beneath their controlled facade but licking its lips in lieu of tonight's meal later.

You let them lead you inside and there she was, sitting on a bar-stool in jeans and a low-cut tank top, a deck of playing cards and a bowl of almonds in front of her, two glasses of wine already halfway done. You moved toward her like she was glowing, like the path your feet took to get there had been predestined. You sat on the stool next to her after Evan planted themselves on the other side of the counter, standing, knowing you wanted to be close to her. You didn't take your jacket off until a few minutes in. Evan looked at you like they were surveying an amusing cartoon, popping a piece of chocolate in their mouth, unable to hide that content Daddy energy.

The three of you played poker a little bit, but a version Evan's family played you'd never tried, picking it up reasonably fast. You didn't have to bluff and you were relieved at that. They seemed to both understand you were the type of bottom that wore everything you felt right on top of your skin, all the time.

You wanted this so bad. Just being in her presence again felt decadent. At certain points, she'd run her nails up and down your arm softly, just enough to let you feel your body moving into it before her hand grabbed her drink again. At moments, you had your hand below her hip and were grazing her thigh. You were having the most trouble looking sideways at her because transparency is a bitch. It was all over you that you wanted her and all of your energy was spent trying to half pretend to focus on the game, half pretend you weren't. All you really wanted to taste was her. There was wanting and there was yearning, this was the latter. You liked that the craving hurt.

About forty minutes in, the game turned into strip poker, naturally. Evan ended up fully naked first; still both of you teased them about cheating at the game and everyone was smiling about it.

"How the fuck am I cheating if I'm losing?"

"It feels like winning because you're naked," you blurted out, mid-giggle and Tina nodded enthusiastically.

"One hundred fucking percent, babe."

There was a symbiosis here: a carnal mischief in the dynamic of the three of you slowly figuring out which roads to turn down and stop at dead. You were all great at flirting, tugging and loosening those little strings that needed tension released but also tightening the ones that were already ready to break.

You ended up in your lace panties, tank and bra, shyly trying to deter the fact that you'd lost more hands of poker, enough to be nude a time and a half over, and asserting silently that this was as naked as you'd get for now. No one pushed you to do more or be more than you wanted and were ready to be.

She tried to adorably help you at first, when you started losing, making your bracelet count, your four silver rings, sensing you were already conflicted and thinking ahead, wondering if you'd lose your pants or the top first.

Except now, it was futile. Each hand you lost was a spotlight back on you, that yes, you wanted to be naked, just not here, not yet, not with cards on a bar-stool in a kitchen and you knew they knew that too. You needed more atmosphere than this, more comfort, soft lights, both of their bodies against you.

She was winning for a while and went to change out of her jeans. She returned in a cute pair of boxer briefs that may or may not have been Evan's; the shape of her juicy ass made your teeth water.

They showed off her hips, the lines of her upper body that complimented them. You wanted to have a slumber party and eat popcorn with her and watch eighties movies all night and be troublemakers together, but you also wanted to slide your tongue against her like you were coming in from the cold. By the next round, she was braless and the tank was gone. You side glanced at her long and caught her eye, giggled and whined a bit about how shocked you were that game was still going, attesting you couldn't focus at all now. She looked so gorgeous. Every time she smiled you felt a lightning bolt hit you, especially when she sipped her drink and purred into it, set it down and was smiling harder at you. She was looking at you now with her hips turned toward yours, her soft legs grazing your own. She was intently focused, the way an animal is right before it tackles something with its jaw.

You asked to put your mouth on her and she nodded and Evan came around then, too. You both started teasing and sucking on her breasts together, listening to her relieved little gasps and soft moans, her nails gripping both your shoulders while her spine curved back. She was luminous. Her neck exposed, with your hand on the curve of her back holding her steady, wondering who she was moaning about and lost on the taste of her skin finally on your tongue. You got so lost you hadn't noticed Evan move up to kiss her deep and you felt a craving for them, too.

You asked to kiss her next and she put her hands along the side of your head under your hair, controlling you and the moment. She kept you there, making you reach for her lips with yours and pulling away until that build of desire stifled her. Finally, she put her tongue in your mouth and her hands found their way over your tank, pinching your nipples and squeezing harder the more you moaned into her. Then you felt that small thing, where you wanted to shrink down into her and be tugged and pulled anywhere she wanted you, wherever she needed you.

They said she'd been more dominant lately with women and something in her eyes spoke to that, something flashed into a wolf-like slyness; she was aroused and it was marinating off her, running off her skin onto yours.

Evan moved back around their side of the counter after. From watching the two of them, you still felt the urge to kiss them too, saying you were curious and complimenting how it looked. You asked if you could, stumbling to find your words, the right ones and way of delivering it. Evan obliged but told you to watch them again first.

They kissed like her; with regulated control but an engine behind it that was waiting on idle until all at once from a sound she made, it attacked, overwhelming. Her soft power made the firmness in her spine and shoulders surrender heavy. They pulled away in the middle of it all and winked at you coming closer.

"Daddy and you kiss the same," she said.

They pulled your stool across the tile into them and went into you deep, tongue-heavy and sensual, aggressive enough to remind you they were leading, giving you what they gave her.

She came up behind you with an arm around your neck holding you there to take it, her other hand sliding up your trembling thighs, putting pressure on your cunt. She purred into your neck feverishly while Evan gulped your sweet sounds down their throat.

They started using their kink language then, discussing you like you weren't there but making you the focal point of the moment. It was making you so fucking wet, and making you feel so small and shivery in that just right way where you shrunk into them like a lost faun.

"I want to taste her, Daddy. I want to bring her to bed with us tonight and spread her open for your cock and watch you fuck her while I ride her pretty little face."

Evan's hand clutched your neck tenderly, feeling the vibrato of your sounds like pearls, cupping you with ownership. "Mmm baby, I want to taste you on her mouth while you lap at her after I make her cum. When she's all swollen and sensitive and needs your pretty little mouth."

You whimpered and pulled away breathless, a frustrated "please, fuck," coming out of your lips.

Tina laughed maniacally. Both her warm hands gripped your naked tits and massaged them, amused and biting her lip.

"Say it again baby, but this time let me hear you beg," she said.

Lost in the heat between the two of them and feeling her turn you to curl into Evan's chest with hunger, your hands wrapped around Evan's neck, clinging and small as Tina's teeth and nails on your shoulders made you tremble.

"Please I fucking want you both so bad! I want to taste both of you too and watch you and feel you open me while I taste her, please."

Trailing off into an almost tremor, they stood you up with them and led you to the bedroom.

***

Before you could reach their room, Tina halted the train of the three of you and stopped Evan's steps behind her in the long hallway. Even in the dark, you could see her eyes were deeply lidded now, sensuality and power emanating off of her. Evan put their hands in her hair giggling in surprise, falling into her lips for some time until the two of them broke apart. The presence of their eye contact felt potent. It felt like a window no one got to see through. Evan took a hair tie off her wrist swiftly and wrapped her soft waves up in it as she dropped to her knees. They stared at each other reverently, their breathing deepening and the static in the air humming with their hunger.

Evan reached their arm back to find your hand, tenderly latching their fingers with yours. They pulled you flush against their back, needy and insistent, trying to control what little they couldn't. They arched against you desperately with their spine bowed, soft and vulnerable. Tina unzipped their jeans and took them in her mouth deep. Your lips sucked on Evan's neck and they whined. You and Tina echoed them with a humming moan, like you'd just broke the skin of a kill together, predators flashing eyes in the dark.

The more lost Evan became, the more of their weight they cradled against you. With this, you could feel them sinking into you both, sense Tina's slender hands grabbing their ass possessively, and then teasing you outside your lace panties. Both of you told her how pretty she looked. Evan's arm fell back around your neck and shoulder, giving in harder now. Tina drew them closer until their boxers and packer were down around their ankles and they had opened for her mouth. All of you moved into one another like a dance.

Her words interrupting the dark, "I wanted to make you come, Daddy. I couldn't wait."

Their lips quivered against your mouth, their body almost levitated against you and Tina's arms were holding their calves and hips. You whispered in their ear, "Such a sweet, filthy boi. You love this, don't you? I can feel how hungry your holes are. You open up so good. Louder. Deeper. Let me hear it."

Your fingers opened their mouth back up, scraping the back of their throat now, making their spit dribble down their pretty little freckled chin, the light stubble on their neck damp, too. You could hear them choke a little, feel them trying so hard to keep you there, to take it and be good. They tried to steady themselves as they ground against her tongue. Their rounded shoulders scrunched into their neck more, fighting between you both.

It wasn't long now, between your cruel teeth, the obscene sound of how fucking wet they were around her fingers, and your hands greedily gripping Tina's curls as you guided her deeper. Her hands caressed the crumbling map of them, used to the way their tension rose and fell. The tremors in their tummy and their pulse under your wrist were racing. They were so close, breaths turning into frantic gasps, soft cheek pressed into yours tight, needing every piece of skin to skin they could manage to find.

Tina gripped their hips like a vice as they started to release, their ass tensing and the two of you riding it out with them, kissing and sucking on whatever tender piece of flesh you could find. Your fingers held strands of their hair tight, marbling soothing words down the curve of their spine. Tina used her lips below gently, raking their soft thighs with her black nails, seeing you behind them and the menace of her hunger silently telling you that you were next.

Then the three of you fell haphazardly, in a puddle on the floor, as if the demons had been exorcised, some of them, anyway. Down the hall a few feet, candles performed a ballet of shadows on the ceiling above their king bed. Twin fans breezed on their vaulted ceiling.

Evan, still catching their breath, broke the silence. "Should we, uh, migrate?"

The two of them laughed in unison and you could hear the giddiness. The three of you slowly stood together like all your legs had fallen asleep and had half come back to life, just enough to make it to the bed.

When you got there, Evan went to stand on what you assumed was their side of the bed while Tina sat in the center on the edge, aware you were the next spectacle, book-ended by two tops. Tragic.

She told you to climb higher on the bed and you watched her lean down and grab a black bag from the foot of their closet. Evan scooted behind you against the headboard and she stood before you and raised your arms in open surrender. Checking in with a deep steady gaze,

"Final round of strip poker?"

You smiled back in the dark, showing all of your dimples, while Evan scooted you back into their lap. They languidly began playing with your hair, and then caressed your breasts and shoulders. Tina asked if you were alright. You said you were, all while you were mind-wondering what exactly was going to happen. You wondered what they'd spoken about before this and if this had been planned or spontaneous; you realized it didn't matter.

The nerves were delicious and you were leaning into this night the way you decided to lean into the invite and let yourself go on the decision to come there, the decision to flow with the evening. You weren't yourself right now because you were the most of yourself you'd ever been.

You were listening again and they both said they wanted to blindfold you. When you nodded, she climbed on the bed beside you, kissing you between Evan's legs. Their hands held you where they could reach, while hers glided along the curves of your body and pulled you into her tight.

She reiterated your safe words, while the friction of her hands on you felt like fire. Her fingers slid under the lace of your panties and circled your clit, breaking away to look at Evan,

"Daddy, she is so wet for us."

She sensually sucked on her pointer finger while they watched her, and they took her middle finger all the way in their mouth. Your pussy pulsed from that. You arched your neck back looking at Evan and they cupped your chin. There was a silent understanding behind your shared eye contact, a rooted trust that made you feel so held.

Tina reached behind her to the floor and put the blindfold on you. Your gut changed as soon as you couldn't see. That drop you needed came on you like a storm. Someone eased your arms over your head but didn't restrain you, and someone's hands massaged them, stretching out your tension more.

You felt a kiss on your foot that traveled up the curve of your calves. You heard her voice and sank into the anchor of it. She came over you then, straddling you and kissing tenderly, softer. She told you if something wasn't alright, to tell her, if you wanted or needed something to stop, or for more to happen, to ask. She asked again if you were feeling alright. You nodded up at her and she kissed you deep this time, and you were grounded again.

For a moment it was almost silent. Then the fabric of the bag moving. Then a wand turning on, making you jump. Before even spreading your legs, she set it on high, directly over your panties. It was almost too much right away, same as Evan fisting your hair and holding you steady. She kissed and licked and bit up your legs while you were getting used to the intensity and you were clawing her back and shoulders, kind of holding onto her other arm while she was giving the wand more rhythm. You needed her gravity, needed to find a cradle in her. The cinders of her lips were on you like a warmth you'd never felt, just right there, slamming into you with decadence. Your upper thighs and calves trembled and tensed, erratic and lost.

Evan's voice was against your neck now. "I want you to make her come, baby. Do you think she'd come for Daddy when he tells her to?"

Tina's wordless response was to turn the wand up higher. Your moans became louder and someone's hand wrapped around your throat. Her voice slid up your body after her nails scraped your tummy, in your shoulder now and the weight of her on you like bliss.

"Are you going to be good for us, baby? How many times can you come tonight? Maybe we'll just wear you down so you can lay here while I ride that pretty little mouth, while Daddy fucks you deep, hmm?"

She slid down you like a feral snake, spreading your thighs wide. She gripped the band of your panties, dropped them to the floor in one swift motion. The cool air hit your swollen cunt and then her body lowered. The wand was handed off to Evan and the rhythm of it changed to a pulse and her tongue slid inside you deep without warning. Almost immediately, you came, and then in waves, two more times.

Your shoulders left the bed and your thighs subconsciously closed from your last orgasm. Your bliss was interrupted by stinging slaps of Tina's palms on your thighs, and Evan covered your whimpers with their hand, brusque and rough. Your dripping cunt took two of her fingers in deep. You felt like they were feeding off you, feeding each other. They were relentless and had total control, bullying you further into your pleasure.

Evan turned up the wand again during your breathlessness, hovering it over your clit while she put her tongue in deeper.

"Daddy did not say you could stop."

"Don't cover her mouth, Daddy. I want to hear her," Tina said.

Evan's hand pulled away and slapped your cheek eliciting, a cry. They hit your tits in unison multiple times as you got louder, while Tina added a third finger, making you squirt. Your body was wracked with tremors and her hands slid up your thighs to find your own, so you could hold onto them. The tenderness and aggression together sunk you deep.

You leaned your neck towards Evan when things were becoming more intense, borderline crying, nuzzling their chest and kissing them, biting down when you came. You shook and your fingers pulled Tina up by her hair, silently asking for a kiss.

She indulged you immediately and the taste of you on her drove you wild.

The next time your mouth reached for hers, she pulled away and continued fucking you while Evan described how hard they were for you both, how they wished they could fuck you both at once, how they wanted your little holes all sore tomorrow when they ripped the covers off you and woke you up with their cock again. You came again, squeezing Tina so tight it hurt when she pulled out of your body.

She slid back up curling around you with Evan's legs trying to wrap her up, too. The three of you kissed and Evan tightened your blindfold forcefully. Tina bit your damp neck hard enough to bruise while Evan swallowed your cry and you felt something primal emanating from their skin. Tina left and there was silence again as Evan caressed you all over, as they sucked on your tongue and nipped at your swollen lips. They smacked your ass while you wrapped yourself in their lap facing them now.

Your back felt chilled until the heat of Tina's skin found you again from behind. Evan broke your kiss and growled low over your shoulder at her. She pressed against you tight and took your small hand, placed it on the thick strap on she was now wearing.

'You ready for more, baby?" She asked you.

Her arm came around your throat and she held you by the hair viciously, cheek to cheek.

"Daddy is going to watch me fuck you now. And you're going to be good, aren't you? You're going to squirt all over their cock for me, the moment I tell you you're allowed to? Right, baby?"

She wrapped her palm around your neck, squeezing while you answered. Evan bit and slapped your breasts hungrily and you were gone. Gone until tomorrow, until you woke up and passed between and through each other's pleasure like comets.

I Like It When It Hurts: Lover Letter #7

biting, blood, boot play, choking, daddy/girl, pain play, rough body play, D/s

I like it when it hurts, when my pained knees finally feel the bass of your boots. I like the way the hanging sheets graze my shoulder from your air in the room suddenly, gentle, dream before the nightmare. The echo of my screams from last night are still hiding under the bed. I feel you seeing me, like how the sun knows there are seeds in the dirt that need savage tending.

I love your hands, how they're firm and vicious. I love how they know where to paint me purple, tie my bones in knots and pull me out of myself like syrup, always sticky and sweet for you. I love pulsing back against the metronome of your mouth. You know me, where I need it tender and where I need it turpentine. You know my spit, the break of my crics, my blood. I love knowing there are pieces of me sleeping in the bed of your nails when it's all over, after my cheekbone always finds it way to spoon the sweet crescent of your shoulder.

Your presence announces itself. Your fist finds my scalp and the sweet cream of your tongue finds me harder. You kiss like your mouth is a knife slicing into something holy, like the communion is the sin. The drum in my belly had been banging all day for you, aching for this. You pull away and the hum of your hunger feels like a sonata. You slide your fingers down my throat like rain trickles down a leaf in a storm. You meet me like screaming traffic on slick oil, too much, all at once. You make my mind burn to keep up, plucking at my tension.

You had me. This wasn't about fucking tonight. This was about how far we could go without it. It was about how long before the begging came, when the rise would become the fall. I moved into you and my cheek nuzzled against the denim of your jeans, feeling the length and shape of you. My skin warmed the cold zipper while your neck leaned back and you licked your lips, amused at this. Letting it go for a bit, you noticed how the curves of me sought closeness in the sharp edges of you, always bricking me against your firmness. You could already taste the pulse of my clit between your lips, feel the tension from squeezing my thighs shut, cloud shaped bruises you left there last night that kissed each other.

"Pretty girl," you murmured.

You pulled back abruptly and I faltered forward on my knees. Moving to the bed, you hooked the D-ring on my collar with your thumb. You pulled me into a crawl seating yourself in a chair in a corner. Before I could exhale, your teeth found the swollen pout of my lips and sucked. The kiss was gentle at first, then desperate with your shadow over me like an eclipse. I tried to follow, tried to arch into you like I was worthy. You met this and put the lifelines in your palm flush around my throat, straightening my spine further than it could reach, watching me fight to breathe.

The urgency in you needed it now, to overwhelm, to have me sputtering and spinning as you pushed me away. You flashed me a lidded gaze while I watched you stroke yourself.

"Watch Daddy. Show me how good you are. How long can you wait?"

You Like Me Broken: Lover Letter #8

D/s, pain play, rough body play

S pread my thighs and show me the sky. Show me how you see me with your tongue. Put the poetry of your palms on me like sonnets I can see in the morning. when it's over and I am climbing back down to earth with you. I will show you who I am. I will break my spine to rise up to you, curl my limbs around your body. I want you to pocket my pulsing ache, deep and always humming, always reaching in the direction of you.

You like me broken, in pieces after. You like me wet and messy, stained with the rouge of your power, smeared with your demons. I see them in your eyes when the cage opens and it's now and it is brutal and I can't find a corner dark enough to run to. You are in all of them. growling against my skin and holding me down. You pummel me with your cock while you swallow my cries like you're storing them up, to last until next time, to keep your swollen hunger at bay.

Then we sleep and it is dawn and you are against me with your t-dick. You are standing over me white-knuckling the headboard grinding deep, digging only to take. My tongue is high off you, savoring the sweet guttural boi sounds you elicit in the morning of the room. Something in me blooms while you open, while that luscious bend of the back of your knees accepts the cradle of my palms. I bend with you. I stretch your pleasure long, your spine a string of pearls that come apart and fall down my chin with brutal grace. Your broken words trickle down my neck while your come runs past my past my pulse, cleansing the bruises on my breasts in alabaster. The shape of the hunger at the back of your jaw is licked like a wound now, while my skin purrs and we are soft, while you slide down into me and I hold you tenderly. Tonight I know my chest feels like a home for your sighs. We are here and the river in your gaze is carrying me away like a current that broke me into being.

Paint Me Indigo

D/s, primal, strap on

Kissing you felt like breathing fire, like a rollercoaster of cinders falling down the track of my tongue. The haze and fog of you swept over my body, curling around us in thick wisps, between our fingers and down my throat.

You were smaller than me, had to stand on your tiptoes to meet my mouth. I liked that part, that you had to always reach for me. I loved watching you waiting for me to allow it, and then consume you like what happens when lightning splits a tree. I liked splitting you in half. I liked showing you the patterns of secrets that rested inside you deep. I loved how the concentric circles of your hips made their home against my thigh in the dark. I loved feeling the lines of a brick wall jutting into your back when I slammed you between my soft body and cold stone. I loved the moment when you opened to me and accepted what my eyes reflected back at you.

***

It was morning and I was yearning again, from that dream I'd just woken up from, about you and that raging hunger to have you in my bed finally. I was deep in the ache of anticipation for tonight. The resting quake inside me was eager to find your fault-lines, split them apart the same way my fingers wanted to part your lips and take that first taste of me inside your mouth.

The dreams I had about you were getting stronger, more potent and lingering on my consciousness in the day. You'd left something in my mouth after we kissed the week before, some sort of color I'd never seen, memories I felt like I already had but weren't lived, yet. I walked lighter the past few days, carrying the leftovers of them in my pocket, jangling them between the pads of my fingers like coins I couldn't stop stroking.

My eyes squinted in the early light of the morning and I looked sideways at the pillow next to me, empty tonight but ready for you later. Our third date was later. We'd chatted for a while and met through a mutual friend. There was a fascination on both ends, a foreignness but also something else, a sense we'd been existing in the same realm of life but had been leaning against different walls, not crossing over to each others sides just yet.

You knew about art, poetry; you had a deep curiosity about humanity, poetry, compassion, things I guarded as sacred. The table you sat at seemed settled, inspiring, airy — but deep.

As the sun warmed the blackout curtains in my room even more, I turned into the cooler half of my sheets. I thought about the waves of your hair and how soft they felt in my hands when we kissed. I loved the lipstick you wore that stuck to the blush of my cheek when you'd said goodbye last, turning and wafting your perfume back into my chest once more before my door shut.

Sometimes you couldn't tell when it would be "the night" with someone. Sometimes that delay and yearning pounded in your chest all week like a cannon and by the next time you'd meet, it was a collision. The air felt thick with that as I stood in my shower, touching parts of my skin and imagining where your hands would go. I thought about how I'd unfold you, make you bloom below me, find your depths. My favorite packer sat on the counter neatly folded, the one I'd decided was too soon to put on last week. I caught myself staring at it in the mirror and smirked a bit, searching for that thing in me that was hungry for taking, for pulling and pinning a struggle, juggling nerves at a tempo while I paced someone's novel form with my eyes.

I wanted this tonight, wanted you. My neck turned back to my bedroom on the far wall, surveying the neat lines of kink implements that hung by size.

We'd met through kink friends, but didn't know those corners of one another intensely yet. I wanted to find out tonight.

You were definitely submissive. Had I met you on the street or through our friend, it was obvious. It mixed on you well with your charisma, when you went on about things you were passionate about. It was endearing, how you'd give intermittent direct eye contact to me, boldness blanketed by shyness. You fidgeted a lot, looking down or sideways briefly when my steady gaze was too much. Your knees bounced a little when I could feel you pushing yourself to stay on that road of confidence you had going, trying not to falter, to meet me. My calm unnerved you. My control spotlit your jitters and the flush of your fast pulse climbing up your clavicle, the sweet rounds of bare shoulders I wanted to bite, suck, bruise.

Your tells would have banned you from any poker game anywhere ever. You even had certain smiles reserved for what I was sending back to you, a responsive one that was overeager when I grinned, a deflective one when I flashed my eyes at you. There was a small rise in your breasts and tap of your nails on the table when you didn't know what to do with your hands. You sighed and gasped a lot, hyperbolic in your expressiveness at moments when I pulled the floor from you with my words and body language. My eyes stilled in those moments, trying to row you back to being present in this, in us.

Even my coffee seemed to taste more rich when you were across a table sharing one with me. The animal in me was at bay but stalking his door, starting to claw and rake at a light coming in, the sense of your want close enough to taste.

I set my hair product and cologne back on their cedar shelves and wondered how the hell I was going to get through the day with this urgency. I was damn near wanting to cancel tonight, call you for brunch. I licked my lips after pushing my leather belt through its last loop, hooked it firmly hoping I could use it later on you, hoping you'd let me. I woke up hard and knew I'd be all day, for you, for this. I wandered into my kitchen and looked grimly at the whiteboard on my fridge, an entire agenda of things to be done mocking me.

I poured myself a cup of coffee slow, indulging in the steam rising up and over my senses. It was the smell of morning, but also of us. The creamer you liked was already in my fridge for when that could and might happen. It was a quiet manifestation to share breakfast with you here, my four walls and home and its patient vulnerability open to that.

The text alert of glasses clinking interrupted my daydreaming, I looked down and saw your name on my phone. The sound startled me as my cock strained in my jeans. Tonight was the night. Tonight was the night.

I stared at the text on my phone in awe. *I took off work today. I'm too anxiously excited for tonight. I was wondering are you free earlier? If not, that's totally okay. We can keep it to dinner. I feel flustered I probably sound so silly wanting to change plans. I'm rambling now. Also, good morning.*

I smiled sweetly and the butterflies came back while I scanned the whiteboard a second time after reading my phone again. None of this was particularly imminent, it could wait until tomorrow. I could feel your nerves from here, but also your desire. Your hunger felt the same as mine, it was just disguised by that submission in the tells and language you used. It made me hard, that primal growl inside my stomach deep waking back up.

I texted you back. *Good morning. I was considering the same. How soon can you be ready to come over? I'd like to cook us brunch.*

I didn't feel like sharing her with the public. I was greedy today, wanted her to myself, wanted these walls and this quiet to be ours, just for us. I'd cleaned my place in lieu of her being here tonight, and I always had all the things to make brunch.

I looked around my apartment, surveying the places I wanted her, the curved arm of the couch that was just the height to bend her over on, the blanket I could wrap her in while she lay naked in my lap, the length of the hallway I hoped she'd crawl down, toward me. My fists were hungry to tangle themselves in her hair. My chest had that gasp in it that waiting for release, my nerves like seltzer, fizzing under my skin.

I leaned on my counter thinking of the change she'd bring to this space, and rubbed my packer with my palm. I wanted to make her dance, tremble, whimper below me, reach and strain. I wanted to put fireworks inside her body that came out of her mouth into mine when our tongues touched. I wanted my teeth buried in the soft cream of her thighs.

My phone beeped again and I exhaled a breath I didn't realize I'd been holding.

That just sounds ... so lovely. Be there in twenty.

Little Deaths

daddy/girl, choking, crying, dirty talk, edging, nonbinary daddy using he/him pronouns

I try to remember what my life was like before you touched me, before your cock opened me, before your tongue spread my cunt open like petals that wanted to bloom below your heat. I try to remember how it felt before you filled me deeper than anyone has.

You are in your office finishing work, making me wait. It's been days since you let me come, days since you've taken only your pleasure. You only recently let me wrap my lips around you, looking up with my lidded eyes. You praised my mouth, my hand, my hungry tongue. Then you'd leave me, shaking and wet, burning from your power and telling me how you knew how bad I wanted it, after you finally made me stop.

Tonight was a replay of all of that, followed by a tender kiss goodnight. You held me between your arms while my fists bunched and lips reached for yours, desperately trying to change your mind. You hold your ground and I both hate and love it. You rest your hand on my cunt, a squeeze in your grip, possessive. You stare at what you own and remind me it's yours, not mine. You bite my tits and smirk against my skin. My impatience grows, more desperation in my moans like a smoke signal from my clit. You revel in my unraveling; my singed nerves are barely able to take this.

My eyes are watering for you tonight. I'm whimpering like a lost puppy, a flinch away from sobbing. Your hands and mouth and voice and presence are too much; they make me tremor when you graze certain spots on my skin and I am past the point of being able to take another night of this.

You climb back up and give me your mouth, hold my throat still against my trembling, bite my lower lip that's wavering. You kiss the corner of my eye before a tear can fall, look down at me with mercy. "Alright, baby. Daddy will let you come tonight."

I wrap my legs around you, like my limbs almost doubted your choice. My fingers fly to your scalp holding the roots of your hair and whimpering into your mouth with a deep exhale from hearing you say that.

"Shhhhh. Daddy's got you tonight baby. Whose hole is this?"

You slap me and wetness clings to your palm. I buck away from the mattress from the abrupt yet welcome sting. I am quiet and still against you and subconsciously grinding against your hand.

You plant yourself there, adding pressure to my need. I grind against you, long deep circles of my hips, rising off the bed with my deeply bruised ass. We breath into each others mouths, and your hand slaps my pussy again, harder this time, You circle my clit, hard and sensitive and my body almost curls away from the direct touch.

"Daddy gets you so wet. I saw every pair of panties you wore this week. Walking around every day desperate for me inside you. Did it take everything to not touch yourself?"

I moan my answer. "Yes."

Your slick fingers trail up my tummy, over my nipples, pinching and then slapping them. I respond in hungry gasps and my legs open to the glorious weight of your thigh. You caress my lips with yours, pull away and feed me my arousal. Fingers down my throat. My eyes close, lost in you.

"Did you touch yourself this week? You can tell Daddy. He'll keep your secret."

I moan around you and try to shake my head no.

Pushing further down my throat, you ask, "You sure about that? Liars get punished. Good girls don't lie. You weren't in the shower thinking about my cock and your pretty little hands went over Daddy's clit, secret and quiet. Or when Daddy was sleeping, you tiptoed to the living room with your toy, like a bad girl. You can tell Daddy."

Sputtering around you as you thrust in and out and nodding about being good.

"Use your words, baby."

Your fingers leave me, scrape my teeth and you grip my chin, press your forehead against mine hard.

"I was good. I promise I was good!"

You slap my thighs while you listen. You watch my small cheeks redden and shivers run under my skin, holding onto you wherever I could.

"Then you think you earned Daddy's cock? Because you were good. Because you waited and didn't play with Daddy's pussy, like you were supposed to."

My lower lip trembles out a mewl. "Yes. I think I earned it, Daddy."

You smile down at me, tender, proud, seeing me in that way no one else ever has. You kiss me deep and long and take my thighs and wrap them around you tight. I hear your belt come off. Your zipper slides down. You try to hold me still, look in my eyes. You hold me in your gaze like a hammock.

"Daddy thinks so too."

I Dream About You: Lover Letter #9

biting, boot play, D/s, crying, oral sex

I had a dream about you last night. We were at a play party. Hours had passed and I'd circled the halls and rooms many times, gave brief eye contact to some, noticed pleasantries being exchanged, sometimes more. A crowd had gathered over the hours and the nooks for me to retreat to were sparse, not enough space for my thoughts. The noise was starting to overwhelm me, same as my tolerance for large crowds.

I followed a long hallway that turned into another almost empty one, and a carpeted ramp into a sun-room.

At the back of that, I pushed a pair of doors open to an deserted courtyard. The sound of fountains trickled and the air smelled like fall. Some amber leaves were scattered on the ground and a slowly dying fire-pit with orange embers were whispering to me in their final glow.

I exhaled loudly as the door whooshed shut behind me. Now the noise was gone, the people. I sat still in the moment, gathered myself back up.

Minutes later, you came outside for a cigar, your back to me but your energy still potent. You sat with your legs straight in front of you and crossed. from the corner, behind my sunglasses I drank in your form. Black jeans. Black t-shirt. Black belt. Like when you're a jet you're a jet. You looked like you could pull James Dean over and commandeer his car. You looked like your hands knew work, and your mouth knew more. You looked like you had leather in your bedside drawer.

I watched you intently, a cloud of smoke fixed above your table now, on the opposite end of the patio. The iron legs of your chair on the stone below scraped the concrete disruptively. I watched your shoulders stretch the fabric of your shirt when you bent your body down, scratching your calve. Your hair was styled in a simple fade, just enough at the top for me to pull.

I watched you puff more curled wisps toward the sky and tried to inhale deeper in each of my own breaths. Something about the eroticism of that turned me on, having something scratch my throat dry that had just been in your lungs. a taste that had escaped between your lips. I wondered what your lap felt like. I wondered how I'd feel with your boots on my shoulders, resting your weight on me while you billowed your cigar around my eyes while they watered up at you. I locked in on the glass of whiskey jingling in your hand, found myself shamelessly wanting to sip it after you, just for a taste of your mouth in mine.

I had headphones in, but no music on. My fingertips fidgeted against my clothes and the shared but quiet presence of both of us out here alone, twenty feet apart had me pulsing against my panties, breathing slow and deep.

My eager curiosity mixed with your quiet confidence; I was like the dew on your glass, a body made of dripping, still shy like the bend of the tree giving your table shade.

I wanted to wear lipstick for you, feel your hands creeping under my dress, rip my thong off with your teeth abruptly. I wanted you to take me down so hard it would knock the wind out of me. I wanted to stare up at you small, feel owned from your fingers in my holes. I wanted my mouth around your cock, exactly where it belonged. I thought of my earrings resting on your bathroom counter, next to your cologne, the sheets halfway off the bed and the morning sun hitting the deep bruises on my body while you held me, let it happen. I thought of my neck soothed with your lips, burning twice for you.

I want you more than wanting warrants. I want your kerosene and your flicker. I want my wet lashes wavering on your cheek in the dark, and your mouth on me like fireworks the sky has never seen.

Watch While I Hit You

daddy/girl, biting, boot play, breast play, choking, crying, dirty talk, pain play

Days later, and still the jets stung your skin; the hot water may as well have been falling icicles, transparent spindles reminding you of who you really were, remembering their hunger. They kept secrets behind their soft demeanor, what was was under their shirt and inside their jeans and beneath their boots. They kept you under their skin, kept you in the obsidian of their piercing eyes.

You liked knowing that you could speak in this tongue together, just a channel for the two of you. Your skin was welted, inflamed and raw. Their knuckles were red and bruised and the dampness of your tears still sat on the back of their neck. You didn't cry easy. You fought it until your lungs were heaving and your lower lip was trembling like a child, your muscles spasming and cramping from the inability to escape, from their arms holding you through this, pushing you further in.

Your strength came from somewhere else, somewhere that wanted to prove more next time, to show them how far you could go, to challenge their own power to burn out first, even though it never did.

Plans had abruptly shifted and normally when they came home, they needed a half hour of quiet pause, of decompression from the drag of the day. They needed soft light and you sitting by their chair, waiting to be summoned, eventually with your head in their lap. That was what you'd grown to expect, what you anticipated when the deadbolt unlocked swiftly.

Not today. Today the door slammed closed before you barely heard it open. Today they came into the living room looking at you with the coal in their eyes lit deep. Their steps were heavy, their bag tossed on the ground to prove a point and they stood a good ten feet from you, a pointed gaze that told you more in words than what they were about to say:

"Strip."

Righting yourself to whatever energy shift this was, and looking at them quizzically, hesitant even, you brushed the hemline of your jeans and blinked back at them.

They advanced on you and put both hands around your throat until you were between them and the wall. Their forehead found yours, breathing you in like an animal inhales before ripping into flesh. They met you with a flash of softness when you reached for their lips, kissed you gently, not giving you their tongue and pulling back the more you tried to find it.

"*Strip*. You do not want me to ask again.", they spit at you.

Silently, while they gave you about a foot of breathing room, you quickly pulled your tank over your head, unhooked your bra, and brusquely slid your jeans past your hips, so fast the scrape of the denim almost burned your skin.

You never wore panties. They liked you accessible and aware of how little was truly between your body and theirs.

Their stare still unwavering, they came back and flipped you around so their chest had you pinned back against the wall. Their hands grabbed your ass like the meat of you was dripping with blood, a growl at the back of their whisper made the atmosphere darker than it really was.

Kissing and biting your neck,

"I want you to look at me while I hit you tonight, while you need me to stop, while you will try not to. I'm going take you past the edge, while your tears make me hard, make me wet."

Their hands spidered over your skin in a brief but rushed effort to warm you up. The insistence of their energy dissonant between getting through this moment to the next, but knowing the sugarcoat would push you further, too. Your knees buckled slightly when their boot kicked your legs open, when their fingers felt how swollen and soaked you already were.

"You think this is still for you, don't you?"

Slapping your cunt and swallowing your little gasp with their mouth. "This is for Daddy tonight. Say it."

One hand in your hair, the other on your throat nodding your head for you as you repeated them, contrived bravery flecked with timidness, just what they fed on.

Kissing you one last time and biting your lip so hard you cried out into a staccato whimper, they swept you to the floor on your knees abruptly. Their closed fist reached out at a sharp angle and pointed to the sectional couch impatiently.

"Crawl," they simmered.

In the twenty seconds it took you to reach the furniture, they crept behind you objectively, staring at the lines of your ass, the sweet arch of your back, the delicate glisten of your cunt they wanted to slam mercilessly into later. They kicked you into the sofa before your last step, dragged you up onto the couch and then flipped you on your back abruptly. Your lips quivered from a mix of fear and arousal, the scent of you obvious as all hell you wanted them in all your holes.

You looked so fucking perfect: a little breathless, doe-eyed, scared, on the brink of wincing. You were wavering between trust and fear and trying to ping-pong your overthinking mind to the right side of the net.

They looked down at you like they'd been starving all day and had one bullet left, like their eyes were pulsing panic into your own and then swallowing it like mercury down their throat.

Their full weight on you, their knees tethered your hips and your skin sinking you lower on the fabric of the couch, no way out. Then their fists came raining down, along with their rabid teeth. Their mouth covered yours the louder you cried, swallowing the taste of your bravery shrinking, of your pale skin giving way to deep colors and your limbs trying to cover spots that had almost had enough. Still, their strength and resolve were bigger, bullying you more knowing you had nowhere to run. Your eyes closed as you tried to disappear and their hand hugged your throat almost too tight as their knees dug into your ribs.

You watched. You watched them become and watched them rise and they felt you fall, for them. They felt your heat against them slick and grinding on their thigh, desperate for any small piece of comfort. You kept trying to take their fingers down your throat so they'd have one less hand, kept trying to suck and kiss skin so you'd melt them into acquiescence.

Then the moment came when the ramp grew too high. You couldn't climb anymore. You were sobbing and shriveled, sunken and trembling, cheeks salty from your own tears and their sweat, unable to even beg anymore because you were crying so hard.

Their current slowed, the ocean of them listening to your body. Their hand reached for your clenched fist to open it. Their lips found your breasts and shoulders and neck, thigh pushed into your dripping cunt. Your hand found their cock and your eyes looked up, so whole in your brokenness, so lovely in the cradle of their wicked smile.

I Need You More Than Breathing

being loaned out, biting, blindfolds, blood, bondage, D/s, dirty talk, edging, flogging, pain play, femdom

T his was the game we'd play, but tonight there was no softness, no pillow to hold onto, no candles to add warmth to my shivering skin. There were no smells I was familiar with, no "you" to reach for.

We'd negotiated this. We'd reached a stage of trust where loaning me out to someone else was a new comfort level. I understood deeply you knew what I needed, sometimes more than I did. The solace of that confidence you had in me, that trust I felt in it, bled into me deep and I grew taller for you.

Still, this was the first time. I'd spent today shaking, fumbling on my words, completely unable to focus on any task seriously. I checked in with you briefly in text to share all of this, and then we had a connected video chat while I dressed for tonight. Your voice grounded me back to us, to the depth of love I had for you.

I hung up almost immediately after, went downstairs where a car was waiting for me and a nameless driver placed a blindfold over my eyes, closing my vision to the world. With only the unknown ahead, my mind scrambled with dissonance of you orchestrating all of this, knowing that would make it good, keep me safe. Still, I felt like I was faltering into this. Despite that, I wanted this push; I hoped I could fly for you again tonight.

Still, there was an ease to doing this, because I knew it was for you, because I wanted always to be the spark to your dynamite, the light in the charcoal in your eyes, and the reason the world could roll off our shoulders from the potency in ourselves we sought.

Now here I was, cuffed by four points from each tense limb to a St. Andrew's cross in a fully cement room. There was chill in the air, the only familiarity to my nakedness apprehensively waiting for what was to come. I'd been led into a building blindfolded, then a hallway, then a turn down another hall, then through a door that closed behind me with solemn menace. The vibrato of some sort of finality echoing in my chest made me jump slightly. I was following someone who pulled me rather than led me, an impatient insistence in their stride that made me feel like a number on a list.

I didn't know how long I'd been waiting. Blindfolds always make me lose a sense of time, even though the rest of me was stretched to be acutely aware of my surroundings. There was either a pipe or faucet dripping, a bladed fan high above my head on an even higher ceiling methodically humming. The floor was slightly uneven and cold. I could hear doors outside of this room's door faintly closing, a tone of voices further away but nothing coherent enough to understand.

It smelled like an unfinished basement back home, coupled with the stain of the wood against my skin, my own sweat, and leather. The air was foreign. Despite this, I knew I was alone in the room since the door had shut last. I knew it was just my body in overdrive, missing you dearly, my mind pushing to be present, my calves trying to root their place in an open stance. My breath struggled to right itself before it all began.

What I didn't know, was that you were here too, watching, intently. You were quietly sitting less than five feet from me, stroking your cock from the outside of your jeans already throbbing from my fear. If I could only see you, those eyes of yours were viewing the spectacle of me with a lidded smirk like the frothy animal you were.

I had been given the bare bones of information for a reason. All I knew for sure was you would "be here to take me home after it was over."

That and whoever this person was, this familiar top, had been a respected confidant of yours for years. As an overthinker, this was already torture and as you watched me pretend to exude the "I've got this" facade, and then waver back to "oh fuck, I'm here," the pads of your fingers tingled to be inside my holes. Your teeth watered for that spot on my neck where I would shrink away and into you at once.

The door opened abruptly, with a vacuumed whoosh of air announcing another presence, heavy boots coming towards me, perfume that already made my head swim with hunger. Next I felt the texture of a corset and breasts on my naked back. Slender fingers gripped my hipbones possessively like they belonged to only her. Lips sucked on the curled edge of my ear and a throaty but feminine voice hissed,

"So, I hear you haven't been allowed to come in three weeks. What a shame."

She started grinding her body into mine and craned my neck as far back as it would go, biting me so hard. I was thrown off balance immediately.

"Let's see if we can make that worse for you," she snickered.

I elicited a pained moan and she laughed louder. She broke away and fumbled around somewhere to the left of me at what sounded like a table of implements she was thumbing through. I heard small pieces of metal rubbing each other, what sounded like a clothespin dropping to the floor, a zipper being pulled quick. I heard her exhale with the smallest pleasured moan at the end of it, then at once a heavy flogger slammed my shoulders back against the cross, cutting through my curiosity bluntly.

She stayed there until I was almost past broken. She was relentless, pushing me to where my body was trying to twist away. My heels had left the ground and my hands were balled into fists so tight my nails had imprinted my palms. Was this a fucking warm-up or the actual event?

My breaths came out erratic and a sheen of dampness coated the goosebumps on my neck. The weighted stings finally ceased and her warm palms caressed the lines she'd made, sensual as she moved her hand down to grab my cunt,

"If only your Sir could see how bad you need it. You miss them filling your pretty little holes? Has it been ages? Have you stayed up at night squeezing those thighs together for some sense of relief?"

Before I could respond, she slapped my pussy in rhythm with her words and took her hand away just when the contact started to feel delicious. Her nails dragged down what felt like the worst part of the marks she'd left on my back, and my skin tried to run away in what little space I had to negotiate.

She laughed again and kept going, slashing me like a cat, both hands and then just one. Then the weight of a curved cane pushed against my ass. There was no comedown, just a sensory warning, and two fingers between my lips that tasted like blood, my blood.

"Your blood is so pretty. I might have to bend you over my bench after this and give you some relief, hmm?"

I moaned around her fingers desperately, my lips trembled while the first blow of the cane landed and I bit down on instinct.

Pulling out of my mouth, she beat me in a rhythm only a seasoned top would understand. She edged me to a cliff, until she sensed me about to fall, then pulled me back, and finally shoved me forward harder. This was when the tears came, my calves now convulsing. I sniffled as a signal for mercy and wondered how dark and welted my ass would be. I was dripping and terrified and just missed my Sir.

Finally, in my haze, I heard the sound of the cane dropping, and her body rushed flush against mine; her breathlessness heaved her tits against my shoulders and her soft lips sucked on my neck. Tenderness in her demeanor and maybe a tinge of pride, her tongue met mine commanding every piece of energy I had left to follow. Her arms rose up my own gently unhooking my cuffs, rubbing my tingling nerves back to life sweetly.

What I didn't know was that you were standing even closer now, and that when she had come in the room, you had sauntered onto the spanking bench as a contented spectator. I didn't know that during the loudest of my cries, you were stroking your cock, biting your lip, and dripping with anticipation.

I was dazed as she led me to the bench, my limbs loose and unsteady, my body lost and aroused and vibrating from the pain.

"Do you think you deserve relief? Was that anywhere near worthy for me? Would they be happy when they pick you up to know how long you lasted?"

Too many questions at once, demanding immediacy. She expected too much sharpness when all I had was languid malaise. I felt faun-like, and hungry for my Sir. Before I could answer, her boots shuffled away and the door closed harshly. I sat kneeling and draped, worried I'd been a disappointment, worried I'd cracked too soon, wondering if she was done, scared she wasn't.

Then a hand cupped my chin and the growl of your energy fed me too many of your fingers and my stomach flipped sideways. A wave from the presence of you rushed down my spine like a waterfall.

"Hello, pretty girl."

The room was warm again, with the scent of everything familiar in you, the feel of your skin on mine. I need you more than breathing.

Control

biting, blood, bondage, boot play, breast play, choking, D/s, crying, dirty talk, fear play, slapping, strap on, femdom

I like it when the boy's eyes beg like this, when they're dilated and cloudy, gone on me. My wicked whispers reflect the malice I've grown inside all week, for this moment. His spine hums from my black nails on his scalp while I pinch his short, textured hair up by its roots. I keep him below, glued to the floor on his sweet knees and I ground him with my lowered gaze. I like him desperate, on the brink of a flinch, uncertain, overthinking. I like him balanced on that tightrope between hunger and fear knowing I hold the knife to slice it.

I notice his fingertips behind his back are curled and clenched. He is tingling for touch, his back and shoulders tensing and releasing nervously. His bravery wavers, sinking and coming back to rise up. His thoughts race against the quiet of the room, trying to read me while I view his body, on display so well. I snap my fingers when I want him to watch me, like tapping on glass to bring him closer.

I pace him in a wide circle while his eyes follow his favorite cock, slightly bouncing between the leather around my hips. It highlights my pale ass and thighs in thick stripes. I am wearing only that and my boots, and a bomber jacket I had on when we first met, open and holding my tits to my skin. We objectify each other in similar ways, knowing we've been here before, knowing the pressure valves in both our bodies are clamoring for release. He is sweet and still, shoulders slightly rounded down and trying to focus on his breathing. I continue my silent viewing, offering no words. I watch his chest rise and fall, goosebumps forming on his neck from a mix of me studying him and the chill of the room, no doubt.

He likes this almost as much as me, needs it, the build and crescendo. He revels in the ticking seconds that drag on while I circle him like a meal, while I test his sturdy body with my boots, kicking in his soft spots, poking his fear, licking my lips. I stroke myself above him while the filthy things I say land on his tender shoulders. They run down his neck like marbles I plan to put back in his throat later. He is so good, my boy.

He is pliable and aching, with little tremors in his muscles popping out here and there from how I draw them out, scrape against his sweetness while I swallow his soft cries. He is nectar between my fingers when he opens his holes eagerly, letting me in so deep, swallowing me while I chew on his moans. I feel him want to run when it hurts too much, while I command him to come when it does. Then, the brutality of my teeth make him bleed; his tears are moist on my shoulder while he shakes and I hold him, while I carry him through my fire.

I need this just as much.

My lips are rabid for his skin. I can feel my god complex ripe for his prayers. I will make him cry in bursts tonight. I will be his altar, his sweet holes, my sanctuary. His tears will be the holy water I bathe in.

I kneel in front of him finally, one knee bent and the other bumped up against his own on the floor. I cup his chin and he gives me his eyes. So good. They are searching, curious. They try to discern which type of storm I have inside tonight. I stay there while our breathing regulates together. I am slow with him, building the deep, soothing his nerves before the roughness.

I love pretending the scream of me is really a whisper. I love waiting until he's settled inside of my softness., feeling his anticipation breaking, edgy and wavering between standing up and cowering down. I watch the waves of his energy change, remember and forget, his eyes glazing like the fog at the bottom of the cliff, lost in me.

Until it's time. I shock him the hardest when a slap lands across his cheek. I admonish him for losing his posture. My boot finds a resting place on his thigh and I dig until I know the tread will leave a mark, until I see his wince wrinkle in that deeply pained way. I plant the deepest kiss while the sting on his cheek meets the air, while my hand finds his throat and I can feel his pulse knocking on my palm. His spine rises up higher in a jerking reaction that almost feels like stuttering. I pull away slightly, swallowing a brief whimper while I rest my weight heavier on his other thigh, digging again to make that sweet symmetry I love on his tender little skin.

I take my cock and graze it across the redness my palm left and he nuzzles it, exhaling a breath he must have been holding for a while. His brow is slightly furrowed, half trusting the gentleness again, knowing it won't last. I slide three fingers in between his lips, too much, too fast. A small gag escapes before I even push them down, fear of what's to come. His eyes are closed, almost like he doesn't want to see, can't handle knowing.

He settles again as I hold still and I feel his pretty little jaw stretch. His tongue is thick the further down I go and his body is so tense.

"Can you take it all for me, boy?" I whisper.

I push further, at his molars now and spit falls down my wrist, running down his chin. His breathing has escalated and the heat of it warms my damp hand. I know he can't do it, at least not all the way, but I love to watch him try.

He looks up at me stunned, eyes incredulous I'd expect this so soon. He sputters as he tries to open more from that last push past his tongue, no room to go further until his throat caves closed in another gag. His eyes well up staring at me still, fighting for me.

My cunt pulses as I pull my fingers from his mouth, grab the d-ring on his collar and pull him up from the floor. I kiss him while I wrap my arms around him, uncuffing his swollen wrists. He wraps around me with a need I can feel so deep it makes me shiver. I kiss him until his lips are sore, until my nails make enough stripes on his back I can feel flecks of blood, until he is breathless and gasping for air and his muscles are melting like a lullaby into mine. We land on the bed at some point and he buries himself in my breasts, making me lose my mind. His hand wraps around my cock and he grinds against my thigh, shaking.

His teeth chatter around my nipples while I cup his skin between my hands. I bruise and pull and stretch him out like he's a landscape that doesn't end. He slides down until he's between my thighs kissing and biting, looking up at me from time to time with pleading eyes. His strong hands grip my calves while I rest my boots on his back.

My own spine leaves the bed and I pull his handsome face back to me. "Let's see what that mouth can do. Maybe you'll earn my cock, boy, if you do it just right."

He is wordless as he dives between the sweet folds of my cunt, tongue warm and hungry on me like he's never had me before. I raise my arms in sweet surrender and hold onto the curved rails of my headboard, the ones that still have black silk strips from when I tied him last. He is so eager, stroking my clit with his tongue and then sliding it in my hole, deep. The rhythm he gives me feels like an opera in my body, soft notes moving upward in crescendos. His hands hold my thighs possessively, gripping me through his desire until I can't stand it anymore, until my palms fly to his scalp and push. I grind off the mattress into his face, that starvation to release already building deep in my belly. I talk down to him, while he whimpers into my warmth.

"Such a good boy, give me those fingers now. Harder. Maybe you can earn your fucking like this tonight. Would you like that, boy? A reward? Keep going. I'm going to have all of you when you're done. Bend you over every surface and mark you from the inside. Good boy."

I'm close and he knows it. He moves into me with his full weight while my thighs shake against his strong shoulders, the cream of me milky against his skin. His voice matches the murmurs I exhale in the dark and his arm drives into me the same way I fuck him with my cock, the one he is so needy for. I can smell his wetness now, even through my own. I think of that small layer of sweat I always make on his neck while I've got him on his knees and he's stroking his little dick so desperately. He moans that same moan against my cunt and as I release, he pulls out of me and shoves his tongue back inside, taking every drop of me down his pretty little throat. I shiver against his caresses while my body follows the sweet paths he continues to lay down for me. Urging me not to stop with his mouth, I fall into that bit of power he has over me, just for now, just for my pleasure.

My fingers find the sweet silver ring on his damp collar and I hook it like a predator, pulling his body above mine. His weight is a savior and every nerve of me feels it at once, little lightning bolts from his brown eyes looking at me in quiet worship. I wrap my legs around him with ownership and he whimpers as I bite and suck his lips. My good boy. My sweet, aching, darling boy. My nails slither between our stomachs. I graze his cock and the tension in his tummy becomes taut; he leaves a gasp against my neck and I grin against his ear.

I suck on his tongue like I wish it was his cock and give him a squeeze with my warm hand. My boots click against his hips in synchronicity and he yelps as I smirk harder.

"Get on your hands and knees, boy. Time for you to take your reward."

Be Good, Spread Your Legs

biting, bondage, D/s, crying, dirty talk, edging, fear play, fucking, oral sex, primal

H e was behind me in our basement. On my neck with his words. I could smell the musk of his body, his shirt damp around the collar. His hand gripped my throat with ownership, while I was there, dangling for him. The suspension beam that ran the length of the room held me, just enough space between my toes and the floor to get a soft grip on gravity.

***

My thighs were damp and your hands were tender in their comedown, massaging the knots on my ass you'd just made with your cane, and then flogger, and then again, cane.

I had cried some today, had more to let go of than I realized and the nerves under my skin were unwound by you, your lips and teeth. Your whispers made me bloom. Your presence down here was always kerosene over velvet, saccharine underneath, hiding in the dark. You were against my skin like a vice, feeling all of me coming out from the inside, holding me like I was precious, like you could lose me if you did it wrong.

You answered me with a menacing laugh as I whimpered, arched back into you; I could feel you fucking with me. You loved me like this, when my desperation climbed past hunger and dove into brazenness. I clawed the air like an animal, trying to pull back the bits of control I had let go of.

Your palm slid down my stomach and hovered over my cunt, tantalizing me. My neck turned as far around as it could to find a home in your mouth, moaning both for and against you, delicate on vicious, I crumbled against your power that gathered me back up in fistfuls. I arched my hips as high as I could, trying to meet your fingers, just barely above my clit and not giving me what I wanted.

I bucked my hips up against your hand, insistent. I tried to show your tongue how good I'd been, how I knew where I belonged. I wanted to prove myself so hard to convince you I deserved a reward.

You bit down on my neck and I cried out louder than you expected. I was unraveled, hitting a brink of want that almost hurt. I was running only on my need, by the pain on my skin from all the blows you'd delivered. My muscles reached for you like tendrils, for any sense of relief your mercy might grant.

You knew it, could feel it. As you let go of me, you melted away, making me believe this was over, that I'd get nothing. Sometimes it was just for you. Sometimes I was forced to accept it and by the next time we'd fuck, you edged me until all I had left to give you were my tears. This was the game.

Alone now, I hung by the beam pathetically. My thighs squeezed together while I arched my neck, trying to hear your movement in the room above the sound of my racing pulse. My own arousal was the newest assault and all of my senses stretched to their edge, desperate and dripping.

I could feel you watching me, noticing which muscles were taut, which ones were screaming, which ones had thrown up their white flag. I could smell the musk of your sweat nearby, intuit your eyes on me. I could always feel your gaze. It was relentless, designed to consume.

Then your hands coiled around my thighs, your lips climbed up my legs like a ladder to the sky. The slight stubble on your chin scratched where your mouth had been. Your tongue opened me, your fingers teased. My desire ran down your skin, shaking under your touch.

You were kneeling below me and my legs were resting against your back, then your shoulders in former spots I loved to hold onto and rake. The bud of my clit rested between your velvet lips and my calves trembled.

"Don't fucking come until I say so. You're not done until I say you're done."

My neck flew back with full abandon from the sensation of you. Your fingers buried and curled inside me deep. You pulled me out of myself, into you. Your other hand gripped my ass hard, especially where the bruises had risen. My hunger under my skin was still so thick and pulsating under your touch, leftover fear in my nerves still there. Rabid, you pulled my hips flush against your face like you hadn't breathed until now, like you could threaten your law with my pleasure.

I was on the brink of begging for it. Your fingers were relentless and knew how hard I was working to not let go, not give in against you. The rope in my belly unwound and I tried to use any leverage I could to swing myself away from your mouth, while you grabbed me harder. Your nails dug into my hips, marks for me to remember this fight.

You pulled away long enough to remind me,

"Don't forget to fucking ask. If you come without permission today, I fucking swear you won't be allowed again for a month."

Then you rushed back into me harder, fucking me faster. Every fiber of me focused on holding back against your touch.

Then the tears came and I was begging, shaking. A litany of syllables and sounds fell over your shoulders like hail, while you shoved me towards my release. You ravaged my clit with your tongue, brazen in your control, unresponsive to a word of my desperation. I cried harder, tried to run against my suspension, my limbs tired and tingling and my ache looking over the edge ready to give in and jump.

"Come."

Violence against your mouth, your strength held me through the quaking of my muscles. I felt a guttural relief leave my lips while your mouth met my release. Tongue soft, my face exhaled from relief as I ran warm down your throat. The murmur of your giggle against my cunt was a signal of your triumph. The vibrato of it made me let go again. My orgasms were almost tantric, one into another, into another. Your warm palms caressed me to tell me how good I was, your kisses told me you knew how far I pushed tonight.

You slid up my skin and cupped my swollen pussy with your hand and kissed me. The taste of me was thick on your tongue, met with the dampness on your cheeks from my thighs. I felt owned and possessed, spotlit and cradled, injected with your power. You reached up and unhooked my cuffs and my arms fell around your neck like a rag doll. The weight of gravity on my legs was too much for my exhaustion as you held me and slid down with me to the floor.

My final resting place fell into that nook against your chest where I fit so perfectly. My fingers flexed lazily in your short hair, eyes came back to yours, unwavering. The room was quiet now, except for the hum of your praise against my skin, the only lullabies I ever wanted.

Breaking The Rules

D/s, daddy/girl, punishment, oral sex, orgasm control/denial, cage confinement, cuffs

*L*ucy:

A shiver ran through my body as I heard the mattress creak with your weight, the bones of the frame over my head aching harder in spots, trying to regulate itself. I was doing the same.

There was always a hope that the locked cage your bed rested above would be slid open by a swift reach of your thumb and forefinger, and sometimes you did change your mind, but it was rare. I was sensing tonight wasn't one of those times.

When you came in the room you ignored the fact that I was under here, my collar locked a notch tighter around my neck for the long night ahead, a blanket over me not doing a great job of avoiding the floor fans you kept going until morning. They were the loudest thing in the room right now, aside from my racing pulse that hoped for mercy.

You were supposed to be working late tonight, at least that's what you'd reminded me when you left this morning, directing a nod to the list of chores on the fridge I was meant to acknowledge and complete before then.

The list wasn't that long today and I'd surmised I'd be done quite a few hours before your return. I was antsy, suffering, bored having just finished a series I enjoyed and a longer novel you'd suggested to me. Beyond the menial tasks that were part of my protocol, I wasn't sure what to do with myself today. You had me on limits; orgasms only on weekends when you were home and only if I'd proved myself that week to be good enough and earn them.

It was only Tuesday and considering the days I still had to go, my thighs squeezed together in hope of relief. Maybe if I did everything extra well today you'd reward me early? Not likely. Your power was always so measured and more often than not you didn't stray from what you said you'd do, what you told me was coming, how you'd deny me.

I thought of the toys lined up in our play closet, thought of how hard you'd fucked me this weekend and the taste of you in my mouth, your fingers gripping my scalp urgently while my tongue twirled around your dick and I kept my hands behind my back.

You knew this weekend protocol thing wasn't enough for me. It was something we were trying anyway, a new challenge for me to see how far I could go for your rules, for you.

By 1 p.m., I'd fit in a movie, a lunch that took over forty minutes to prep, all my tasks were complete, and I still had three hours until you were home. I sighed in frustration for the dozenth time that day and decided to walk upstairs toward the bedroom. Maybe if I just looked at the various toys that would be enough and flush out the desire.

I padded down the hall listening to the o-ring around my neck bob slightly up and down and I squeezed my fists by my side when I opened the well organized toy closet you kept for us.

You didn't keep it locked but truthfully, whatever access I was granted to the implements in here was usually by abrupt direction from you telling me to fetch something quickly. I left the door wide open so the light from the day filtered through the closet. For whatever reason, turning the switch on felt even more invasive than just standing in here.

I felt myself keeping my breathing more shallow while I eyed the shelves; your various sized cocks lined up neatly, hooks on the back wall that held crops and floggers by size, different plugs, a tens unit with the white cord zip-tied neatly. My clit throbbed more as I scanned your leathers that hung along the higher rod. It smelled like you in here; it smelled like shoe polish and the tread of your boots, your sweat, a tinge of lube and silicone combined, cold metal and fabrics that had swallowed your scent that drove me wild.

I almost hit the ceiling when I felt my watch buzz and saw your name pop up with a text that read,

"How's your day, babe? Getting those chores done for Daddy I hope."

Flustered, I sent a voice message back, hoping I'd sufficiently hid the crack of surprise and arousal from you, answering obediently.

"Yes, Sir, all done."

"Very good. Hope you're behaving. I will be back around five or six still. Things to finish around here."

I sighed in deep relief and my shoulders lowered and my jaw relaxed, tension easing away from me and my hand now reaching to touch my favorite dick of yours.

I knew it was wrong. That wasn't the issue. I got to the point in that small space where I just felt more intoxicated, the visual and sensory having the reverse effect on my body I'd hoped for. It was 1:30 p.m. by the time I laid myself on my side of the bed and had started sliding it inside my pussy, calves shaking from the relief of being spread wide again and my eyes closed, lost entirely in my pleasure.

***

Dylan:

A half hour before I texted the girl, I'd gotten a cancellation from a client for a project that was to take up my entire afternoon. I had an extra week now to finish things and the idea struck me that I could rush home early and surprise her. Maybe I'd get some flowers, her favorite comfort meal. I was feeling romantic tonight, missing her, thinking of her naked and following my rules in her pretty little collar, all alone and waiting for me.

I was even considering breaking my own rule tonight, give her a surprise fuck on a Tuesday because she'd been so good lately with our new protocol. I enjoyed rewarding her, surprising her with more pleasure, almost as much as I enjoyed enforcing my rules when necessary. Granted, no one was perfect and I didn't expect perfection. I expected intention and effort, as well as trust and devotion, same as her. My cock stirred as I shoved some things in my leather satchel and I shut down my computer for the day.

When I texted her, I was actually parked in front of the house. Usually she heard me pull up and opened the door for me, peeking her eager head from behind it, bashful about the neighbors accidentally seeing her body.

Maybe she was upstairs in the bath, hadn't heard me pull up. I pulled my keys out and unlocked the deadbolt and walked inside. Things looked more immaculate than when I'd left this morning. I saw dark lines through each item on the list of her tasks, signaling completion.

Instead of calling her down to me, I took off my shoes quietly and headed up the stairwell in my socks, opting for a sneaky approach to catch her in the shower or bath. Maybe I'd join her. The roses in my fist were still heavy and thick and had that velvet wick scent that reminded me of her cunt against my cheek. I was already hard, and then at the top of the steps, I heard no water. What I did hear were her wild moans from breaking my rules and when I advanced to the bedroom, the open door revealed her duplicity quite clear. The sound of the flowers hitting the cellophane when I dropped the bouquet was actually what made her jump, stop, and stare at me.

As soon as our eyes locked, the hand she had wrapped around my cock loosened and pulled it out of her body swiftly. It rolled onto the floor off the curved edge of the bed and she lay there, terrified and staring back at me. She sat her body up clumsily in silence and noticed the roses and then me again, putting two and two together.

***

Lucy:

Daddy was more than mad. I'd never thought or expected to be caught like this, let alone him coming home mid-day without telling me. When I saw the flowers, something in my stomach lurched inward and I felt nauseous, sick from my own desire and knowing by the look in his eyes I was going to pay for this. I wasn't sure what to say because there didn't seem to be any words that could matter to him in this moment. I stayed silent and hung my head and knelt on the bed in one of my protocol positions with my hands resting on my lap. I couldn't look at him anymore, couldn't see his disappointment and sense of betrayal and hurt mirroring itself back at me. I ached to rewind the day and take this back. My breath was coming out in panicked bursts as he walked toward me, a silent plea for mercy I knew I wasn't going to get.

***

Dylan:

My head swam with ideas of how to deal with her doing this, breaking protocol and lying to me, trying to get away with something while I was at work. I looked down at the flowers and felt my chest puff out. She wasn't looking at me anyway and I could feel the fear radiating off her skin, stuck in that place of regret and terror for what was to come. No going back now.

I didn't sit on the bed. I stayed above her and talked down to her in a firm and clear voice, making my decree for the beginning of a very long night for her.

"You are not to speak. I know you aren't sorry for this. I know you thought you'd get away with fucking yourself while Daddy was at work. Greedy fucking girl. Like you don't get enough of my cock. Maybe I'll have to starve you of it so you remember how lucky you are to be fucked by me."

A mewled whimper at that last sentence.

"Shut up. I don't want to hear anything from you. Get off the bed and hand me my cock. Use the bathroom and get a drink of water. When you're done you're going to climb in your cage and think really fucking hard, alone, in complete silence. Bad girls don't get to sleep on the bed.

Cock. Bathroom. Water. Do it now before I have time to grab my fucking belt. Now."

***

Lucy:

I hated the cage. Hated the padded bottom that feigned comfort but delivered none, the cold air of the ground and the fans in the room, the darkness and the hours I'd spend struggling to position myself to find any comfort. I was taller than its length so I had to sleep crunched into myself, if I even did sleep. It was rare. I'd hear you above and miss your skin, miss you waking up biting and kissing my neck, miss your hands caressing me calling me your girl and my body arching into you tight and satiated.

You had a tone in your voice tonight I'd not heard before, a numbness that felt like miles were between our bodies and you were talking to me like you didn't know me anymore. I wouldn't let myself cry as I handed you your cock and you took it from me brusquely, careful not to touch my hand with your own. I wouldn't let myself crumble until I was down there and alone and could sob in the silence of the room. Sometimes I think my tears made you more upset, mocked you in their regret and the more I cried sometimes, the more you'd leave me to it.

I was glad I'd had lunch. I gulped the glass of water down on the bedside table I'd brought up earlier and as I set the glass down, you grabbed my wrist and put your cuffs on me abruptly. I let out a breath I'd been holding and you seethed,

"Clearly you can't be trusted with your hands so they will stay locked to the bars, ensuring you don't touch yourself again."

The lock clicked and I felt like you pushed me down a hill as you shoved me to my knees and waited for me to climb inside. I lay on my side, not fully positioned the way I had hoped to be while you pulled one wrist and locked it to the cage, then locked the door of the cage with a key you kept on you at all times.

***

Dylan:

She looked pathetic laying there like that, under my bed in her cage with just the thin blanket I'd given her. It was half the size of her body so every corner of it, her naked skin was jutting out in frustration, unable to stay quite warm enough until she exhausted herself to sleep.

She'd cried longer than usual tonight, after I stood back up turned my back to her with a chill. I'd locked both the cage and the bedroom door, adding that extra slam to make her aware I wasn't caving tonight about her punishment. Some nights I'd come back in late and hear her still sniffling and something inside me would pang to soothe her, be a sweet Daddy who was sorry about being so firm.

That wasn't tonight. Tonight I had that boil in my blood, that scarlet of rage in my stomach and chest where I wanted her to suffer. This was her fault, after all, her decision to be punished when I walked in and caught her fucking herself in the middle of a workday and breaking protocol behind my back. I was still seething, still shocked, still cracked over how duplicitous she'd been thinking she'd get away with it.

When I closed the door and locked it from the outside, I went downstairs without a second glance. Let her feel that wall between us, this growing space she longs to have closed.

Downstairs, I let myself lean into a head space of living alone. I watched a film, called some friends. I went for a walk and slammed the front door shut loudly so she could hear me leave the house, wonder in fear when I'd be back, if I would. I got back after 20 mins or so and thought of her up there, probably crying, cold, uncomfortable in her limbs and the smell of dust and carpet in her lungs as it got darker.

The hours passed quickly for me. I meandered and made a conscious plan about what to do with her tonight, deciding which alley of punishment she deserved and I wanted to give her. Mostly, she *was* a good girl. Sometimes she'd brat at me and need minor correcting or she'd need me to remind her why she has things so good. Sometimes I'd deprive her until she resorted to begging, sometimes I lavished her so much she'd beg me to stop. She was always so reactive and present and she always wanted her holes filled by me, day or night.

I wanted to slap her ass until it bruised purple, hear her cry. I wanted to see her wriggling under the swell of me trying to run while I pinned her, against the wall, over my desk, on her knees. Her silence irked me, the lack of apology in words with the sorrow in her eyes. Those big brown eyes were so pretty and needy. I looked at the clock then, noticing the windows were dark now and it was almost nine.

I rose off the couch and stretched and started back up to the bedroom. Once outside the door, I put my ear to the wood and listened; she was sobbing in that quiet way, not full-bodied any longer but her throat dry and exhaustion evident, that scrape of her crying making her tender. I slowly unlocked the door and noticed how dark it had gotten up here, I'd decided not to turn on any lights as I made my way to the bed.

I hung my legs over the side and slid off my socks and then my jeans, lastly my boxers. I yawned loudly and walked nude toward the other side of the room, knowing she was watching me intently. One not so quiet sniffle was uttered as I reached the bathroom and began my nightly routine; shower, brushing my teeth, getting things laid out for the day tomorrow like always.

When I came back, I stood halfway between her and the bed and started using my vibe on my t-dick, standing to make a scene, taunting her. I rarely came without her mouth these days, and I moaned theatrically, like this felt better, like I'd missed it.

I spoke into the air about how fucking hard I was, how I wished I had a dirty little hole to fuck, to fill with come use up just right. I edged myself until standing became too hard for the tension building in my thighs, my calves shaking with need. I plopped my body above her on the bed and writhed extra hard. I was loud and obscene in my pleasure, and knowing she had to hear it all but not touch me made me harder than ever. I came , more times than usual and let the vibe fall to the floor just feet from where her pouty little tear-stained face was.

My dick was still throbbing, that feeling where the nerves of it had spread up and down all my limbs in that radiation of pleasure, one desire unraveling another.

Jacking off amped me up sometimes and I knew after the third time I came, I'd need to let her out tonight to use her.

***

Lucy:

Daddy got off so violently above me I was worried the mattress was going to bend or break the cage. The rattling of the frame scared me and I could smell his scent and my body ached to taste him, to clean his dick off, to feel him fuck my face and shove inside my holes, the ones he owns. I was exhausted as a rag-doll, my limbs hurt and my tendons were sore from compressing my spine to fit in here and stay mostly still. My cuffed arm tingled and longed to be stretched out straight.

He was quiet for a while after and I was afraid he'd fallen asleep, scared I'd have be here all night. My head hurt from crying, the muscles in my eyes were sore and my cheeks were still damp and mouth dry. I was more sorry than I realized I could be and when his breathing became deeper and slower, I started to cry again in defeat.

I wanted this to end, to show him I'd never do it again, that I was sorry, that I was wrong. The muscles in my stomach tensed and released and were sore from how much of this I'd already done for hours. I hoped he'd wake up and take me out of here. I hoped he knew how much I regretted what I'd done.

***

Dylan:

I was too hard to sleep, so I let her think I was and listened to her break back down below me for a little. I knew she hadn't meant it, knew her little cunt had been deprived more lately from being fucked and that bad girls can get into trouble when they're left all alone with their own arousal. Honestly, I was shocked I hadn't caught her sooner. Those last few minutes I listened to her, I slid my harness up my body and stroked myself, thick and pulsing to shove into her sweet little holes, wear her out until she was shaking and I'd need to hold her after to still her skin, put my hand over her cunt while she squirted from that sweet pressure.

I slid off the bed and allowed my body to be on the ground, laying beside the cage close enough to touch her but far enough to build that want even more.

She started writhing through her tears for me then, knowing my closeness might mean an end, knowing my presence could close this gap of hurt between her sore little body and mine. She was frantic now, her skin flush against the bars like they were thick dark stripes against her pallor that she wished she could wiggle past.

She was still sobbing, her cuffed hand sliding up and down the bar rabid for me to release her. She'd had enough and had reached her limit, needed to be held now and fucked and tenderized by my power, even if was brutal.

I tried to soothe her with my voice as I inched closer, grabbed the cuff her wrist was still pulling on and noticed red marks had formed from her tugging so hard.

"Shhh. It only hurts because you're struggling. Hold still, Daddy's got you."

She simmered to a shivering calm after that and tried with fail to wipe her soaked nose and face on the pad of the cage. Her fingers were trembling against mine as I unhooked her and then slid my key into the lock and let the cage open back up.

She stayed put, surprisingly, still caught between that deep submission where she wanted my permission verbalized to leave her confinement. I told her to come to me while also wrapping around her sore limbs and sliding her out until she was against my warm body tight.

We were spooning close on the carpet and her cries had come to a slow but her breathing was still trying to catch itself. I brushed her hair with my fingers and kissed her neck and squeezed her ass reminding her who owned it. She exhaled in pleasure and sighed against my body like she was lost, like she had swallowed a sunrise and it was settled right inside her throat. My arm wrapped around her neck rough and she bent back into me tense and tight, my cock was between us and I felt her ass start to grind back.

"There's my girl, that's what you've been needing in all your holes, isn't it?"

I slicked the tip with the wetness of her cunt and teased her with the head of it, barely.

"Are you sorry?"

Her hand reached back and she turned her neck awkwardly to kiss me, to pull me back in. I pulled away and used my cock to slap her ass a little.

"Are. You. Sorry?"

Woefully with her lashes still wet and a nod of her head,

"Yes, Sir. I'm sorry."

I crushed my mouth against hers and shoved my tongue in deep, just as I slid every inch of my cock in her greedy little hole.

"Good. Daddy likes it when you're sorry."

Charcoal: Lover Letter #10

choking, masturbation, rough body play, oral sex

I woke up in the dark, my window still open in my bedroom and the blinds shivering from a small breeze outside. It smelled like spring in my room, the limoncello candle I got when we fucked last, and the wetness between my legs.

I woke up frustrated, antsy, my calves too sensitive to touch the sheets and my shoulders missing your furious fist, the way it claimed me from the outside in.

I keep thinking of the way your eyes look like two pieces of coal when they flash open at me from above, look down in lost focus when my tongue is on you like you're the last thing I'll taste. I think of that moment when your thighs desperately squeeze my neck and my hands slap them back open because I'm nowhere near done with you. I think of you whisper-shouting my name in slow staccato that ascends. I bite my own lip from remembering how perfect the swell of your t-dick rests against the warmth of my mouth, like I'm the sun and your need is leaning in, like your legs are two petals and I know exactly how you need to bloom tonight.

I miss the way you move, violently right before it's over and then that softness shuddering back into you when I encircle you. I miss the way your hair smells, the way I eat a meal later, and can still taste you on my tongue. I think of the way you have to hold my pillow with both arms, because you need more than gravity to hold you still.

It's 2 a.m. and I'm writhing in the dark for you. I'm waiting until you're here again soon, when I can turn into you instead of the morning sun that finds the cracks between my blinds. I am missing your naked back and the way I press my body into you to wake you. I am longing for the way my fingers bow down your spine and the humming inside of you becomes louder than my touch. Mostly, I miss the scent of morning coming in the room, complimenting the honey blossoms in your eyes when you look at me, and the smell of us is on the sheets, from how hard we danced last night.

I Want To Taste You On My Fingers

daddy/girl, pain play, fear play, primal, fucking, oral sex, crying

I want to taste you on my fingers, feel them opening your mouth after you come. I want you to suck the leftover pieces of skin, sleeping in the beds of my nails just like your exhausted body in the next room.

"Daddy has to work, baby."

I lay with you as long as I can manage to, after. Your body was all saltwater and sighs. The tendons and muscles of you were stretched from the crescent waves of my hands knowing just how to kiss your shore. Your head rested tenderly against the cay of my chest, anchoring you like the wake of a river that can hold any weight.

I love this tangerine sky of us just as much as I love the storm that births it. The way you fold into me is so languid, the way you wrap your limbs in mine, starving for tenderness. My saccharine whispers stroke you while you purr. One of your palms still grips my shoulder from when you ran violently down my wrist.

You were so good for me today, so open, so wanton. You pushed past thresholds, tried so hard when I know you wanted to run, but instead you cried and pulled the brutality of me closer.

I caress the thick knots under your skin gently, I soothe your shivers back to sleep. I press my lips against the dampness on your cheeks, my hand on your soft tummy feeling you flutter. My cock is still hard, remembering the talent of your tongue and how gorgeous your bruised ass looked while I came down your pretty little throat, held you there until I let you breathe.

***

I hear you moan sweetly in your sleep. I am in my office now, after throwing boxers and a t-shirt on. I smell like you all over, the perfume of your skin and cunt. I notice the small vessels on my palms that popped from how hard I hit you. I stroke my chin, knowing we aren't done for the night. This is a pause, not a bedtime for you.

I set the mug of coffee down next to my laptop and press my fingers to my lips, shamelessly feed them to myself and suck on the leftover drug. I love tasting you twice. I think of what I still want to do to you, then try and push it out of my mind so I can work. Hours later, I shut my laptop down and see my reflection on the screen, then see your form behind me, startled.

My office chair swivels and you're in the door-frame nude, hair disheveled, sleepy little face stirring something in my cock. You are wrapped halfway in a blanket, more of your skin exposed than covered, splattered in bruises and bite marks.

I stand silently and move toward you without words. I kiss your swollen lips like I'm still starving. I slide two fingers into your cunt and growl when I feel you there, soaked for Daddy, desperate again, like your body forgot.

"So greedy for Daddy."

Your hand strokes me outside my boxers and I slap your ass, pushing you back to the bedroom. The blanket around you falls to the floor and my naked eyes are all dressed up in you.

A Case Of You

D/s, primal

"Oh you are in my blood /like holy wine
You taste so bitter
And so sweet, oh
I could drink a case of you darling, and I would
Still be on my feet."
– Joni Mitchell

I had been wanting you, for a while. A lot of time had passed, as friends, confidants, tender support. Sometimes the topic would shift, where one of us was broaching something closer to what we really wanted to discuss, like we were sitting on a bench with that honesty only children have, sliding closer as the connection grew high, branched out. It never got there completely but we were becoming deft at skating closer to what we really wanted to say.

I was a dog for your voice, when I heard you being authoritative to your kids in the background on my calls, during my walks. I'd think about it later, think about you repeating "eyes on me.", except into my face in the dark at a party where I was undressing for you and you alone.

Some of your photos you sent me have that look, like you knew something about me I didn't know myself yet but you couldn't wait to show me, couldn't wait to put a hand around my throat and mirror me back to myself clearer. I showed you things I'd kept on the back of the shelf. I told you stories I forgot I had to tell and they came out sharper, more observed and real through telling them to you. I wanted you to know me like that. I wanted to have the pages I tore out and put away to hide. I wanted them shoved past my lips so I could taste them moment to moment, reliving them with you and tangoing into your changing tones. You needed that too. You wouldn't ever say it, but I knew you did.

We took our time unfolding. Nothing was rushed. Nothing felt immediate. We had time to bloom and we both understood that. We both knew that we were growing something and we both admitted even when we weren't texting or calling, we missed one another, despite not yet meeting.

Then one day, we finally met. We didn't have to wait anymore as soon as we knew that there was a bigger stadium of feelings present, more to gain, pieces of one another to touch, things to swallow. We both had such a desire to unveil ourselves and we were more than ready to feel the presence we'd been stacking high.

We met on a Tuesday at a cafe. We sat in small metal chairs outside on a patio and the sun was too hot but I still ordered warm coffee and it made you laugh. Hearing that sound in person made the bones in my arms hurt from not touching you. Seeing that and not climbing on the table against your body was harder. Everything felt measured in, scaled back, even my breathing while you were here.

You had ways about you now I had imagined but could see. You turned your head down toward the end of a run-on sentence. You fiddled with the edge of the napkin making folds in it absentmindedly when you listened to me. You focused on my mouth and my eyes hard, and my chest felt like a kick-drum I was trying to throw a blanket over. Your eyes were blue and then green but also blue depending on the shadows that were being cast over your face from the changing light. I wanted to kiss you whenever you squinted and kept offering to change spots so I'd have your shade, but I was insistent, stubborn even. I wasn't used to someone else's comforts being diminished by mine and you understood that enough to change the topic quick enough to distract me. When you looked at me directly I had trouble meeting your eyes, but shoved myself into doing it because I wanted you to see me. I knew you felt me trying and feeling that felt good too. I knew there was a power in you and you were aware I understood. You kept trying to highlight mine back to me in conversation, reminding me that's what that was. I felt like I was dizzy in that beautiful way when you did that.

You were more sensual in person, the curve of your hips and spine, the way you moved through space and the fabric of your shirt and jeans, how you chose pieces that hung along the lines of your body and then went away. Your hands were graceful but knew work. Your lips were thin but spread wide open when you laughed. You were dainty in how you drank your coffee but in control when you set the cup down and came back to looking at me. Your legs were crossed and you had boots on that showed attitude against the colors you wore. There was an edge there peeking out, but not obvious. Your hair was finer than mine but looked just as soft, and sometimes when you spoke I was thinking of what it would feel like against my cheek in the dark.

We couldn't get enough of this. We had been starving for the novel, the sensory things, the kinetic buzz of raising the curtain to reveal. We'd been hungry for these talks to finally be here with our bodies across a table. You let me know after coffee that kids were at a neighbors and you had more time to spare. You offered to drive me home now, but also offered up a hang at your place, and could bring me home later.

My chest had that feeling of tension from excitement and the reverb we had manifested. We weren't giving the air any space to breathe between our words. There was a flow here, an ebb that picked it back up and cradled it against some quiet spaces; ones that we leaned against like pieces of shade on blacktop.

I wanted to know what your perfume was because your car still smelled like you'd secretly sprayed it before meeting me. The sunlight and your dark interior made it stronger while we'd sat outside chatting and I felt heady. When my head bowed to buckle my seatbelt I was inches from your shoulder and I wished I could nestle into you for a moment.

I wanted more of you, however I could have it, so we headed to yours. You winked at me when i decided this, blushing, joked to me that we could make up for time lost. I sat with my legs towards you and felt smaller in a good way. My seat was lower than yours slightly or your posture was better, or maybe I'd slid down to move how I felt beside you.

I liked the feel of being in your car, the way you drove was more aggressive than you seemed. I kept trying to hang onto those ways and the words you said because that assertion turned me on. The road and other drivers were things to overcome, to surpass, not to be confused or muddled up in where you were going or placed there to distract you from your destination. You were headstrong, flippant even, with them but not me. I had your spotlight for now and I felt what that meant.

You switched the radio on and finished the bottom of your drink. You talked with your hands and made comments on other drivers while still looking sideways at me as often as you could. You were capable; you were assertive but somehow still soft enough to make me want to be between both of those tides, smashed and grabbing for each energy as hard as the other.

We pulled up to your home and there were toys on the lawn. Small shoes littered your front porch and I heard wind chimes made of wood. I felt hollowed out by your standing next to me so close as you opened the door. You motioned for me to go inside past you. I hesitated briefly and awkwardly, and it was all I could do to stop myself and stay still right there, against your body There was a breeze that followed us in that smelled like freshly mowed grass. Your street was quiet and I felt like a tangle of desire. I was trying hard not to be perceived and in that, I knew you read me even more.

Standing in your living room scanning it discretely, there were signs of you and your family, signs of your life and clutter, smells from my own childhood I'd forgotten, crayons and cheerios and apple dish soap and plastic neon bowls in your sink with sideways pools of leftover milk, colored pink by something from the morning. You had hanging plants in your dining room, different remote controls on different couches and one missing it's back to hold the batteries inside of. Much of your furniture looked like it was made of walnut or cherry, sturdy and beautiful with stories, like you.

I forgot you were behind me emptying your arms and checking your cell for text updates until I felt your breath on my neck. I wasn't here for a tour and didn't want to be. I wasn't an onlooker or even someone meant to be shown, not right now anyway. Your head was on my shoulder and we had run out of words finally, or I had. I had run out of anything that was keeping me inside myself.

My body melted, not leaned, back into you, like a current, like bending was a sport for my bones and like the nights alone I stayed up yearning for it. Your chin on my shoulder was sharp, angled wide and my fingers clumsily found your own and I pulled them against my hipbones, making them grip me. You clenched me like rope, tugged me into you tighter but slow. I felt the angle of your jaw change against my collarbone and knew you were smiling. We were done with pleasantries. I didn't care what dates were blacked out on your calendar or what size your TV was or whose doll was in the corner of the room left tilted on its side, half watching you swallow me, flush with your own body heat.

I didn't need to think. All I needed to do tonight, was feel.

Criminal: Lover Letter #11

D/s, edging, oral sex, rough body play

The first crime you ever taught me was how to jailbreak your thighs. Your body ripped through the air to meet my mouth while I held you down, kissed your cheeks inflamed with bemused frustration. Your moved below me like a spirit, punching my gut with your smile.

I couldn't contain you, and you bowed back into me with your violin curves. My grips found the sweet bones of your hips and you didn't know if you should run or scream for more. I felt both coming off your body like shock-waves. I loved you desperate, loved you clawing for me with just your eyes, cappuccino dark when I had you pinned. Your sounds changed with my voice, as I commanded your body to soften and tense until you didn't know air from touch, teeth from lips, fingers from pain, shadow from form.

Tonight, I was a whisper of my breath on your ribs, climbing. Tonight I was the pulp of your pulse beating like a broken metronome under my teeth.

I had you, losing yourself like sand falling through my fingers, like my tongue was the only strobe-light that could make you dance like this. I unlocked you with a look. I swallowed your sounds like a demon, like I was the one pushing you off a cliff, but also the water below cradling your curves every time you fell.

Late at night, I can feel your ache changing colors under my palms. I want you tongue-tied and turbulent. I want you tenuous, violet in your palms from how hard you need to hold me. I want you to flicker like a hot wick from my breath right over your cunt.

You were all of these things as I stood in the frame of your door last night, your body naked on your sofa under the only soft light in the room. You were catty-cornered from me, but the doorway to your busy hallway was wide open. Any passerby clueless to how gorgeous you were with that candy-red gag between your lips, glistening like your fingers, like the thin sheen of sweat on your tummy from edging yourself.

I watched you hard but silent. I watched the sacrifice of your unhinged shaking. I watched you like a predator, the juice of you already running down my throat, tasting just like black cherries and wood-smoke.

Sofia

D/s, edging, riding crop, gags, oral sex, strap on

"**I** have a fuck machine at my house."

That was the last text she'd sent you and admittedly, it made all the blood in your body rush straight to your clit. You felt a flush come over you when you read and reread it, and you lay in the dark at 1 a.m. trying to figure out how to respond, how to sound like the most nonchalant, under-enthusiastic, cat in heat as best you could. This was hard.

***

There was serendipity here. For a newcomer to the bay area and someone from Iowa where there had been such a lackluster scene, the small events you attended in town so far, she was at eight out of ten of them. Every single one, you'd successfully avoided interacting with her and tried to just sip your coffee, stand in a corner behind a group of three other strong personalities, or meander against the wall leaning into your phone with your gaze half-preoccupied. All of these were less than perfect guises for the crush you were developing, and the intimidation you felt from her energy, even across the room. You sometimes held your breath when she got nearer to you, without even noticing. You'd made a few acquaintances so far, even ones you could see becoming close to. You hadn't felt lifted by anyone yet though, or moved for that matter, except by her.

She was always in leather combat boots, the kind that had weight to them, that could make your skin feel your bones closer, good for prowess and aesthetic that served this all-business-with-edge purpose. She had one dimple in her right cheek that was super pronounced. Her voice almost didn't match her presence. It was soft, almost saccharine, tauntingly so and very juxtaposed with the energy she was trying to exude. This made her presence feel more intense when she was silent and you couldn't read her. When she did top, it was sensual but harsh, overbearing but empathetic. She was too much at once, book-ending it with a gentleness and measure to keep her partner on his toes.

She was statuesque compared to you, not in the way a model is, but just someone who had some sturdiness to her body, equalized with grace. She smiled more than you'd expect someone as dominant and withholding as her to do. She seemed warm, but to a limit. She kept her cards close and even what she gave away in groups seemed calculated. Her friendliness was almost terse, but forthcoming enough to make whoever she was with feel spotlit. She didn't give away what she didn't have and when you observed her at your first two play parties; what she did give away was sacred. It was all of herself at once and no less. It was the room's walls melting into the floor, and just a bench or table and her lover, only the moon watching. You were transfixed, in an admiring way of her power and how she chose to wield it, but also in a cautious way to not be so openly in awe you gave your growing fascination away.

There were other players that manipulated and melded into one another, but her scenes were different. They had history behind the touch. They had stories she knew below skin because there was symbiosis and connection there. There was patience and practice, but full agency and abandon. It felt special to even witness it.

Growing up in Iowa queer and having tried to explore the scene there one last time, you'd found and seen nothing to keep you rooted anymore. You had no partner. You had design skills that could employ you wherever you landed because you had your own business, and a pregnant list of clients you'd built over the years. While you had friends there, some of them had started to stifle you. Lots were starting to settle; buy homes, have babies, Feng-shui their living room.

You were a fringe-dweller. You cared about things that seemed fruitless to their existence and you wanted to spread your consciousness further. You were morphing into something new since coming out and finally getting comfortable in your identity, a struggle that had been years overdue. You'd since had a small number of kinky relationships under your belt. Even so, you knew there was more than this, much more.

With these seven square-miles you chose, and two purposefully orchestrated roommates (a pair pf gay men who happened to be into puppy play and leather), who were kind enough to show you around some local dungeons your first weekend in town; that was all it took for your hunger to grow. The air in your mouth knew it now, and you wanted to be enveloped in and by kink, and sponge everything you could in measured gulps, as much as an anxious, shy, overthinker could muster up, anyway.

By your eighth event (half of them phenomenal play parties), you were still wall-flowering like a kid at the edge of a pool; you just didn't know how to dip your toe in quite yet.

It had been building. You'd been watching spines arch back into someone, listening to moans from crops, watching fingers shoved inside mouths, gags tenderly placed around cheekbones. You were yearning now but needed the push (maybe even a shove) to really act on it.

You liked what you saw, even understood the energy behind much of it, but you knew not to settle. You never did. You waited for a bright green light always and then purged your being into that until it was part of you. You wanted to feel something more than what everyone else feels. You wanted to hover against it and then fall into it. You wanted a voice in your neck that scared you and made you feel cradled.

Then there was tonight's party. It had been a few weeks since this dungeon had thrown one. One of the owners had had minor surgery of some sort and it was a celebration of their recovery and their locale being back on the map to host again. The night had started strong, everyone eager with extra weight to their play bags and less clothes than normal worn when sauntering through the door. The air had that buzz that was humming louder than usual. Everyone had been waiting for this for a while.

You were perched around the corner from a partition that separated a social room from a playroom, following a particularly brutal spanking scene. Solitary, you were sidled up in a crowded hallway checking the time on your watch, trying to discern if the night was winding down or up. You knew less than a handful of who were here and most of them had either come to scene with their partners or were finishing a plate of food hovering close to where they'd hung their jackets.

You felt flush from replaying what you'd just watched and thought about going home, squeezing your legs together with your mind on your new vibrator you'd bought last week. This party like all others, had already put you in a mood. You were getting off more than ever, and an electricity in the air at the events always coursed through you during and after, lingering for days sometimes where you'd come so many times you'd had to buy a second set of sheets.

You smiled softly to yourself unable to contain your own mischief and afterward, pressed your styrofoam cup to your lips. Even through your drink and halfway down the hall, your back bolted tighter against the wall as you heard her, laughing with the host, and the front door closing boisterously.

Others in the crowded hallway moved past you, one queer boy pulling his pup by a leash, smirking too hard from seeming to know her. You swallowed a gulp of your soda and felt the bones in your arms vibrating, thinking of the last time you watched her cuff her boyfriend's wrists. You envied him and craved what they gave to each other. You wanted to be a portal in the same way.

"I have to piss *so* bad! Is this the line, fuck why do you always run on queer time, Jack?!"

Close to your ear, no, at your ear, you turned and she was there, with about six inches on you in height. She was already staring at you before you could put up a shield. You knew your face was pink enough to be a tell. You shared a flash of eye contact with her, noticing hers were fucking green. Did the universe even mean to make that color? Fuck.

You swallowed awkwardly and almost reactively tried to set your cup down, knowing you had no surface to do that with. Fuck.

She was intensely staring at you. "Hey love, are you in line? Cuz we just hit ridiculous traffic on the way here, and ..." She was open and smiling but already adopting the energy she would need for play.

"No. This isn't the line, I was just standing here, chilling." God.

She looked down at you again and you met her eyes and she winked and squeezed your shoulder. "Fantastic. I remember seeing you before, if this place empties out you should be our audience, 'kay?"

Finishing her sentence as the door shut, the scent of her wafted past you, leather and espresso beans, expensive salon conditioner. a tinge of cologne from her guy (probably from trying to devour her in the car), and she was gone.

You turned your neck back and he was obediently removing his shirt and jeans, already had his infinity collar on. He was doing that slow breathing the bottoms all do in the moment before a negotiated scene. The room had emptied some and both crosses and benches were unoccupied. A few folks lingered in the living room leaning against one another, expelled from play or engaged in intense conversation from the atmosphere of the night.

You were absolutely fucking staying.

***

This is what I wrote for you, because you asked. Because you saw me.

I wanted to call her "Sir" as soon as I watched her top him. She came out of the bathroom in a ripped up mesh bodysuit and a second black spandex one over it, covered just right to not see her breasts or her pussy, but somehow accentuating them more. She had a chest harness on, which served as a bra, and a leather harness on without a dick in it. The o-ring just did more to highlight the gorgeous cut of her hips and curves. Her skin was fair and laden with tattoos, all black ink and no color whatsoever. I hadn't really comprehended inside what desire was until I watched her. It hurt to want her, and I liked that there was pain behind the wanting.

I liked that I would never know what she was saying to him that made his entire body, now spread out on a long table with her straddling him, rise up into her. I liked that I'd never see what they ate together for breakfast or what toothpaste they shared between his and hers sinks and who slept on what side of the bed, but I liked that I could feel that in their energy. There were sacred things behind it that were untouchable to anyone else in their presence, things that had work, practice, and trust. She had a terrifying sort of grace, withholding to all but a few, and when it was released, it was incredibly erotic and subterranean.

I wanted to be her man on the table being sucked off with the tread of her boots in my face. I wanted to be his tongue against her cunt, hungry and heady. I wanted to be the joints in his fingers that were struggling to find anchors to cling to in the fabric of her clothes. I wanted to be his bated breaths and his shrinking inside himself when she laughed to the room about edging him.

While I was there and attending all the functions, and seemingly meeting those I felt drawn to on some or many levels, I had been feeling problematic about the scene at the same time. I didn't want to just lead with kink. I was exhausted of others doing that to me and constantly feeling like I had emotional crumbs but never the bread itself. I didn't just want my body scoped into an idea of surrender and projection placed onto it because of it. I wasn't an A=B equation. Seeing someone else play in such a poignantly connected way like I desired, felt revelatory.

I didn't know it yet but I was looking and seeking the D/s connection over kink, and kink was a placeholder for the intimacy I craved, the kind many seemed to misconstrue at parties as something it wasn't. It was the kind she had with him, the kind I saw during aftercare when a top would cradle someone in the quiet and knew what they needed before they asked, knew when to slow touch and knew when to push and they saw with their heart instead of their eyes. I wanted to feel the eros and the pull of gravity that wasn't just a Friday night dopamine fix. I wanted the arc and the stories behind the touch, I wanted every brick that built the tower.

For a while, with a small few who had stayed around in the room behind me, I was their audience. I was a passerby in their universe and entranced because I felt what was there, there against the implements and their bodies and the words. The touches with just her voice and the way he sighed in tremors; they were real, and they were achingly beautiful.

When she climbed off the table, covering his eyes with the gloves she'd been wearing coaxing him to stay still, she turned and caught my heavy gaze and I saw her seeing me. I felt it. I felt the floor under me fall and the weight of my eyes fell to the floor in a deeply perceived fight-or-flight response. I wasn't used to being seen that way, not yet.

She withdrew to the corner table where she had already put cool water for him, sitting him up to take slow sips. I stood up awkwardly, suddenly very aware I hadn't moved and people were now cleaning up in the kitchen.

I saw her whisper something to him intermittently out of the corner of my eye. I bent down by the short stool I'd been on to grab my own drink cup from the floor, and rose back up. Suddenly she was there, breath on my shoulder and a soft hand against my mid-back, to turn me toward her and move my body into her words.

"I want you to add me on Fet. I'd very much like to know what you thought. I was watching you watch us and I could feel you. I've never felt someone seeing us like that before. Have a good evening."

Sticky And Sweet: Lover Letter #12

daddy/girl, D/s, choking, fear play, primal

The hunger I have isn't like anyone else's, because it's for you.

It's for your mouth, the exquisite way your lips part and press together, suffocating mine. I want to hollow myself around your fingers, feel you swallow parts of me I didn't know I even had to give away. I want to give you those things, parts where I'm tender and too close to the surface, parts under my shield that are soft like porcelain, waiting for your grip to break me in half.

I want you to deep throat my cries so I can talk to you in tongues. I want the tremors of the skin above my stomach to quiet with your warm palm, when I sense you moving into me from behind.

This was when I felt you the most, the moments before the moment. I felt you before this happened, before the back of my neck was damp from your drug. I dreamed about this, the way you held me down, the shades of purple I hid between my thighs from the world, days after.

You can have all of it, my forehead against yours all sticky and sweet. You can have my halted gasps, the ones you cover with your hands against the hum of my pulse, the ones you silence with your violent tongue. I want you to make me scream louder, make me feel like crushed cherries between your teeth. I want the black bulbs of your eyes the clearest thing I can see in the dark when I call you "Daddy."

I want to feel like I'm made of pieces you can crumble, like you're the rabbit hole, like I don't have enough arms to reach up and hold on, like you're turpentine and torture, like I'm a knothole and you're the wind.

I want to call you Daddy. I want to nestle into you like you're a cradle when this is over, want to feel like I'm your sugar in the morning. I want your hands to splash me with the meaning of control, the deep measure of it. I want to feel you spreading my thighs and hear you taking a knife off your belt, then listen while you take your belt off next and wait for it to fall to floor, never hearing it happen. I want to know it's still in your hand, and know every stripe you paint me in is a color I already have inside.

I want to look somewhere in the room and see that silver is gleaming while I feel like the weight of gold under your touch. I do love your touch, the one that follows my ache, that pinches and gathers me into your darkness, sometimes shoving me into it before I'm ready, to test, to see what key I'll cry in tonight.

I want you to display me like a doll, to fight against your current and even more brutally, acquiesce. I want to bow and buckle at my knees, claw into your tunnel made of echoes, rest against the swirl of howls you keep in your belly, and release in the dark, on me.

I am squeezing my legs together in the quiet of my bedroom thinking of it all. I am molding my body into the memory of you. I know the lines of you are harder than my curves. I know your bones are stronger than mine and the sweet bend of your fingers can curl too far down at the back of my throat. You know where to go. I know where to follow. I know how to throw my head back like an animal for you, know how to make my shadow dance with yours on the wall and flicker my eyelashes against your cheek, as I hold on, as you made me feel like a hot wick, crackling in the air to show you just how good it feels to quiver in oranges and blues.

Greedy Little Thing

daddy/girl, blood, crying, edging, masturbation, mild degradation

Y ou looked down at me on the bed like you'd been chasing me all day, like you had one bullet left to make me drop, like the devil had spit turpentine in your eyes.

We'd spent all day together as foreplay. We hadn't seen each other in weeks but kept our social commitment with friends during the relentless sun, the constant noise, and the sweat on the back of my neck falling where the last bruise from your vicious teeth had faded.

Everything felt too bright, too long, too exhausting. The a.c. never got cold enough before we left your car. The hum of the summer crowd never let up. The asphalt all day was rigid on our calves, for miles. We came back to yours and showered one at a time, on your insistence, on your rules and your control, frustrating me even longer, squeezing my thighs together when you decreed that was the plan.

I was laid out on your bed when you went in after me, steam coming off my skin as the fan above wisped above my ass. Not in your control for a moment, my fingers felt jittery for you. My stomach felt hungry. I waited, while I was wet, while the sheets against my skin had your scent that intoxicated me. I started grinding on my hand, relieved to be touched, but still impatient. This wasn't you, wasn't the same, wasn't me anticipating and trying to follow where you'd go.

I thought of your body, your shoulders. the razors of your teeth that burned my thighs. I thought of the way you'd lean your face on my bent knee, watching my eyes flash back at you while you added more of your fingers inside me.

I remembered the way you'd push my head down on your cock begging me to keep going. I thought of the zipper of your jeans, how it felt cold against my cheek and the other side of the strapon vibrated for your pleasure. I wanted you. I wanted to worship the taste of you in my mouth, after. I don't think there was a spot on you I hadn't kissed, or a spot on me I didn't want dark purple from you.

You were taking forever. I wanted it harder tonight. I wanted it for hours. I wanted you to be cruel and hold me down. I wanted to fit against your body with your arm still around my neck when it was over, when we were breathless and spent and I could turn into you and kiss you so you could still taste my ache, the one that never filled for you, that I always tried to show you on my knees and back.

I'd left just my panties on. They were your favorite pair, red lace in the front and caged strips of satin in the back, just for your eyes. I wanted your soft hands and brusque touches, my teeth on your shoulders. I wanted you to make me whimper and bend me over everything. I wanted your roommates to hear us through the walls and cover their mouths in shock. I wanted you to wake me up while you insisted on cooking breakfast for all of us, making me sit on the one dining chair that didn't have a cushion for specific reasons, making me face them and knowing in silence they'd heard. I wanted to eat my hashbrowns and burn a hole in your back with my eyes while you played your game and whistled while whisking our eggs. I wanted them to leave so I could climb under the table and suck you off like last time.

I wouldn't let myself come; I wanted it from you, dancing on the edge and drawing back. My sighs still weren't loud enough for you to hear me in the shower.

I was angsty, agitated you were taking so long, taking your time, making me wait. I wanted to get caught, to look over my shoulder and see you naked and in that stance I loved, the one with your belt in your hand in retaliation.

I inhaled your pillow like an animal. Your room always smelled like your skin, like autumn year round, like pine trees after a hard rain, like a forest of whispers and me being so small below you. I craved your hand over my mouth so the whole neighborhood wouldn't send sirens for my struggle.

We had a candle lit with the window open and the lights off. We had thunderstorm sounds playing and I felt like a hurricane between my legs.

When you saw me laying on my tummy I heard the shower stop abruptly. The pipes squealed briefly, a waft of humidity and the smell of your body wash rushed over me like a fog.

Then I heard it, the sound of your towel dropping to the floor as you growled low. You sucked in your lower lip and smacked it hard about what you saw, about you weren't happy about. What had I started? We hadn't made any sort of agreement about my orgasm control, not today at least. Still, you stared at me as if I'd broke a promise, as if you thought I should always wait without testing you.

You abruptly grabbed my ankles and pulled me lower on the bed, simmered at me and told me to stay quiet, hold fucking still. I felt your teeth on my neck before anything, your fist tangled in my hair to keep me pressed into the mattress. You knew I'd fight you before you'd let go. You waited until I was close to screaming, until I was sure you'd break skin. Then you licked the heat of blood that almost broke the surface, just before tears came.

You raked your nails down my back, until you could see those halted speckles of crimson appear, until my whimpering gasps became more hysterical, while you slapped the same spots with your hand.

The air stilled again as all the heat of your punishment rushed my skin, the cool dew of your body kissed mine. You grabbed the narrow wooden rod you kept on the wall letting me hear it slice above my body in the air, giving me a warning. I exhaled something between a cry and a vocal shiver and you laughed, said I'd started this, said you were just going to go to bed but now I was in the way. You asked me if I forget who was in charge, not really wanting an answer. Later, you left a whole novel in my mouth with your tongue while you turned my chin and held me by the scruff of my hair possessively, like a predator that ate for fuel, not taste.

You took the t-shirt you had on and abruptly wrapped it around my eyes from behind. You tied it tight with one of my hair ties. I breathed the cotton in shamelessly, drunk on the scent of you from the day. Your sweat mixed with the grass-cut freshness of the summer air.

You flipped me over and I shrunk smaller. I was yours tonight, because I was yours always.

Here's What's Going To Happen

D/s, daddy/girl, anal, strap on, dirty talk, primal, blood play, oral sex

When you get here I'm going to sit you on my couch. I'm going to pull out my dick, rub it on your lips, and slap your face with it. I'm going to control your head with my fist in your hair, put just the tip in, pull out, and eventually push my way past your gag reflex. You will keep your hands behind your back, look up at me while I shove it deep, your sounds helpless while you take it and suck on me while I take your breath away. Your lungs and throat are going to burn, the same way your pretty eyes do when I look down at you with my praise, my pride of being your Owner.

I know you miss me in your mouth, girl, I know you need me there. I'm going to make your jaw nice and sore, so next time I can hear you whine even louder, ignore that bit while I take even more from you. I will empty you so good, while I fill you even better.

I want the taste of me in your mouth all day, girl. Your little pink tongue savoring what Daddy left you until next time. I want to catch you staring at my cock through my boxers on the couch later on, your throat still swollen, but your holes still hungry. My slutty girl. Always needing it. Always wanting me deep and firm and rough, like that. Always like that.

After it's over, we will be close and tender. My chest is for your cheek, my arms and lap long to be a nest you can sigh into. I like you like that too, when you are quiet and small against me while the television is on. I can sense your hand fighting itself to not start stroking me, biting your lip to distract yourself in that way you try and always fail to hide your desire.

I'll grab your little fist and shove it inside my shorts, your warm little hand that's unable to close around the length, poor small thing. I can tell you're already soaked again, hiding a little that your want is there still, louder in your body's shameless hunger and begging me silently to rail you the way you need it.

I'll order you to the bedroom to strip, where I'll cuff you to the headboard urgently, half sitting up so I can straddle your eager little mouth, grind my t-dick on you and use my hole again. All of them are mine, aren't they? Nod so I can tell you're listening. Good. You're so good.

I am rough and wet and hard against the warmth of your tongue, your full lips accepting my thrusts; they're deep and strong, tender and tumultuous, while you pull at your cuffs wishing you could touch that throbbing cunt, the one I own and keep and take from and give to and slap.

I will be relentless with your mouth, while you realize the couch was just a warm-up. You'll lay there like the toy you are, scared and sputtering with the back of your head digging into my hands. I will fist your hair until you try to swallow and suck it all down, until I'm running down your chin all warm and thick and you're shaking for a kiss, for a reminder that you did good this time, too. I talk dirty to you while I kneel over your body and undo your cuffs, your lips kissing my neck and shoulders still whimpering sweetly for more heavy contact, while I remind you how lovely you are, when you're obedient and eager and I can put you to good use. Like that.

Later, after I feed you and give you slow sips of cool water, watching your lungs catch up with the air in the room, you collapse into my chest and I soothe you down until you're a quiet little shadow, simmering and warm and still against my heartbeat. Your nerves are tired and limbs are limp and pliable while I wrap you in mine. I tell you how good you are, fill you with praise as much as I filled you with my cock.

You fall asleep against me soon after and I turn you to your side, sleep some until I feel the salacious curve of your ass jutting back against me. I'm hard again, my hands want to spread and take and hurt. My teeth throb to break your skin. You are sweet and silent, dreaming and still and I feel like a monster that just picked up the scent of blood. The room is dark and the house is silent. I slide my strap over my hips and I stroke the head to the base, eager for the moment I decide to slide it against your ass while you wake up slow. It's thick and it's too big for you, and I place a hand around your mouth telling you to shut up and spit. I lather my cock with your warm saliva and invade you deep, it hurts in that way you need it to, your shoulders tell me that story as they shake.

I grind against my still damp hand against your swollen pussy a little, to relief you the force that' coming, pushing you open wide to make my dick fit. One hole is clenched while the other wants to take my fingers, desperate little hips reaching for pleasure I hover over you until you still. My decision.

Your ass is tight and sore around me and the pillow is holding your sad little moans while I start thrusting, forcing it all the way in and out.

I'm insistent, impatient, uncaring you've still got sleep in your eyes. You made me thick and hard and this is your fault. I remind you to say thank you, tell you what a fucking lucky girl you are to be woken up by such a strong cock, to squeeze it nice and tight like a good little slut, lay still and take it. My fingers dive into your cunt and holy sounds come out of your throat, obscenities and my name and gasps and whimpers. Like that. Keep going.

I remind you while I quicken my pace they are my holes and I feel you nod over and over, writhing against my shoulder. I remind you that I'll take them wherever and whenever I please. Whenever I'm hard and my dick needs some relief, even if it's the middle of the night and your sweet pussy is still sore from the pounding I gave you only hours before, or I haven't fucked your ass in days, you're gonna take it. Your thighs and calves tremble in that way they do just before you ask to come, and fuck do you ask so good, so desperate and small and starved.

Your hand finds my hip and holds on and I find your pulsing little clit and I tell you to let go. My teeth break the skin on your shoulder and come instantly, screaming while the iron runs along my tongue. The tension around my cock is unbearable and I follow right after while your spine curls back into me tight. My lips suck the wound I made and I stay inside, buried where i need to be, holding you like you could melt from my burn. You're mine. Just like that.

I Got Off To You Tonight: Lover Letter #13

D/s, dirty talk, masturbation

I got off to you tonight, threw the covers off my damp skin after, breathless and running my hands along my body imagining them as yours. My thighs were still tense and I could feel my pulse in my clit, my body raging from thoughts of you. I like lying between these walls knowing you're right up the street, that it happened, that it will happen again.

I'm shivering with my comedown from remembering last night with you. Last night on your porch, your tongue was between my lips while your hands scrunched the fabric of my dress further up my thighs, raking your nails on my skin, like dream follows nightmare.

You kiss like you have to be in charge, like your tongue is a knife to remind me I'm the worthy object you're slicing into. I am fighting to breathe against you, to keep pace with your teeth sucking on the plums of my lips. I want to wear the lifelines in your palms like the they're the only choker I ever want.

You are amused, entertained even by my whimpers, my tactile fingers confused if I'm grabbing you for safety or holding on for life. The growl in your chest is brief as your mouth curves up against mine, each time I flinch, each time I grind against your thigh desperately.

My limbs are starved to pull you into me, as close as I can get before we're melting, until we are. We forgot the road you lived on had traffic going by, and that you had neighbors ten feet away, that your queer partner was in bed after telling us to, "Have lots of fun!", with a hard smirk.

You taste like whiskey and leave my cheeks flushed. Your eyes burn me just as hard whenever we manage to pull away, to push air into our lungs, to recognize the sense of reality flooding back into our faces simultaneously. There are trees blowing in the evening wind. The air is cold. Damp leaves after the rain from earlier are littered in your yard. The moon is somewhere above and all I want to be is below you, always.

You feed me a sip from your watered down drink, watch me scrunch my nose at the taste and put two fingers down my throat while I sputter and suck, that lidded look in your eyes hunts and holds my vulnerable gaze. Keep it deep. Keep it safe.

My hair is wild from your fingers gripping and pulling, scraping me toward you like an animal. My lips swell from your teeth and my shoulders are striped from your nails. You had me. This wasn't about fucking tonight. This was about how far we could go without it, how long I could take this before begging, how much I wanted to nuzzle my cheek against the bulge below your zipper. I never wanted to stop until you stopped me, I never wanted to go home with this pitting ache for you.

"Enough for tonight," you whisper to me.

You pull my head into your mouth again, one hand on my neck and the other bunched in my hair. The porch light is so bright and the assault of the air that isn't the smell of your t-shirt and your sweat leaves me weak. As I walk away, your shadow hangs over me like an eclipse.

You stand on the porch and the silhouette of you gets smaller as I walk down the gravel drive while my ride waits.

You lick the fingers that were down my throat and wink in silence and I shiver. I want to fall asleep with the taste of you in my mouth, take as much of that with me as I can, keep you for later like a secret on my tongue.

Seconds after you break our last kiss, you put your cheek against mine and whisper to me in the dark. "Go home, so you can get off to me all night."

Communion

D/s, oral sex, religious references

She wanted to fuck slow today. She wanted to reach me like a light that found every corner in a room. This would take all night. She would take her time, but only after my hunger was filled.

I looked up from my knees, heard her speak in that slow whisper, "Show me what's under your dress."

She had me on the floor before we made it to the bed. The impatience inside me was wringing it's hands for her body. Her pussy tasted like saltwater and coconut had fucked in the breeze overnight, and she slid down my throat like rain runs down a leaf in a storm. I felt like the birth of a howl when I was with her, like I'd been born to make her a canvas of earthquakes and sunsets.

The lusciousness of her thighs rattled like something broken around my shoulders and softly, her fingers crawled against mine to find a cradle. She rested her sweet cream against the spoon of my tongue. Parts of what lived inside of me intersected with parts of hers, meeting like a collision people stop to watch, and her spine rose up like she could feel it, too.

She was paper-thin with me, her clit throbbed in pulses against the metronome of my mouth. I wanted to show her what worship meant, wanted to sing the rage in my belly that had been screaming all day for her. I just wanted to reach her deep enough, leave her bruised inside with just my tongue.

I ached for this, to take her in like communion, all body and blood savoring what was left of her, all over me like a perfume for the next night of sin.

Divinity: Lover Letter #14

blindfolds, blood, crying, daddy/girl, fear play, primal

I want you to feel divine, kiss you onto my bed and show you with my eyes you're about to be shackled, about to be lost, about to bleed demons. I want you to feel like squeezed fear between my teeth while you wrap your sweet arms around my neck like innocence. The silk ties I wear are deliberately here to circle your eyes, while my hands speak in cursive along your skin.

I want to streak you with my crimson, feel your knees drop more weight into the bed when the stinging bleeds into more stinging. I want you to feel the air in the room is the only causeway between your body and my deliberate strikes.

I want to pull you flush against me when it's too long, too hard, too tense before the next blow lands, exhale into my lips, ice-skating my tongue ring against the tracked stripes I painted on you.

I am holding you into it, through it, my arm around your neck and voice against your ear. I have them, all the tender words trickling down your shoulders like warm water. I'm here, baby, caressing your back and neck and devouring you with my teeth, hungry to hear the beautiful music I can pull from your lungs with the rake of my teeth. I will kiss you while the fever spikes, then bite down. I will tangle your softness between my fingers, let you suck on my lower lip. I will listen to that sweetness in the air from your halted gasps, now louder than the flogger, pushing your head back down into the bed.

You're my crime tonight, my soft violence on canvas. I am here baby, I am holding you after, my lips against your neck, a love letter to your tears.

Let The Simmer Steam

D/s, blindfolds, masturbation, primal, threesome, voyeurism

I touched myself tonight to memories of you, of us, and the first time I watched you with her.

We were in a car riding toward your house to meet her. I was holding your hand and letting the simmer between us steam the lid until it got pushed off the pot. There was no real plan, but we both had choreographed this in our head long before. There was no law of the evening, no edge to push past or shy away from. I was hungry from seeing you this way, from feeling it. We were all close and I thought about the layers of it all, knowing her while seeing her bend into you, feeling you knowing her, seeing me feel her. My desire to be there with you and watch you take her was almost overwhelming.

I knew so many of your facets, so many pieces of your past, your shame, your fears. I liked the anecdotes you told to new friends at a bar when you were comfortable and I was against your shoulder with your arm draped haphazardly around me, protective. Pure. I wanted to see you from the sky, and know it's you, but different, know it's you without me, within her, against her, around her, invading and scratching to be let in. I couldn't wait to be there after it all slowed to just shadows on the walls, taste the sounds from your throat she swallowed off your tongue, find the pieces of her body after, where she trembled the hardest for you.

Once we got to her apartment, the light in the room was soft. She answered her door naked and our eyes were dancing. The silhouette of my body was facing you both in the doorway, quiet on the surface. My nerves were already incendiary, pushing through my skin towards the poetry of this, this sonnet in the dark while I began to watch. You tethered yourself between her limbs, coiled around her throat like a boa. Her palomino hair became tangled in the firmness of your palms. The softness of her against the power of your thighs was gorgeous. You're making sounds both familiar and foreign and your body is driving hers, her noises are desperate, then devious; she's all train-off-the-tracks, until you settle her back down into rolling steadiness.

I'm quiet and wet from what's in this room, from what's growing from the crumpled wreck of the two of you, and how bad my lips and fingers are humming to feel your skin after, damp from her, steam coming off you like a midsummer night that starts to breathe again in the coolness of the morning. The dew of her on your body and your sadistic laugh fills the corners of the room. Your words to each other hover on the ceiling above, drumming on the silence of my skin perched in the door frame. I catch your eyes every time they flash open, like the sword of you is swallowing me.

You're touching her and pulling her like taffy and I want my shadow on the ceiling alongside yours, alongside hers. My mouth is watering like I can't wait to chew on her gasps, like she will miss me inside when I'm through, like my teeth and hands will hold her hostage in those sheets.

While you are both gone, you're both still here in the euphoria of seeing me, tasting the air of my uneven breathing. You smell the shivers in me wanting your teeth.

Then I am there moving into you both. I am being pulled in that metaphysical way where my fingertips need the stardust in hers and yours. My hands entangle in your hair hoping they get stuck there forever, tasting what her tongue left in your mouth. I slide my face down your body to lick her sweat off your torso, still shaking from just a graze, from the small warmth of my breath traveling down. My cunt waters for her mouth to leave dark rosebuds on my thighs.

I want us this way, too — the seconds that make up the hours and the storm that shows up as lightning before sound. I want the drop in your body before a fall, the way water crests in rhythms against a shore. Tonight, the burnt cinder of my lips is on you both, like a filthy haze of cinder-smoke and twilight.

The Exquisite, Holy Ache: Lover Letter #15

D/s, oral sex, rough body play, crying, boot play

I want the mindfuck to be profound. I want your presence around me like a cloak, the burn of your need on my tongue. I want the change you put in me to jangle around in my pocket between my fingers the next day, while I reminiscence about how rich your moans make me feel. I want to be taken away quietly, thrashing on the inside. I want to lap dance with your demons, want your palms to frictionburn my curves. I want to swim in the steam coming off you, want you to breathe for me while I go deeper.

I want to be peeled to the core. I want your palms on my pulse, pinning me into the sheets, commanding surrender. I want the walls to remember this tomorrow. I want your whispers to seesaw the pain, want your lips parted on mine so I have someplace safe to leave my screams. I want to feel you walk into a room, interrupting the air, want to sense it with my eyes shut. I want to catalog the sounds only you can bring to silence, I want the way you look at me to feel like marbles in my throat. I want the way you touch me to feel like cinders when they're blue.

I want the skin on your neck a waiting cave for my teeth. I want my chest to feel bricked in by your voice. I want to think about the freckle on your lower back at four am on a Tuesday. I want to be followed by that thought all day.

I want your thighs to be my pulpit. I want to go to sleep with the taste of you in my mouth. I want your teeth to teach me regret, disbelief. I want you to cover my pretty little lips with the heat between your legs. I want to suffocate in the smell of your hair.

I want to lay by your feet while you work, wait for you quietly, my knees sore in that holy way. I want to live inside the tension my muscles get from the hardwood, want to feel dragged through the long minutes while I'm trying to be still for you, while I'm trying to be good. I want you to rest your boots on my chest while you blow smoke in my soft hair. I want the burn to last around my eyes, like the first time I saw you walking towards me.

I want to dig in until I become.

I want to find the small things that make big ripples in you, be a muddled canvas you can splatter them on. I want your hands full from taking everything I have. I want your nails on my tongue, and the love lines in your palms, book-ending my throat. I want your presence draped around me like a cape when you're gone.

I want to be small enough to fit anywhere below you, against you, behind you, near you. I want the back of your hand cradling the dried tears on my cheek when it's over, want to feel dizzy from the way you move closer, before you even touch me. I want to watch your eyes pickaxing my body, deciding what's next. I want to wish I had less nerves, the right language to explain what this means to me, the right look to show you how much that is.

I want the moisture of your whispers on my shoulder when you're making it hurt worse than I ever thought it could. I want your hair to brush against my cheek like warm rain. I want the muscles in my calves to have seizures on the sheets, open my eyes after and feel like I'm breathing through yours looking down at me. I want to cry so hard I look as mauled as you make me feel. I want my curves cradled and trembling against your lines at the end.

I want to be pushed so far away from myself the strings inside my heart split and rip at my rib-cage. I want the knife of your voice to slice through the air when you tell me you're nowhere near done.

I want to floor you from how much I can take. I want to wiggle out of this but feel squeezed harder by the trust. I want to hear your boots on tile and tense up, shake like a branch the first minute of a hurricane. I want to be pulled around on a leash behind you, want my soft to be pelted with your steady.

I want this to feel sacred, want the litany of vowels I drum out to land on you like fireworks, all over. I want your demons to lick the tears in my eyes, only after they make them. I want the marks your belt left on my hipbone to light up like hot pokers the next time I put on jeans too quick. I want you to feel like a prayer I'm slowly memorizing.

I want this to haunt me later, want this to hold you like the wake in a river that keeps a boat still, want your heaviness to fall free from this, like the ease of a crane tossing rocks.

I want my bruises to swell the way my chest does when I forget to remind myself to breathe with you. I want to hear you laugh when I whimper. I want to reach out for you and feel swallowed whole from when you finally decide to touch back. I want to crane my neck, stretch my spine, squeeze your hand, break myself to be near you.

I want to know how deep this cave in me goes. I want you to carve into it bluntly with no apologies, showing me it doesn't stop anywhere near where I thought.

The Sharp & The Soft: Lover Letter #16

D/s, biting, oral sex, crying, choking, rough body play, primal

I: Undertow

I write about you lately, a lot. Sometimes I keep the thoughts to myself, secrets under my pillow while I dream, so I can touch them in the dark. I love palming the pleasantries like coins I carry in my pocket on a Tuesday when I'm watching the clouds go by on my patio. I wonder how you like to be held, what you're doing in this moment. I wonder how close these arrows will get to pinning you down.

When I wake up and spread my legs open I imagine what you taste like between yours. I think about how I'd get you off, how you'd take me down, how much of you I could fit inside me. I wonder what you smell like. What are your rituals? What things do you keep quiet about? How you take your coffee? What was the last thing that made you cry? What did you love most when you were a child? What would the cappuccino of your eyes feel like running over me warm, from above?

Sometimes I want to hang my thoughts about you on walls, like pressed flowers between glass, like delicate letters on a page only the writer ever gets to read.

I am torn in half at times; do I keep you sacred, just for me? Do I keep you in mind like this with the sweet landscapes of your body beneath my eyelids, where I am pressed against you in my slumber and you are crushing me with the bricks in your voice. I think about you thrashing me with the undertow in your quiet smile.

Sometimes I want the spectacle of this. I want us existing in the eyes of strangers, the moans I hope to birth from my hunger for you.

Sometimes it's a message to you between the lines. Sometimes the lines are you. Sometimes my wickedness can't hide at all and it bites into the fruit of you with my jaw wide open. I dream about the thick nectar of your come running down my chin, my thighs damp from your full possession, like you are here with your hands on my shoulders while my fingers fly on your skin. The froth I feel for you boils high, just like I want it to.

I write about you, darling, your ways entangled with my wants. I write about the brutality of your mouth sucking on the petals of mine, how I want be the branch that holds your rope swing, the captive in a cage beneath our bed. I like thinking about the knife on the bed-stand that never made it back to the kitchen, my thoughts shining strong in crimsons and blues, azure violence dancing between our frantic shadows on the walls.

I write about you and you are here, too. You are in this one like a moment that stretches further than it should, shattered glass on clocks and the ticking of my fear beneath your soothing palm on my stomach. Keep me on your hands and I will hold you in my mouth for later. I will hold you in my mind when it is quiet, when the world is sleeping and I am breathing in the night air of you deeper than I can take.

The burn of this want stings my eyes with tears and I just want to rest below you like a begging question, like the pulp of my skin still on your teeth, like the cool frost of me, licking you back to life.

II: Them

Sometimes it's about their dark corners, their sharp edges, their primal gazes, the starved way they kiss. With others, it's about how three of their fingers fit in your mouth just past that sweet spot where your tongue meets your throat and you know they're watching you try for them. They're watching you even though this room is dark and the only noise nearby is the hum of the lamppost a floor below outside, the only brightness on the street attracting all the summer mosquitoes at once.

They were too much, a pill you bravely wanted to swallow but once it got to the back of your throat you panicked, having no choice but to convince yourself to keep going, keep coaxing your body to take it and once it went down, sideways and awkwardly scraping the inside of you, your cells fizzed in relief. They felt the way fairground lights do, that illusion of the ride slower than it's really going.

Their features were sharp and yours soft, and even you thought your voice sounded best when it was caught in your chest for them, same way your palms would clench their clothes like you were falling off a cliff, like this was the last thing you'd hold onto. This was that specific breed of too much you always craved.

It was never about sex with them, until it was and then it was always about plummeting into them, violently, like a free-fall where the air rushes over you so fast you can't breathe.

They tasted like a mix of bourbon and the honeysuckle you used to pick on paraded walks you'd take as a child, down a street that ended in a creek-bed. They tasted like the first time the skin of a black cherry broke between your teeth. They tasted like the pit of a plum you sucked on while the juice still ran down your chin in the summer, sticky, warm, and decadent.

Their straightforward with your cryptic made the sex feel like you were both puzzles, made your fingers feel like you were getting away with it when their boxers finally slid past their knees and you were hit with their scent. Sometimes you'd lay in bed after and just remember how their shoulder felt to lean on, and wonder if when your corpse was studied, there'd be a hollow in your cheekbone from doing that all the time.

You were full of those spaces, those caves that waited for someone to pickax hard enough to make you come so violently your calves shook against their sheets making their own vibrato. As for them, those spaces you knew you needed to carefully explore, almost deftly like you weren't even there until they bloomed below you, recognizing you were making yourself a soft shadow, or at times, a dark scream. Sometimes they wanted that, too, wanted to tangle their hands in your hair so furiously that when you pulled away your scalp was sore. Sometimes they'd let you deeper than anyone else had been and you'd bury yourself there for languid moments, holding their sweet thighs against your shoulders as their hand found your knuckles and you'd root yourself further; trying to prove to them you understood what it meant.

Sometimes you'd wake up and think about the way they walked down a hallway towards you, and then you'd forget it again when their teeth were pulling your left nipple away from your body while they looked at you like you were a prayer they purposely forgot to say, because the caramel of sin tasted better.

When you fucked it wasn't ever measured; time would crawl at first and then run from you both, the bedding would slowly unfold and then be everywhere around you on the floor at once. Their room would smell like them when you walked in, and then the rest of the night, like you.

Their face would be over you seeing you and you would be below being seen. Neither were ever taken for granted. Things they did with their eyes made your soul flinch. Things you did with your hands made their body fit against you like water finding cracks in rocks, traveling down a cliff, ending in a trickle.

Sometimes you'd slow yourself down and drape yourself beside them, giggling about something mundane neither one would ever remember, but because you had those slow moments, it felt like walking out of a forest when you'd leave them.

You let them do things you never had done and you were almost always scared of who you became in that room. You were almost always wondering who you were later on and felt like you had more selves than you realized, like a mirror you could open where you became infinite but the same, or at least the most of yourself you'd been so far. Sometimes you growled and jerked like an animal, sometimes you were so soft you were barely there, sometimes you were so lost in their body your fingertips felt like your lips and your lips felt like your hands.

III: I Could Fall Into You Like A Crash

I could fall into you like a crash, like the open space between my lips were meant for your nipple, for your clit. I know the stardust in the universe convened to make the bone of your hip just for my teeth. I want my palms full of your thighs, my nose buried in your hair while I inhale and cover your mouth with my fingers., desperate to try to show me what you want. I want the words you keep secret, want them falling over my skin with broken syllables you run down my neck like rain, when I'm inside, when I'm against you. I want to run through your mind like water; finding the cracks you hide, lighting every corner you keep with the warm candle I have for you in my eyes.

I want you more than wanting warrants, more than the bones in my arms ache to hold you, unravel you. I want to wind you down with my tongue, wrap you in the ribbons of my palms, like taffy stretching through a candy shop window, pulling away from itself to go back inside.

I want to taste you all day long, feel the pressure of your eyelids when you you self destruct, when you come and shake into my mouth, violent like a door slamming in a storm. I want you to lose gravity just because of me, give you a second pair of lungs to breathe with. I want you to see the sky with the eyes of a God, find us in every constellation. I know my fingers were born to curl against all your fear and caress it into relief.

I want you rabid. I want you filthy. I want you the way I can taste your heartbeat from my palm over your pussy. I want you with sweat on your back and your bones stretching further than they should to pull me back in, to have me again, to triumph past sleep into something else. The hours after midnight are there for us, love, only us.

IV: Our Other Hunger

I am lying here thinking of you, your slender fingers cradling my hipbone, the smell of your hair, how your skin feels like summer in the morning when I first open my front door. You hit me all at once, so hard I feel like squinting.

Your voice is feminine but husky, with strong, bold tinges of your sensuality but this other thing, this measured way you grace yourself with softness, vulnerability resting on the back of a razor.

I miss the flash of your nails on my back, the purple poems you leave on my thighs. I miss the violin shape of you when you'd bend over your bed, holding onto the metal frame while I fucked you from behind.

I miss the way your skin tasted like saltwater and smelled like cocoa butter, and we'd only leave your room on bowed legs giggling from exhaustion to inhale something together, the end of one hunger starting the next.

The taste of your sweetness was still on my lips mixed with whatever it was we were downing in gulps, sometimes vanilla ice cream bogged over by butterscotch. Your microwave would sit quiet at times, full of leftovers from a foreplay dinner we barely touched because we were thinking too much about our other hunger.

Everything between fucking was just everything between fucking. The warm tea I'd bring you came before a massage, came before my lips pulling the hem of your skirt off with my teeth. The jokes I'd tell you to get that full-bodied laugh that made your neck stretch to the sky, came before me getting wet from the way you showed joy on your body, like electricity flowing into me.

Then there was the full way you looked at me sitting behind you, from the mirror while you were getting dressed and how I'd pull you into my lap to run my hands against the fabric on your skin. Why was it still there?

Jazz was always playing in your room, Erykah Badu if you were purging something deep, Misfits if you wanted to remember your youth in Philly when you used to duct tape your boots that fell apart on your way to school.

Sometimes when you were gone, I'd crawl under the covers and sleep on your side of the bed just to feel like you were still there, humming against me and all my senses, inhaling that smell of your sweat and hair and body wash you used that smelled like peaches.

Sometimes when you'd get back home, we'd pace the night, pretend we didn't know where it was always going to go. Sometimes I felt like when you were inside me I could see god.

Tonight, you're behind me like a ghost in bed. I smelled you when I turned my lamp off and felt your matte black nails curling into that grip around my hip, pulling me back into you with a rage, a fever. I wanted to nestle into that brutality, that way your breath on my neck would turn to a bruise from your teeth and make my blood boil. You were jagged, leaving your sharpness everywhere on me and my spine bowed against you like a cello.

You didn't touch me sometimes until I was desperate. You got off on that, on my craving and raucous whimpers and the slow avalanche of my hands holding yours and then trying to push them down.

Until defiance took over and I'd just put my own hands there and you'd punish me with your nails, turn my decision into more restraint. I'd move my ass back, circling into your warm thighs and giving you the sounds that made you weak for the same thing, made you weak for the way I'd offer my neck up to be choked. I'd stretch my jaw wider for your hand and hold my breath longer while you came and kept me tight between your thighs.

It's three a.m. and that's all I fucking want.

V: Between My Teeth

Lately all I think about is kissing you. The way you part your lips after you smile is so subtle, just enough to let an air of quiet laughter out and drive me up the walls from joy. The loudest volume I've ever felt is from that one dimple you have; I hear it so hard in the small of my back. So many of your ways throw me into other worlds, ones made entirely of the purples of dusk.

I want the pulp of your thighs between my teeth. I want to pull away when you lunge at me for a kiss so I can feel the exact heat of your want emanating between the shape of our bodies, screaming, but waiting for someone to squash it with a sudden spark of touch.

I want to chase you back, swallow that need of yours in desperate gulps, the way a wolf takes in water after a hunt, tongue full of blood and ripe meat between its jaws dripping, needing to wash the feral down with the pure.

You are something pure, but also something full of turpentine and kettledrums. You are something like ivory clawing to be seen as onyx, the howls in you greater than any silence the world has. Those sounds you bring to the dark rooms we exist in destroy me, the same ones I know you give away only to those you trust, those who hold you back just as hard as you hold them.

I want this to leave blood on my tongue. I want to wake up with burning slivers down my back from the way growls raked me back to life. I want to make you laugh because I know it's how you giggle when you get fucked, guileless and unashamed, with your neck thrown back in ecstasy.

I want to assault you with that, bring my demons to square up with yours and see how long the battle can last.

Last night we were on your couch and the static of the television wasn't the movie I was watching. It was the veins in your neck stretching into the plot from the film, the way you leaned closer to my body heat. The flash of your eyes in the dark reminded me how I want to stretch you out like stars, show you with my mouth.

You're made entirely of moonlight.

Acknowledgements & Appreciation

This book is for the fringe-dwellers, the unashamed perverts, the lascivious lovers, the folks who are doing it despite. This book is for you, babe, the queer that feels alone but isn't, the future drag king who's about to take the world by storm, the advocates, the comrades, the allies, the ones who have to hide to be safe. This book is for my LGBTQIA+ family and I truly hope it can hold, ignite, and spark joy and consensual filth in your lives. I love you. Keep going. You are a beautiful treasure.

This book is for the nervous kinkster, the newbie at the munch, the solo rope player, the top looking for a safe mentor, the experimental switch hoping to be visible, and the bottom that's looking for the respect and care they deeply deserve. I've been you and I hope you find the safe spaces and people that ARE out there. Take your time. Breathe. Journal. Commune. We are delicate and glorious, and capable of so much consensual intimacy and I hope your exploring leads to bliss and revelations.

This book is for the found family I've had in my corner. I truly hope I am able to encircle you with the same amount of love you've poured over me in buckets. To Alan, Alex, Carly, Jon, Key, Kortney, Lore, Michelle, Rae, Zander: I love you endlessly and thank you for being there for me in more ways than I can type. You are my heart.

And last but by no means not least, this book is profoundly dedicated to Sinclair Sexsmith who was my first inspiration to write erotica, the first author of erotica I ever read, a mentor, and a lovely queer human I respect deeply. I am beyond grateful to know you and I hope you understand and feel how much your care and support has meant to me. This book wouldn't have been possible without you and you believing in me has meant the world to me. I hope in this life you get to feel the love and care you give to so many and it rushes over you with abundance and makes you swell with joy. You too, are my heart.

About the Author

J ezebel Jett (she/her) is a white, queer, kinky, disabled femme living on Miwok land in California. She has been educating herself and participating in risk-aware kink since 2018. She is published in The Lantern, wrote a music column for 3 years, has published writing online since 2012, and is also a visual artist. Jezebel is always interested in feedback, collaborating with other queer artists and writers, and making heartfelt connections. Visit jezebeljett.com for more information. This is her first book.